THE UNCHOSEN ONES

THE UNLIKELY DEFENDERS BOOK 1

LILY SKYY

First Edition: May 2022

ISBN 978-1-956525-04-5 (ebook)
ISBN 978-1-956525-78-6 (paperback)

Published by Books to Hook Publishing, LLC.
www.BooksToHook.com

CONTENTS

PROLOGUE

Kire ran past towering Sequoia trees with dense leaves that shaded the forest from the sun overhead, making the forest dark, humid, and uncomfortably cold. As he ran, he felt like his lungs were about to explode, but perhaps his body was waiting to fail him just as the thumping getting closer and closer finally closed in on him.

When the chase first started, taking in long breaths and then holding them in proved to be the best breathing strategy. But it no longer mattered whether he held his breath in his belly or exhaled until his soul escaped through his nostrils; every single breath of air he took left a trail of fire burning in his throat down to his chest and belly.

He leaped over giant roots sticking up out of the ground and fallen branches the size of trees. The smell of rot and moisture hung thick in the air like fog on a misty morning. He could hear the gurgling sound of a stream merging with the river somewhere in the distance. The forest was treacherous territory—twice he slipped on rocks covered with moss, leaving him covered in mud. Another fallen branch presented itself before Kire, and he leaped over it, landing on a carpet of dead leaves.

This felt like a game of Temple Run or Danger Surf, except not fun and full of dread because he couldn't respawn if he died. It was he, Kire Hunter, who would be killed. Kire's surname was Hunter, but today he ironically found himself as the prey fleeing with its tail between its legs.

St. Bernard High School's two apex predators, Trace and Kaos, were two of the beings chasing after Kire, and who could forget Trace's girlfriend Amberly McHenry, who was the special angel sent to Kire from the darkest pits of hell? Kire would never understand why she was always out to get him, just to make his life as miserable as can be.

Kire fell again after running into a clump of moss and ferns hanging from some hemlocks. "Ugh, how do I get out of here," moaned Kire. "Oh! I can call for help." He felt around all of his pockets, searching for his phone before groaning in disappointment. He then remembered when he punched Trace Henderson in the face earlier, he quickly threw his backpack aside and started running—the backpack, of course, had his phone in it.

Kire noticed a very familiar girl bending over something a little too late. Before he could stop himself, he smashed into what looked like a pot, but pots don't break to pieces, do they? He muttered hurried apologies and scurried to his feet just as Trace boomed out in that rich bass voice of his.

"There he is!" the tyrant called happily. "We have to get him! I can almost taste him!"

Trace's words "taste him" filled Kire's weary legs with adrenaline and he found himself picking up the speed he didn't know he had in him. How could Trace say, 'I can almost taste him,' as though Kire was a warthog being chased by a pack of coyotes?

The thumping of the trio's feet drummed a scary echo through the forest and Kire thought someone had joined; when he risked a glance over his shoulder, he saw that someone *had* joined the pursuing party. He scoffed in disbelief.

"Kire, if you stop right now, I promise I won't lay a hand on you," someone called. It was Kaos.

"That's right, Kire," Trace bellowed behind him. "You'll only lose an eye for that sucker punch you threw at me!"

"Oh, stop talking," Kaos snapped at Trace. "You're good at using everything but your brain. Don't you think luring him over beats the chase?!" he exclaimed.

Kire scoffed; fat chance he would stop at Kaos' request. That kid was as sly as a snake and as cunning as a fox.

"I got him!"

Kire's eyes were bulging as Amberly came straight at him from out of nowhere.

"No!" Kire yelled as Amberly crashed into him, bringing them both down into the gorge. The last thing Kire thought of as the world of green leaves and black rotting wood swirled in his eyes was his mother smiling in the kitchen—then the day snapped into darkness.

1

Gabby Drive was a long street with a narrow two-lane road braced by towering pine, spruce, and fir trees on either side. What made the neighborhood that Gabby Drive ran through unique was the age of the homes. The youngest block was fifty years old, and though its owner had two Ferraris in his garage, he refused to replace the old Victorian-era windows of his house. The same went for nearly every person living on Gabby Drive; young people, old houses. Most houses on Gabby Drive were built during the Victorian Era, so many had that Victorian architecture look to them—the homes that weren't brick were painted in pastel or jewel tones, and the homes had ornate features and details decorating the window frames and lining the rain gutters. The homes were mostly all tall and thin and had ancient trees growing all around them, making Gabby Drive a very shaded street.

The house with the address 7 Gabby Drive was made of red brick and had an old maple tree towering over the front yard. The house, built in 1904, had four bedrooms, three bathrooms, a kitchen with a separate dining room, and a living room. Only two of the bedrooms were in use—one by the owners, Gerald and Emma Hunter, and the other by Kire, their seventeen-year-old son. One of the other bedrooms was made into a guest room which rarely saw any guests, and the other bedroom was an exercise room, which was also rarely used.

Gerald Hunter, the father of the house, was very set in his ways. He was a stubborn man with old-fashioned values. Growing up, Gerald's family was poor; they always had just enough to eat, but not enough to spare for collection at their church on Sundays nor to put their ambitious child Gerald through college. Gerald's father dismissed his son's ambitions as a waste of time and encouraged him to work in his jewelry business. Upon graduating from high school, Gerald started his career as a jewelry salesman at his father's store. Abandoning his ambition to succeed academically as a child, Gerald, like his father taught him, now viewed higher education as a waste of time, as can be observed in his apparent success in the jewelry business. He was a tall, big man with blond hair, pale skin, and light eyes, and his face was usually scrunched up into a scowl.

Emma Hunter, the mother of the house, was as different from Gerald Hunter as an apple was from a cup of milk. She had tanned skin, dark eyes, dark hair, and a small smile with thin lips. She was a college graduate with a master's degree who was employed at the mercy of the economy, against the wishes of Gerald who wished she would stay home instead. She was kind and sweet and was the glue holding the tumultuous family together.

It was an unusually bright morning in the typically dark and cold Montgomery. The birds had risen and were chirping noisily from one tree to the next. The sun was up, warm and yellow-white, eager to make up for all the days it left the city dark and wet. Kire was in his bedroom, stretched lazily in his bed with the blankets over his head to shade himself from the intruding sunlight to which he wasn't accustomed. He was basking in the sweet bliss of ignorance of what was to come.

His big brown eyes were wide open under his blanket and his ears tingled hot with the expectation for what was to...

"Kire! I know you're awake! If you don't get out of bed, I'll be calling your father!"

...come.

That got him—it always did. He kicked off his blanket angrily and got out of bed. He made straight for his door, opened it, and then slammed it hard so his mother could hear downstairs; he was similar to his father in this way, his aggressive way of telling his mother that he was out of bed now. Kire's father insisted he communicated using more 'manly means' which is just what he chose to do—his mother hated it.

"I don't need that from you, young man!" shouted Emma.

Groaning and rolling his eyes, he got ready for school: brushed his teeth, took a cold shower, and got dressed before going downstairs. "Good morning, Mother," Kire said, planting a kiss on Emma's forehead.

"Did you even try to use a comb today?" She flashed a look at his messy brown hair that had the tendency to stick up straight and sideways and refused to sit neatly atop his head. Even if he cut it shorter, which is how he had it as a young boy, it would still look stupid.

Kire settled into a seat at the dining table. "I *did* use my comb, but my hair refuses to stay where the comb tells it to."

"You're more like your father every day," Emma said, handing Kire a piece of toast slathered with raspberry jam.

"Cool," Kire said dully.

"Just eat so you can be on your way already."

"School is just a waste of my time; can't I stay home? Mr. Fischer doesn't even know the seventh number in the Fibonacci series, and I'm supposed to believe he's a genius?"

"Kire, you being exceptional doesn't make everyone else less human. Now quit messing around and eat so you won't miss your bus."

As a rule, the school bus never waited for him; it had done so every day for three weeks, with Kire still in bed each time. The bus driver had called Kire aside one day on the bus ride home from school and assured him through gritted teeth that the bus would no longer do as much as take a drive down Gabby Drive again, an agreement that suited Kire just as well.

2

St. Bernard was a thirty-minute bus ride away from Kire's house but only a nine-minute sprint away—the latter is the method he chose to use most often. When coming up on St. Bernard, one could recognize it because of the huge signboard the graduating class of five years ago made, wherein they wrote all of their names to spell out 'St. Bernard.' The school was just like any other high school in the area: they had a soccer and baseball team, as well as a swim team, tennis, basketball, and the like. Aside from the sports teams, there were a number of clubs one could join at St. Bernard; for example, Kire used to write for the school editorial with a group of socially awkward kids until he quit because he didn't feel like doing it anymore. There was also a science club, a French club, a volunteering club, and a club called Guardians of all that's Green and Living, a group composed only of the founding member, Charlie Rose, the invisible.

Kire showed up to school late that day, as he had missed his bus as usual, and felt the weight of twenty or so pairs of eyes pressing down on him as he slumped into Mrs. Goody's class with his head held low. Mrs. Goody was an older Army Veteran who taught literature. She always wore her black and white hair in a tight bun and kept her lips tightly pursed most of the time. She was scribbling furiously on the board when he walked in, so he managed to get in without her noticing him—at first.

"Mrs. Goody, I believe Kire Hunter was trying to tell you something," a thick male voice called from the last row of seats. It was Trace, the bane of Kire's existence.

Kire froze. He had almost made it to his seat when she stopped writing on the board and turned around slowly and rather dramatically.

"Mr. Hunter," said Mrs. Goody, "halt right there while I address you, please."

Kire gulped. "I've halted already, ma'am," he said, "I cannot halt any further."

"Feeling smart today, are you?" she said with her hands clasped in front of her. "I want you to face this class and tell us why you thought it was okay for you to arrive thirty minutes late."

Kire shrugged. "There was—"

"And don't you say traffic—"

"—traffic."

"You will report to room 112 at 2:45 this afternoon. You won't leave until an hour after school is over. Your parents will be informed, and you will wait outside the front of the school until they come to pick you up."

"Fine," Kire said, slumping into his seat at the back of the classroom.

"How did you like getting ratted out like that, huh?" Kire's spine crawled as he heard Trace's whisper.

Some facts about Trace Henderson: One, he's always with his girlfriend Amberly McHenry and his best friend Kaos Miles. Two, nobody ever messes with Trace, but Trace can mess with you relentlessly. Three, he was handsome, with blond hair and blue eyes, popular, athletic, tall, muscular, and all the girls wanted to be around him—that is, if they could get past the incredibly frightening Amberly McHenry.

Trace Henderson wasn't born the ruler of St. Bernard. A kid named Alfred Graham used to top that most dangerous chart. The rumor is that one day, Trace challenged Alfred to a battle off-campus. Whoever lost was never allowed to show their face at school again, ever.

Alfred couldn't have shown his face in school again anyway; Trace reduced the lad's detention from thirty-two to about twenty-eight. Alfred couldn't report Trace to the police because it was a pre-arranged fight—Alfred would've found himself punished too. So instead, he lied to his parents and told them that some men nearly seven feet tall had attacked him. Then he convinced his parents that he was too traumatized after the attack to return to St. Bernard. He's never been seen again.

Amberly McHenry, on the other hand, was the most popular girl in school, but she was loved mostly because people feared her. She was the head cheerleader and her looks fit the bill—she had long, thick and smooth blonde hair and piercing blue eyes. Her lips were plump, and her build was athletic. Amberly and Trace both have mysterious home lives that they rarely discuss, which is what makes them all the more interesting.

Back to Mrs. Goody's classroom.

"It wasn't exactly ratting out," said Kire. "She was going to eventually see that I came in late anyway."

Trace snorted. Oh, and one more thing—he was unpardonably proud.

"She wasn't going to notice you, weirdo. It's Trace that gives you a face in this school." Trace turned around to Kaos, who was equally proud, albeit bored. "Did you hear that?"

"Yeah," said Kaos dully. "You should consider a career in rapping."

"Oh, please," muttered Kire.

"What did you say?" hissed Trace menacingly.

"Nothing," said Kire, pretending to try to pay attention to Mrs. Goody.

"That's what I thought," said Trace.

KIRE'S last class of the day was botany—the only class he didn't share with Trace.

"Now, ladies and gents," Mr. Donnie began, "this here is a special plant which I like to call Edax Animae, which is Latin for soul eater."

The Edax Animae stood about three feet tall. It had a flower the shape and size of a small jar, and it was bright green at the base and red at the top. Despite the height of the flower, it only had three large leaves and the single jar-shaped flower— nothing more.

"It's a carnivorous or flesh-eating plant," Mr. Donnie contin- ued, looking proudly at the plant. "My colleague in Brazil sent me this two days ago. It hasn't been formally named yet, nor is it in any textbooks."

Murmurs of "cool," "wow," and "impressive" started among the students. However, Kire wasn't impressed.

"Mr. Donnie," Kire said, "if this plant has just been discov- ered, then why is it here? All carnivorous plants eject a form of neurotoxin to incapacitate their prey. Do you know what sort of toxin this plant here emits?"

Mr. Donnie grunted, clearly displeased by Kire's attitude and cockiness. "You kids these days!" Never eager to learn or gain any new knowledge by trying new things," he said. "Always waiting for someone else to figure it out first! I say we don't wait for the scientific community to give us an evaluation of the plant; how about we give *them* an evaluation instead?"

The short speech given by Mr. Donnie triggered a round of cheering from the enthusiastic students.

Mr. Donnie walked up to Kire and said quietly, "Now, would you like to participate, or would you rather sit out and then regret not participating later on?"

Kire smiled sweetly. He wasn't going to give Mr. Donnie the satisfaction of seeing him worked up. "Is this the only specimen we have to work with, sir?" Kire asked.

"Ho ho," Mr. Donnie laughed heartily. "You must not know who you're talking to. Everyone will have their own toy to play with. Put on your gloves, people!"

At first, the students were all having a lot of fun, until things started to go wrong. The plant's jar-shaped flower was triggered by the slightest touch. The plant's first victim was Angela, a blue-eyed girl who loved to remind everyone she was *the* cheerleader until Amberly came along. So, Angela listened to the devil standing on her shoulder, took off a glove, and touched the trap of the carnivorous plant with bare hands. The jar snapped closed on her hand and she giggled. However, a few seconds later, she let out a blood-curdling scream that had everyone covering their ears.

"Tell me, Angela," Mr. Donnie began angrily. "Why didn't you tell me you left your senses at home before class started?"

"Look!" one of the other students cried in horror, pointing at Angela's trapped hand. When Angela's skin began to take on a reddish hue, it was clear to see that the redness was spreading like heat through the blade of a burning knife.

"Help me, get me out of here!" Angela screamed, no longer caring about ruining her makeup as tears ran down her face.

"Mr. Donnie, do something!" Kire snapped, but the teacher looked equally as lost and befuddled as the fifteen other students in the greenhouse.

Kire groaned. He should've known the man would have no idea what they were dealing with. Mr. Donnie was hardly the pioneer of botany he paraded himself to be. He fumbled over to the plant and grabbed it by the stem—he was going to rip the jar from the plant.

"Wait!" a small, high voice called out. "You're going to kill it!"

The room went quiet, and everyone turned to look toward where the voice was coming from.

"Oh, really?" Kire scoffed. "And somehow you think that's more important than saving Angela's life?"

The advocate for the plant came forward; it was Charlie Rose, the invisible. The other students parted to allow her space.

"It won't kill her, but she'll feel miserable for a few days. And don't you try to argue with me," she said. "If Angela had her gloves on, the plant would've never sensed her blood and trapped her hand."

"You know the toxin released by the plant won't kill her?" asked Kire.

"I'm certain. It doesn't need a prey as large as she is."

"Then do something!" yelled Kire.

Everyone watched Charlie Rose pat the flower on the top of the jar as though it were a puppy. The plant opened its jaws in response, allowing Angela to jerk out her hand, which was as red as ripe tomatoes in late summer and wet with a slick, slimy substance. Tiny drops of blood oozed out of her pores. Kire got closer to Angela to get a better look at her hand. Apparently, the plant ate by softening its prey's skin enough to allow blood and nutrients from the widened pores.

"Someone, take her to the clinic so the nurse can have a look at her," Mr. Donnie said. Now that everything had returned to the point where he could play by the books, his voice had come alive again. Five students led the injured Angela out, a task one person could've achieved successfully. Kire suspected it was simply a ploy to get out of class.

Mr. Donnie and the remaining students stared at Charlie Rose, who held the plant as though it didn't just trap a girl's hand right before their eyes.

"Mr. Donnie, that's not normal, is it?" Nathan Bury said quietly to his teacher. "She just patted a f—my language, sorry —she just patted the human-eater on the whatever-that-is-called like it was a cute puppy."

Mr. Donnie gulped, sweating profusely. "Well, full marks to Charlie—"

"Call me Rose, sir."

The teacher frowned. "Fine. Full marks to Rose here," he announced. "Now, let's see if any of you can repeat the feat."

"I'd rather fail," Nathan declared, pulling his hands out of his gloves.

The other students began to murmur at this, and the next minute they were all taking their gloves off and putting them on the table. Shortly thereafter, only Kire, Rose, and Mr. Donnie remained in the greenhouse.

"Now, Rose, how did you manage to pat that Edax Animae to sleep? I've never heard of doing such a thing."

Rose shrugged. "I don't know," she said. "It just... happened."

Kire pulled off his gloves and approached Rose's Edax Animae. He put a finger on the same spot she patted it when saving Angela, waking the plant up. Kire jumped back as the plant snapped its jaws and it wasn't until Rose worked her magic again that it managed to calm down.

"That was so cool," Kire said. "I knew the Edax Animae would have a bundle of nerves that could be stimulated for different reactions, but I didn't imagine you'd be able to find it so quickly! You're a genius!"

Rose blushed. "Thanks," she said, looking down at her feet.

Mr. Donnie seemed befuddled. "The plant has nerve bundles?"

Kire shrugged. "It's only my hypothesis. It snaps its jaws closed when it senses movement near its trap, which means there's some sensory organ at work."

Relief flooded Mr. Donnie's features. "I just knew it wasn't in any of the textbooks I read." He patted Rose on the shoulder. "You did well there, Rose. I think we have had enough to do in class today; how about we all get on our way?"

"So long as they see everything as another topic to be conquered, they'll never discover anything," Rose said quietly to herself. Kire and Rose walked out of the greenhouse together silently.

Charlie Rose was an average-looking girl with a petite build. She had long, wavy, untamable brown hair and warm honey brown eyes. She had a small, sweet smile which she rarely showed people, didn't wear makeup and often dressed oddly. She didn't dress the way most of the other girls dressed —rather, she wore whatever she wanted, whether it be something she sewed together herself or a hand-me-down from her great-great-great-grandmother. She definitely wasn't mean like Amberly, but she much preferred plants to people and wasn't afraid to let people know. She was a bit shy, rarely ever spoke unless spoken to, and didn't have any friends.

Kire suspected the reason she wanted to be addressed as Rose was because of her love for plants.

"Everything is another topic to be conquered," said Kire.

"You're one of *them,* aren't you?" she hissed. "You see plants as nothing more than food to be eaten."

"That's not true! I also see them as medicine, decoration, and clothing," Kire said enthusiastically.

Rose stopped walking. "I knew you were just like them. Have you ever seen plants beyond just what they can do for us?"

Kire frowned. "I don't get what you're trying to say. How else am I supposed to see plants? They're plants and that's it. They don't talk or have heartbeats or anything."

"Enough!" said Rose, stomping a foot. "Don't talk to me ever again. Certainly, you don't even see *me* as something other than someone who can do something for you." She turned around and walked quickly in the other direction.

Kire stood there in disbelief. *What does that even mean?* He thought. *I'll never understand girls.* He glanced at his watch and gasped in disbelief. "It's 2:40 already!"

He ran to room 112, where Mrs. Goody was waiting for him behind a desk.

"Late again, Mr. Hunter?" she growled.

Kire glanced at his watch. "I think not," he said. "You asked me to arrive here at 2:45 and here I am. It's exactly 2:45—46 now."

She narrowed her eyes at him. "Just sit down," she commanded.

"Yes, ma'am."

3

The classroom used by St. Bernard High School for detention was a small room with two broken windows covered with cardboard and some broken tables and chairs that ensured sitting was as torturous as could be. It was a little dusty; Amberly and Trace were usually the only two who would ever be sent to that room. On the wall at the front of the class was a square chalkboard with the words "LOOK AT YOU" written in menacing block letters. A CCTV camera looked down from the top right corner of one of the walls. Kire found himself a nice broken chair and took out his books to start working on some homework.

Ten minutes into detention, he heard the door creak, revealing Amberly.

"What is she doing here?" Kire said.

"Be quiet," Mrs. Goody snapped. "Amberly here is every bit as infamous as you are around this school—"

"I'm not *infamous*; I was only late to class," Kire interrupted through gritted teeth.

"Which is a habit you've become rather infamous for," Mrs.

Goody said. "This young lady here was found dancing in front of the principal."

Kire raised his eyebrows. "What?"

"Sit down," Mrs. Goodly barked at Amberly. "You seem shocked, Mr. Hunter."

"Maybe she was showing him some new... cheerleader moves?" Kire said rather slowly.

"Precisely what I told them," Amberly murmured.

Mrs. Goodly scoffed at this. "And the principal has a degree in creative criticism of dance. Just the right audience," she said dully.

Amberly was smiling as though she had just won the lottery but was trying to hide it. Kire knew what this smile meant —trouble.

"Uh, Mrs. Goody?" Kire said, springing to his feet. "You know, I've thought about what I did."

Mrs. Goody nodded curtly. "You realized your wicked ways?"

"Yes," he said, rolling his eyes internally. "How about you punish me by making me clean the toilets?" Anything to not have to spend the next hour with Amberly.

"What?" said Mrs. Goody.

"Yes, you see," Kire began, "what I did was so rude—coming into your class late and all. I just remembered how much I hate cleaning the toilet, so how about instead of making me stay in this room; you just make me clean the toilets instead?"

Mrs. Goody started chuckling at this. "So, it's true then?" she said.

"So, what is true?" asked Kire.

"I've heard people say that you and Amberly McHenry have a cat and dog kind of relationship."

Kire shook his head. "More like cat and rat—she's the cat and I'm the rat. This girl is after my life."

"I don't know what he's talking about," Amberly said innocently when Mrs. Goody shot her an inquisitive glance.

"I think you're being paranoid. Your detention still has forty minutes on the clock. Enjoy," Mrs. Goody said, walking out of the classroom.

"Seems like I struck the jackpot," Amberly said darkly.

"I'd like to warn you that there's a CCTV camera in that corner—" He pointed to the corner. "I'd stay where you are if I were you."

"It's broken," Amberly said, not looking away from Kire. "Trace told me so. It's just for show."

Amberly got up and found a different seat closer to Kire. "You and I have a lot to talk about, my friend," she said.

"We have nothing to talk about," Kire said.

"Have you noticed that we have a lot in common?

Kire snorted. "I'm not obsessed with making Kire Hunter's life a living hell; only you are."

"And you don't think there's a reason for that?" she asked, tilting her head.

"There's no reason, Amberly. You just don't like that I'm a genius and you're not."

She exhaled sharply. "As expected, you're really good at pretending. I wonder if he taught you that, to deny your connection to people. You both must have had all these years together..."

"What are you talking about?"

Amberly sighed. "You know what I think?"

"No, not at all."

"The two of you are just the same. You both think so highly of yourselves that the whole world is beneath you. That's why I try to make your life hell because hell is the only place fit for demons like you and him."

"Whatever stuff you took before coming here, I strongly

recommend you don't take it ever again. You've gone clean crazy."

"I am crazy," she said with a shrug. "I danced in front of the principal to get detention with you."

"W-what?" asked a very confused Kire. He didn't know what he did to earn such reproach from Amberly, but she was absolutely obsessed with hurting him.

"Yeah, I know," she said in a bored voice. "But better a crazy girl than the devil you were raised to be. You had it all growing up, right? Vacations, sleepovers, family game night?"

"What are you talking about?" Kire snarled. "You think you know me? You think I had it all smooth, nice, and easy growing up?"

"Yes, you did have it all smooth, nice, and easy," she said matter-of-factly. Amberly's face displayed no emotion whatsoever at the moment. "I hate you, Kire. For acting like there's nothing between us, I *hate* you."

Kire was dumbstruck. Was this Amberly's weird way of telling him she had a crush on him?

They were still looking coldly at each other when Mrs. Goody pushed the door open. "Both of you out. Now."

Amberly smiled and rose to her feet. "We haven't even started yet, Kire. The fun has just started."

4

Being with Amberly ruined Kire's mood for the remainder of the day. He kept playing her words over and over again in his head and grew angrier with each passing moment. By the late evening, the anger had spread through his entire body like poison.

Everything from the humming of the air conditioner to the neighbor's dog barking next door irritated him on an amplified level. To try and manage his anger, he buried himself in books, working on his physics homework and leaving the answers in such an open-ended way that Mr. Loch would have a hard time understanding. After finishing his physics homework, he went to math and drew out a theory of his own to solve an iteration problem.

Kire's mother called him down for dinner while he was working on his homework. He noticed his father sitting at the table. He was wearing a starched white shirt with the two top buttons undone, with gold cufflinks glinting at his wrist. His hair and mustache were gelled neatly, as he had the same unruly hair Kire did. Nothing could tame it except a lot of gel.

"Look at this boy," growled Kire's father, Gerald. "I've never seen him bring home any friends to play video games or soccer with. All he ever does is read! What kind of man is that?"

"I don't see what's wrong with that," Kire grumbled, calloused to the way his dad treated him.

"See how smart he thinks he is, Emma? Did I not teach him that being smart won't get you everything?" said Gerald.

"Kire is old enough to choose his own path, Gerald. He's so smart and has chosen the academic path—it's his choice," retorted Emma.

Listening to his parents fight in front of him about him was nothing new for Kire. He chewed on the chicken his mother made and pretended not to hear them.

"He's a teenager! He can't choose for himself! That's what we're here for; to tell him what he needs to do and make sure he does it!" spat Gerald.

"You mean, force it down his throat?" asked Emma.

Gerald clapped his hands together. "That's the phrase I was looking for," he said before adding an afterthought, "Or spoon it into his mouth since you probably think shoving something down your son's throat is too violent."

"Gerald!" Emma cried, horrified.

"Oh, spare me all that, Emma. My hard work pays the bills around here and pays for that schooling of his. I should have control over what he does at school."

"And what is it you'd rather have him do at school?"

"Sports!" Gerald yelled, his small brown eyes gleaming with passion. "He needs to join the soccer or basketball team or *something*. So, what if he isn't a good athlete? I have the connections to make things happen. He can at least make the bench of a good team—that would be better than what he does right now."

"The bench?" Kire asked. "Wow, what little faith you have in me. Thanks, Dad."

"Yeah. You gotta take what life brings to your doorstep," Gerald said, talking with his mouth full of mashed potatoes.

"Or, in this case, what you're bringing to my doorstep and breaking-and-entering into my space," said Kire.

Gerald chortled. "You don't have a door yet, kid, or space. And if you're hell-bent on being a full-time academic, I can guarantee you'll never have a door."

"Why?" asked Kire blankly.

"Well, look at your mother: she has a master's degree and struggles to hold a job. Meanwhile, I didn't go to college and I'm able to provide for my family all on my own."

"I don't want to be a soccer player," said Kire, poking his chicken violently with his fork. He had played soccer most of his life, actually; his father enrolled him as soon as he could run, and he played for years until he got into high school and had a big enough argument with his dad that he finally let him quit. He didn't hate playing soccer so much as he hated that his dad wanted him to play soccer so badly.

"Then a baseball player," said Gerald casually.

"Or a baseball player," argued Kire.

"Fine, then basketball."

"Dad," Kire said through gritted teeth.

"There are so many opportunities with sports! You could go pro; you could be a coach or a ref or an agent or—"

"An agent? Like what you're trying to be for me right now? A person who ignores another person's wishes and forces them to take a certain path because it looks lucrative?"

"Enough with the self-righteousness," Gerald said, looking at Kire and reaching for his wine glass at the same time. Because he wasn't watching where his large, clumsy hands were going, he knocked the glass onto the floor, where it shattered."

"Gerald, I don't think you should drink with a glass cup anymore," Emma said, greeting paper towels and the dustpan.

"You want me to drink from plastic cups?" He scoffed.

"Or stainless steel, if you prefer. And not just the cups, the plates as well."

"What?!" boomed Gerald, slamming his fists into the table. "What do you expect? I'm a man, and men have to break things. It shows power."

"You're always breaking things," Emma said. "Why don't you try fixing stuff for a change?"

Kire sighed and got up from the table. "I'm full and tired. Goodnight."

5

Kire woke up earlier than usual the next morning and Emma was pleasantly surprised to see him awake.

"What's up this morning?" she asked.

Kire shrugged. "I want to try out for the soccer team, see what happens."

Emma walked up to her son and caressed his cheek. "You don't have to, you know?" she said. "If this is because of what your dad said last night, he didn't mean any of it."

Kire rolled his eyes. "He meant what he said, Mom. You keep trying to defend him."

"Kire," Emma started, "the things that people go through, what your father went through when he was growing up, change the way they see the world."

"We can all choose how we want to live and treat others, Mom," he said firmly, "and clearly dad made his decision."

Emma frowned a bit and fiddled with Kire's hair.

"What is it now?" he asked.

"You have hair just like your dad's," she said with a gentle chuckle. "Why don't you go up to our bathroom and borrow some of his gel?"

"Oh, what a great idea, Mother!" Kire said sarcastically. "I'll pass. Thank you though."

Kire's school day started out as bad as ever. He saw Amberly first thing in the morning, and she put her hand to her neck in a sawing motion as she stared at him with cold eyes. Trace and Kaos were a particularly grim pair that morning.

Even on the brightest, warmest of days, Kaos always dressed like he was driving a hearse; a black shirt with a black jacket on top, black pants, black shoes, and a pair of dark glasses. Kaos had a softer, more handsome face than Trace did, with a few freckles scattered over his nose and auburn hair, which contrasted with Trace's sharp, angular features and powerful build. He came from a rich family that was heavily involved in the school, and he was the first one in his grade to get his own car. He was incredibly smart and got stellar grades without even having to try—a feature that infuriated his classmates who worked hard and didn't do as well as him. He was sly, witty, and cold and had a way of making people feel terrible about themselves with a glance. Despite all this, he was lovable, and people had a hard time hating him.

Everybody hated Trace because he was the bully, but people tended to view his sidekick, Kaos, differently. Kire thought Kaos was a jerk, just a less violent jerk than Trace, but everyone seemed to think he was nice. His peers sympathized with Kaos and were always willing to do his bidding.

One time, an ex-girlfriend of Kaos caught him cheating on her with another girl. They got into a huge fight, during which the ex-girlfriend got really mad at Kaos, but the next day at school, she was overheard telling him she was sorry for getting mad at him, sorry for not being good enough for him. She ended up taking the same route as the aforementioned Alfred; she never showed her face at St. Bernard again after that.

The class settled in for their first lesson of the day when Mr. Turner, the director of sports at St. Bernard, boomed over the school speakers.

"Good morning, boys of St. Bernard High," he said. "This is an announcement to remind you that tryouts for the male sports teams will be taking place today. Anybody interested should report to whichever field corresponds to the sport you're interested in during your gym period. Have a good one."

Kire became a bit anxious after hearing this announcement. Was he making the right choice trying out for the soccer team? Where's the fun in a bunch of grown men chasing after a ball and knocking each other down for it?

Kire's thoughts were interrupted when Mr. Loch, his first teacher for today, spoke up. "Good morning, class," he began excitedly. "How many of you heard the news last night?"

Mr. Loch was a wiry old man with a short, stocky build and hair that looked like a wig. His eyes beamed and his lips were parted in anticipation for his class to share in his excitement. When nobody responded, his shoulders dropped, and he frowned.

"None of you keep up with your science news? Kaos, do you mind sharing with the class what I'm talking about?" said Mr. Loch.

Kaos stood up and cleared his throat. The whole class turned to face him. "NASA noticed a spike in energy levels within 5,000 kilometers of Earth."

"That's not all!" said Mr. Loch beaming. "Tell us the rest!"

"The same energy levels were replicated in smaller sizes inside Earth. Five of these energy pockets were picked up, and all five of them happened in this town," continued Kaos.

"Does that mean there are aliens around us?" someone asked.

Everyone laughed.

"No, stupid. Aliens aren't real," said Kaos sharply.

"Mr. Loch," Kire said, raising his hand. "May I ask what sort of energy we're talking about?"

"That's the question everyone has been asking, but I'd have to tell you a little story to preface this and—okay, Kaos, you may sit down now," he said to Kaos, who was still standing up beside his desk.

"Everyone, please clap for your classmate here who has just cured all of you of your ignorance," said Mr. Loch. "And as I always say, ignorance..."

"... is the bane of the soul," the class chorused.

"That's right, people," Mr. Loch said proudly. "Now, settle down; let me speak. Two hundred years ago, astronomers detected this energy spike. We didn't have all the cool machines we have now to tell us when there's an explosion beyond our planet while we're all still in bed. People had to sit on hard benches and just stare at the sky. These astronomers saw increased activity in the stars, and right outside our atmosphere, there was an explosion. Well—not really an explosion since there's no air in space and explosions need air to happen. It was more like a slow burst of light wrapping our planet like a shawl. Then the astronomers all swore they saw five comets traveling in the sky together. Now, we have detected that same energy spike again, and I take it that the five energy pockets are the same comets they saw last time. Now NASA is being a bit stingy with the images, but I expect someone will leak them soon. It'll be our next study when they're released."

"What?!" cried Amberly. "That's not in our syllabus!"

"Syllabi are meant to guide us, Amberly, not constrain us," Mr. Loch said.

"Five comets the first time, and five comets the second time," a student said. "Is it just me, or do we have aliens on our trail? How come it's exactly five every time?"

"It's hard to say," said Mr. Loch. "There have been cases

where two dice roll the same number simultaneously. This might be one of those instances."

Kire raised his hand again. "But, sir, you never answered my question. What sort of energy are we talking about here?"

"I don't know for sure," Mr. Loch replied. "Not even NASA has any idea of what we're dealing with. But if this caught the eyes of astronomers two hundred years ago and still holds our attention now, it has to be something significant."

"And those five comets?" a student began. "Did they just pass overhead or crash somewhere? Surely someone must have tried following their movement."

"They simply vanished," said Mr. Loch, and the class broke out into whispers and murmurs amongst themselves.

"I'm glad you guys are suspicious about that," Mr. Loch said, laughing. "That's proof you're all scientists. The data from that time isn't solid, but a school of thought suggests that they burned themselves out along the way. Now, let's return to our work for today."

KIRE'S GYM PERIOD CAME, and he changed quickly into workout clothes so he could warm up on the field before tryouts. While jogging around the field, he heard Mr. Turner call out, "Have you been training elsewhere?"

"No, sir, I just read a couple of pre-match drills online."

"None of that 'sir' stuff, kid. Call me Coach."

"Yes, s—I mean, Coach," Kire said.

"Your calves are quite developed, too. You didn't download those off the internet, did you?"

"No, I typically jog to school since I always miss the bus. That's how I get in my exercise."

Just then, several other boys started pouring out onto the field, including Trace and Kaos. Trace and Kaos weren't there to try out, as they were already established players on the soccer team. Both played advanced positions on the field and because of their relationship off the field, they made a deadly duo whenever they played together. They were at tryouts to scope out the newbies and make fun of them.

"Kire, are you lost?" jeered Trace.

"No," said Kire dully.

"Do you know what we do here?" Kaos said as he and Trace both approached Kire.

"Yeah, it's called soccer or something," said Kire, gulping.

Kaos eyed Kire grimly. "What position do you play?"

"I believe that holding a midfielder or a right-back would be good positions for me," said Kire.

"And you know this... how?" Kaos asked with an amused look in his eyes.

"I read up online," said Kire. "I think I'm going to be able to intercept the opposition's passes and relieve pressure on our team."

"Wow, boy genius over here thinks he has it all figured out," snorted Trace. "Coach, I suggest we put the new recruit to the test."

A loud whistling tore through the air—Coach was trying to gather everyone together.

"I hope you break a leg, Kire," said Trace before walking away.

"I can't promise you anything, but I'll try my best," Kire said with a falsely sweet smile.

While Coach was talking, Kire looked out into the distance and saw Amberly sitting alone in the bleachers, staring right at him. When they made eye contact, she gave him an evil smile and waved at him.

Why did she hate him so much? Kire found it hard to focus on Coach with Amberly staring at him like that. He snapped out of it when Coach clapped his hands together.

"Okay, I'll divide you into two groups. The senior team usually plays for an hour, but we don't have enough time right now. Each team will have thirty minutes against the senior team." Coach began passing around a clipboard. "Write down your name and position here on this list."

As everyone was writing their names and positions on the list, Coach continued. "Now, let me tell you about soccer. You might think you already know everything you need to know, but you don't." He motioned to the field around him. "This here is a field of green grass and on either end of the field is a rectangular goal post. The goal of soccer is to get the ball past through those goal posts. There will be a goalie trying to stop goals with all parts of his body and ten players to defend, play, and score goals with *your legs*. You're not allowed to touch the ball with your hands unless you're a goalie, or punch anyone in the face, or break anyone's legs, or commit any other bodily damage to anyone. Today we'll see if you're even trainable. After a goal is scored, the conceding team will have to restart the game. Am I clear?"

"Yes, Coach!" everyone shouted in unison.

"The senior team should realize they have thirty minutes to spell 'refrigerator' on the scoreboard and they're not allowed to reply at all. It's just thirty minutes against *babies*."

'Refrigerator' has twelve letters. Surely the senior team didn't plan to beat the 'babies' that badly?

Kire noticed Amberly had come down off the bleachers and was speaking with Trace and Kaos. The boys were listening intently, and Amberly had a serious look on her face and was pointing in Kire's direction every few words.

Twenty-three students were at the tryouts and ten claimed they were forwards, including Andrew Longview, the thick redhead who had the power to face Trace in theory but ran away every time.

"You? You're a foreword?" Kire asked Andrew in disbelief.

"You can't even run! How about you give yourself a chance at joining the team by playing as a defender?"

Andrew looked like he was going to argue with Kire but ended up taking Kire's advice and retreated to the rear of the team.

The whistle for kick-off blew and the score line was opened immediately. One of the kids on the tryout team took the ball directly into his own team's goal. Kire frowned in disbelief. "Seriously? Just the right way to start a game. Looking really good out there."

The team was very bad, even for a set of new players. They couldn't string five passes together because everyone was trying to go and score for themselves rather than work together as a team.

Trace rammed into Kire twice and Kaos kicked Kire's leg instead of the ball. Kire then drifted toward the eighteen-year box and stuck to Andrew for protection.

"You all right?" Andrew asked after warding off Trace again.

Just then, Kire heard his name from a female's voice on the sidelines. Amberly was standing just off the field, using her cheerleading skills for evil.

"Kire is on the team; they have chosen to lose," she sang.

"That your friend?" Andrew asked Kire. Kire shook his head sadly. "She's just the devil's gift to me. I must have been a terrible person in my previous life to deserve her."

Kire glanced at the scoreboard and immediately regretted doing so. "Twenty to nothing?" he gasped. "What are we even doing?"

"We have a sissy for a goalie," Andrew said. Kire glanced at the goalie just as he was ducking so the ball wouldn't touch him, letting in a clean goal.

"Do you believe that? No wonder we're twenty-one goals down now. Hey, let's see if we can't pull one up. I'm going to distract the defenders."

"Kire!" shouted Coach. "Just what do you think you're doing having a meeting during the middle of a game?"

Kire continued talking with Andrew. "But we need to get the ball first, so how about you let them play the ball between your legs? I'm sure they won't miss the chance to nutmeg you."

Since Trace and Kaos already knew they were going to win, they decided to spend their energy just trying to embarrass those who came to try out. They would dribble one player until he got too dizzy and fell down. When they got to Andrew, Trace put the ball between his legs, and Kire stepped in to intercept the ball before it got to Kaos. He then drove the ball up the field and bore left.

The defenders on the senior team were laughing at Kire who was trying hard to keep from stepping over the ball and falling. He managed to squeeze a pass between two defenders to Andrew, who had been running alongside him the whole time. When the defenders looked back, they were shocked to see Andrew kicking the ball into their net.

The tryout team all ran to Andrew, cheering and hugging him. Kire rolled his eyes. "Thanks for the appreciation for me doing most of the work, guys," he grumbled.

"Kire! Get over here," said Coach.

"Yes, Coach?" she answered, jogging over to Coach Turner's side.

"I saw how you managed to pull one back for your team. That was impressive, son."

"Thanks," Kire said, panting. "I'm just glad there's no second half."

Coach Turner guffawed. "Soccer is a team sport. You can help make one or two goals, but one man can't be responsible for twenty-one goals."

"Thanks, Coach."

"You should prepare to join the team in training next week."

"Really?" Kire asked in disbelief.

"Really. See you then, kiddo," Coach said, jogging off to talk with some other players.

Even in Kire's excitement, he could see Amberly staring at him from across the field. Chilly fingers squeezed at Kire's heart. Just what had he done to earn such hatred from her?

For the rest of the day, Kire tried his best to avoid his bullies. Even if they had won the game with such an astronomical goal difference, they still resented Kire for pulling one back against them. He could tell from the cold gazes and stares they threw in his direction that they would probably come for him after school. Anxiety filled him for the remainder of the day.

6

When Kire arrived home later that day, he was surprised to see quite a number of people gathered at his neighbor's house. The neighbor's dog, a black Rottweiler with fat brown brows, was tired of barking at the throngs of strangers and sat grudgingly in his cage.

"What's going on at Mr. Burke's?" Kire asked his mom when he got home, pointing a thumb behind him toward the neighbor's house.

She was in the middle of knitting a green sweater when he arrived. It was one of the ways she kept herself busy during the long, lonely days. Every year she knit three sweaters; one for herself, one for Kire, and one for Gerald, even though Gerald would never wear something so *feminine*.

"Mr. Burke went out hunting this morning. I saw him leave, rifle slung over his shoulder, taking that monster of a dog with him. I was out front in the garden and said good morning to him and he just grunted."

"Typical," said Kire.

"But when he returned from hunting, or rather, when he was returned, he was an entirely different person. Gone was the gruff manly man, proud of his gun and his scary dog. He looked terrible, Kire. I've never seen a man so scared. These two men from the forest service brought him home. Apparently, they had to hold him down because he kept trying to run out of his house, still afraid of whatever he'd seen while out hunting."

"Hmm," grunted Kire. "Well, I hope this all keeps that horrible dog occupied for the night. He didn't seem too traumatized when I saw him."

"Kire! Is that all you've got to say on the matter?" Emma cried.

"No, I'm just trying to look at the bright side."

Glancing over at him a bit angrily out of the corner of her eye, Emma continued, "I'm bringing a casserole over to him at six o'clock. I'm hoping that the crowd of gawkers would've dispersed by then. I'd like you to come with me." Emma put a hand to her nose. "Kire, oh my goodness, you smell so bad. I don't think I've ever smelled sweat on you! Go get yourself washed up."

"Yeah, yeah," said Kire, "right after I give you a hug."

"I'll knit your legs together if you get any closer to me, young man!" she said, laughing and leaning away from her son.

Kire took this warning with a good heart and promptly made for his bedroom.

At six o'clock that evening, Kire and Emma set out to visit Mr. Burke with a fresh casserole just out of the oven. Mr. Burke's house was larger than the Hunter household and far messier. The two-story brick house was very symmetrical and had few windows. There was dog poop and trash all over the yard and an old rusty truck with no tires sat beside the house. An abandoned swing set stood in front of the house, swinging eerily whenever the wind blew. The grass was overgrown and there were weeds breaking through the driveway and porch. The light at the front porch kept flickering on and off and made an unsettling buzzing noise. Mr. Burke's dog sat in his cage, eyeing Kire and Emma dangerously.

"Let's keep going, Mom," Kire said, glancing nervously toward the dog.

"You're worried a caged dog will bite you?"

"No, *Mother*, I'm worried the dog's prayers will be answered."

Emma knocked on Mr. Burke's front door with a brass knocker in the shape of a skull. The door opened and a graying old woman with moles scattered over her face entered. Emma flashed her sweet smile and waved. "Hello," she said.

The woman looked blankly at Emma, then glanced over at Kire before looking back at Emma.

Emma held out the casserole. "Uh—" She cleared her throat uncomfortably. "I made this for Mr. Burke."

The old woman widened her eyes in surprise. "You're different from the rest," she said. "The rest just want photos and the story. They think my brother is nuts, but he isn't. He knows what he saw."

"Oh," said Emma, not knowing what else to say. Kire shifted uncomfortably from one foot to the other under the heavy gaze of the old woman.

"I'm Julie," the old woman said after a hefty moment of awkward silence. "Come inside," Julie said, taking the casserole from Emma. "He your gigolo?"

"This is my son!" Emma snapped coldly.

"Easy now," Julie said, "I had one when I was your age, Emma, the same age as yours here." She squinted. "Looked like him, too."

Emma and Kire stepped past Julie and heard the door lock with a click behind them. There was an acrid animal smell in the house, and all of the blinds were shut. There were three couches in the living room arranged to form a U-shape that had all been worn to rags. One glance at those couches and it was clear that there were hundreds—maybe thousands—of blood-sucking bugs hiding in the fabric.

Dirty dishes and half-eaten food piled up in the kitchen, and there were several cats lying in various crooks and corners around the house. Kire nearly stepped into a bowl sitting on the floor of what appeared to be spoiled milk and looked down at his feet to watch where he was walking; he saw a roach scurry by.

He held in his reaction.

Mr. Burke was sitting on one of the couches facing away from the front door wearing a worn-out sweatshirt and old pajama pants. Like his sister, he had gray-blond hair, a long crooked nose, and a tiny frame which seemed odd with his large head.

"Hey, Burke," Julie said from behind Emma and Kire. "Guests brought gifts. Now, you must tell them the story. Take a seat," she said, motioning to the disgusting couches.

Emma and Kire exchanged quick glances before sitting on the far edge of a sofa, touching as little of it as possible.

Mr. Burke grunted.

"Come on, Burke, be nice!" said Julie.

"You tell it. I've told it too many times," growled Mr. Burke. "I'm tired."

"Oh, that's okay," Emma said, starting to stand up. "Don't worry about us."

"Just tell it one last time and I'll never make you tell it again," Julie pleaded.

Mr. Burke shot Emma and Kire a dirty look and Emma sat back down on the couch. He then gave Julie a grimace, who grinned and nodded her head encouragingly. He cleared his throat and began, "This morning, sometime around nine o'clock or so, I took my gun and my dog Murphy and made for the forest to get some game."

"The forest?" asked Kire.

"Yeah, the White Forest—" said Burke.

"You do know that hunting in the White Forest is illegal, right?" said Emma,

"I don't care. The forest is a gift to us mortals."

Kire knew the White Forest very well. St. Bernard was built right at the edge of it, and the administrators tried their very best to keep the students from entering during school hours, but that didn't keep students like Trace and Kaos from doing all sorts of shenanigans in the woods when they should be in class. The forest was densely covered in trees and covered a steep hill that led to the top of a big hill which the locals called Kula Mountain.

"I had been in the forest for about thirty minutes when I saw an animal that looked sort of like an elk, but pure white—bright white. I was quietly watching it, getting ready to shoot, when Murphy ruined it all! He used to be such a fine hunter, but the hunt must have excited him too much this time. He barked at the elk, and it ran away. I tried running after the elk, but those things are fast. I ended up getting lost in the woods after pursuing the elk for an hour. I always know how to find my way home when lost, though. But then the strangest thing happened."

"This is where it gets good," Julie interrupted.

Emma quickly slapped a bug off her dress.

Mr. Burke jumped to his feet. "I saw five bright lights in the air going round in circles," he said, looking up at the ceiling and waving his arms around like a crazy man. "The lights were a dark pink and had some rocks shaped like eggs glowing at the center of them. They floated in the air about four feet off the ground, all in a straight line. When I tried approaching one, there was an earthquake! Apparently, nobody else felt it, though—you guys didn't feel it, did you?

Kire and Emma shook their heads in unison.

"Well, the ground was splitting before my eyes! I must have

been screaming because before I knew it, some park rangers came. They couldn't see what I saw and said they didn't hear or feel anything. Sure enough, everything went back to normal when they came. They took my gun away from me!"

"Hmm," said Kire.

"Well, we must be on our way," Emma said quickly as she rose to her feet. "Thank you for the story, though, Mr. Burke."

"Oh, so soon? We have some milk in the fridge," Julia said enthusiastically.

"Mmm," said Emma, trying not to cringe. "I'm sure it's delicious, but we really must be going."

Emma and Kire hurried out of the house and Emma said, "Throw those clothes away and get in the shower. I'd better not see a bug in this house!" She shuddered.

Dinner in the Hunter household was a silent affair that night. Gerald took a look at his plastic plate and said, "What's this?"

"That," began Emma in a voice that didn't welcome any argument, "is a plate that won't break when you drop it, same with the cups. The only breakable thing here is the ceramic jar."

Gerald broke the jar that night.

7

St. Bernard High was busy as a beehive the next morning, and there were two reasons for the bustle.

The first reason was that in three days, Kaos was having a party at his house for his birthday. Rumor had it that his parents were celebrating their wedding anniversary and would be away traveling for the occasion. This, of course, meant that the entire house was left for Kaos to take over—naturally, this meant that everybody wanted to take advantage of an authority-free house.

The second reason was that Mr. Loch was giving the class a hefty paper to be due in three days—the day of the birthday party. Kire welcomed this as a punishment to Kaos, but Kaos seemed to be unphased.

"How is he going to plan his party if he has to work on Mr. Loch's paper?" Andrew asked Kire during lunch. They'd become good friends since soccer tryouts. Andrew was excited about the party and Kire couldn't care less.

"Kaos is brilliant," Kire admitted, "but I can't see him finishing the paper and planning his party at the same time—Kaos likes to plan his parties."

As they were talking, Trace and Kaos showed up in the cafeteria. After getting their food, Kaos nudged Trace and the latter went some other way while Kaos continued straight toward Kire and Andrew's table.

"Do you think we're in trouble?" Andrew quickly whispered to Kire when he saw Kaos approaching.

"Nuh-uh," Kire said dismissively, "and if we were, you're strong enough to beat him up."

"What?" Andrew said, his eyes bulging. "I can't do that!"

"Dude, I've seen how much you can lift. Kaos can't lift as much as you can."

"Actually, I can," Kaos said, standing right behind Kire. "May I?" He gestured toward the table.

Andrew could only gawk at Kaos.

"If you want," Kire said, returning to his meal.

I want," Kaos replied, taking a seat beside Andrew, opposite Kire. Kaos cleared his throat and said to Andrew, "Would you mind excusing us for a minute? There's something I'd like to tell your friend here."

"He doesn't have to leave; I'll tell him what you said to me anyway," Kire said.

Kaos kept a steady gaze on Andrew, who seemed to keep shrinking with every minute that passed. "Andrew?" he said in a low, menacing voice. "Would you please leave?"

Andrew dropped his spoon on the floor twice and spilled half of his juice on the table before managing to shakily lift his tray off the table.

"Is he always like that?" Kaos asked, smiling faintly.

"No," Kire said firmly. "He's just being ridiculous."

"Is that so," he said, returning his gaze to Kire. "I thought you were great at the soccer tryouts."

"Thank you?" Kire replied, not knowing what to make of this.

"I'll speak to Coach Turner on your behalf. You should be able to get a spot on the team."

"Really?!" Kire asked, excited.

Kaos waved his hand lazily as though it was a done matter already.

"Trace and I can train you on the side as well, help you get on your feet faster," he added.

Kire was taken aback by this, certainly a little suspicious.

"And one more thing," Kaos said. "You know you're invited to my birthday party, right?"

Kire sighed. "What do you want, Kaos?"

The smile on Kaos' face faltered at this question. It was almost as though he wasn't expecting Kire to ask.

Kire leaned forward. "Do you know why I think I can intercept passes on the soccer field?"

"Because you can guess people's intentions by studying their movements."

"Exactly," Kire said. "Same with social interactions; I can sense your intentions by studying your movements. Tell me what you want from me."

Kaos leaned back in his chair and started clapping slowly. The people immediately surrounding Kire and Kaos in the cafeteria went silent and looked at the boys.

"Brilliant... just brilliant. This is why I knew you were the right guy to come meet. This is why I choose you, Kire. You're smart, better than the rest of them. And that's why Trace and I have chosen you for this important assignment."

Kire snorted. "Wait, Kaos," he said. "Please, don't tell me this is about the paper for physics."

Kaos gritted his teeth and forced a smile. "You have shown brilliance once again, Kire. In exchange for that, I've offered you a free ticket to my birthday party, a chance to prove yourself to the school team, and most importantly, Trace and I will—"

"—train me and help me get on my feet?" Kire asked lazily.

"Yes," Kaos said resentfully. "What are you saying now, Kire? Yes or no?"

"No. No, no, never, no. I won't be used by you or Trace."

Kaos smiled darkly and shook his head. "Of all the people in this school, I chose you," he said in a low voice. "And this is your final answer?"

"Yep."

Kaos leaned forward threateningly, narrowing his eyes and seemingly swelling like a frog ready to spit venom.

"You turn me down then? You turn me and Trace down; surely you must know what this means for you?"

Kire's pulse quickened but remained calm from the outside, leaning back lazily in his seat. "What?"

Kaos rose to his feet, a dark smile still plastered on his face. He chuckled and said, "You'll probably come to regret turning me down."

Word about Kire standing up to Kaos spread like wildfire. No one knew what the two boys had discussed, so everyone came up with their own theories.

Andrew approached Kire at his locker after lunch. "Hey, are you all right?" Andrew asked.

Kire glanced at him before returning to fiddle around in his locker.

"If I wasn't, what would you do?" asked Kire. "You abandoned me when Kaos came."

"Not really," said Andrew. "He asked for it politely. And he's frightening."

Kire scoffed. "Just what I thought you would say."

"Look, Kire, this might seem easy for you, but you don't know what I've seen those guys do to some poor kids."

"They're a pair of bluffers, nothing more."

"You saw what Trace did to Alfred!"

"Alfred couldn't handle a few punches."

Andrew scoffed at this. "You really believe it was only a few punches? How do you think the cops were convinced Alfred had actually been attacked?"

"Because he was bruised?"

"Because he was beaten like a bear had attacked him," Andrew said with wild eyes. "Listen to me. You see, Kaos is a talker. But you know what happens? When Kaos' talk fails, Trace comes in, physically."

"You're being paranoid, Andrew," Kire said, closing the door of his locker a bit too hard. His hands were shaking now.

"All right," Andrew said, "but you should be careful. If they ask you to lick their boots, then you get on your knees and lick like a dog."

"Get away from me, Andrew. I have no need for friends who can't face their fears."

While Kire acted brave on the outside, he couldn't stop the fear that was growing inside him. Throughout the rest of the day, anytime he saw Trace, he was staring right at him. There was no doubt Kaos had informed Trace of Kire's refusal to write their papers, and now they were both planning his death.

The rest of the day, Kire was unable to focus on anything any teachers were saying. He could feel his blood pumping through his body and there was a bitter, sinking feeling in his stomach.

When the last bell of the day sounded, Kire jumped to his feet and packed his stuff into his bag. He was trying as hard as possible to avoid any confrontation.

"Hey," a female voice said to him.

Kire jumped and looked up quickly, expecting Amberly's smirking face to meet him, but it was Charlie Rose, an unlikely sight.

"Oh, hey—hi," he said to her, very on edge. "I—uh —what's up?"

"Is it true you defended yourself to Kaos?"

Kire swallowed; just why did her question have to be about this? He returned his attention to his school bag. "Yeah, something like that," he grunted without looking at her.

"That's brave," she said. "I didn't think anyone would ever do it."

"That's because everyone is smarter than me," Kire said. "Only a dimwit turns down a deal with Kaos and Trace."

Rose put a hand on Kire's. His hands were shaking uncontrollably.

"The majority isn't always right," she said. "I think you will be fine."

Kire smiled at her and nodded. "Uh, see you later?"

Rose blushed softly. "See you later."

Today has been a very weird day, Kire admitted, as he started home.

8

____

Kire ended up telling his parents at dinner about what happened today. He was afraid of what his father would say, but he was more afraid of Trace and Kaos.

"See, Emma, you have ruined this boy's life. He can't even handle bullies on his own!"

Kire thought his father was a bully in his own way; maybe he was suffering as a result of the bullying his father had done in his younger days.

Emma panicked and suggested she call the principal.

In response to this, Gerald said, "This boy needs to figure this out for himself, be a man for once! You calling the principal will only make this worse."

Though Kire appreciated his mother's efforts to help him, he slipped out of the dining room quietly as his parents shouted at each other.

Kire woke up early the next morning—far earlier than he's woken up in a while.

"Good morning, Mom," he said to his mother upon entering the kitchen.

"Kire?" she asked in disbelief. "Is this young man who's all ready for school really my son?"

"Ha ha," Kire mockingly laughed. He pulled out a chair from the table and sat on it.

"Did you have a great dream?" Emma asked. "This is totally new."

"I wish I had a great dream," Kire muttered. He dreamt that two boys and a girl were chasing after him with pitchforks. Though he didn't see their faces, he was certain they were Kaos, Trace, and Amberly.

"Whatever Mr. Burke saw in the woods must have really changed him," said Emma. "I greeted him this morning, and you wouldn't believe it, but he actually said good morning when I greeted him."

"I wonder if I can ask Mr. Burke exactly where he saw those five lights. There are some people I know who need a mind-blowing encounter like that."

"Me, too. Do you think it'll stop your father from breaking the dishes?"

"Or make him forget to ask if I have chosen to become a professional soccer player instead of a physicist?"

Kire saw a small booklet on the kitchen counter. It was something that appeared to be about plants, and he immediately thought of Charlie Rose. He felt inclined to give it to her for some reason. "Where did you get this?" he asked.

"Got it in the mail yesterday."

"Do you mind if I take it?"

"Sure..." said Emma, puzzled. "I guess if you want it?"

After a breakfast of scrambled eggs and toast, Kire set off for school. He was afraid if he waited any longer, he would've talked himself into ditching school.

Kaos' car, the car that took himself, Trace, and Amberly to school every day, wasn't in the lot when Kire arrived. He did, however, spot Charlie Rose heading toward the greenhouse, probably to check on the bloodsucking Edax Animaes.

"Hey, Charlie—uh, Rose," he called after her.

She wore a flowing green dress and had her hair in a long braid with a few flowers woven into it and Kire couldn't help noticing her quiet and serene beauty.

"Good morning, Kire," she said, flashing one of her rare smiles.

"Hey," he said breathlessly. "I brought this for you." He handed the booklet from home to her.

"An ethereal flower?" she asked, looking at the booklet.

Kire nervously scratched the back of his neck. "I just thought you might like it, but it's okay if you don't."

"Oh, it's—it's all right."

"Uh, okay, so, later then?"

"Later then."

Kire arrived in his first classroom of the day and sat there alone, having arrived so early. His mind raced with thoughts of how foolish he just looked in front of Rose, as well as worries about Trace, Kaos, and Amberly.

After about ten minutes, students began pouring in and the room got really loud. Trace and Kaos arrived after most of the other students had arrived, and a sudden hush swept around the class. They walked up to where Kire was seated and looked down at him. Kire returned Trace's cold glare with a bored glance and Kaos gave an evil grin.

"How are you today, Kire?" Kaos asked. It's important to note that neither held a pitchfork or any likeness of it in their hand.

"I'm fine, fit as a fiddle," Kire said, raising a corner of his mouth.

"We should all do well to keep healthy and out of trouble, which can be done by *pleasing* certain *people*," said Kaos. "Take, for example, a former classmate of ours, Alfred. Andrew saw him once after he left the school. Right? Andrew, how many teeth were Alfred missing?"

"Uh—I-I think five," Andrew muttered shakily.

The class gasped.

"You hear that, people? He was missing five teeth. And that —" He let his voice drop. "—is why we're offering everyone a chance to keep their teeth intact."

"Since when did you become a dentist?" Mrs. Goody said when she walked into the classroom.

"Good morning, Mrs. Goody," Kaos answered while Trace marched off to his seat. Kaos then grabbed Kire by the shoulder and gave it a squeeze. "You know where to find me, Kire," he said, "and I sure hope that you change your mind soon enough. Time is running out."

"Who died?" Mrs. Goody said with a frown. "Why is the class as sober as a graveyard? You all aren't usually like this, though I wish you were."

Kire disagreed. If he had to go through this much stress every day, he wasn't sure how long he was going to last. Nevertheless, he wished the class would never end and that he could be under Mrs. Goody's protection forever.

In the hallways, everyone who walked by Kire gave him a look of pity, as though he had just been sentenced to death. At lunch, while eating with Andrew, slender hands with red nails slid a note on their table. He glanced up and saw Amberly McHenry smiling at him.

"Word from Trace," she said, spinning around and waltzing away.

Once again, every pair of eyes in the cafeteria were on Kire. Kire glared around before picking up the note and reading it.

"What does it say?" asked Andrew.

Kire crumpled the note and threw it away, drawing gasps from those who had expected him to burst into tears and cry for mercy.

"What does it matter to you?" Kire spat. "You're just going to run away anyway."

"I know you think I'm a coward."

"I know you're a coward."

Andrew sighed and looked down at his tray.

"Listen, Kire," Andrew said after a while. "When I was in elementary school, there was this kid, Billy, who would always beat me up after school. My mom used to pack these cookies for me every day, and every day, Billy would beat me and take my cookies from me. Then one day, I tried to stand up to Billy and we fought, and he beat me up as usual. I stood up to him again the next day and he beat me up and took my cookies. This continued for a while. He only stopped beating me up when he left the school."

"What's your point?" asked Kire impatiently.

"Listen, some bullies are there and there's nothing you can do to stop them," said Andrew. "Kicking against them is like striking a rock with your foot; only you will get hurt. There's nothing we can do about them."

"Really?" Kire asked coldly.

"Kire..." Andrew called when he saw Kire rise to his feet. "Where are you going?"

"Away from you!" Kire said harshly.

"See, everyone knows this is a lost cause, Kire; just give it up already."

"'Observe the masses, and do the opposite'—James Caan," Kire loudly replied.

9

He didn't go to class when he left Andrew in the cafeteria; instead, he went to the greenhouse. Ever since the Edax Animae incident last time, most students had been avoiding it as much as possible. Kire was expecting to be alone in the greenhouse, with the only other living things being various annual and perennial beddings, as well as plants with strange flowers of varying colors and sizes, cacti, and herbs. The place was *hot*, being made to simulate the more tropical climate most of these plants preferred. All of the Edax Animaes were cleared from the house but one. Kire saw he wasn't alone—Rose was leaning over the remaining Edax Animae.

"Kire?" she said, hearing his footsteps.

Kire dug his hands into his pockets. "Rose..."

She rose to her feet slowly. "I haven't seen you here, I mean —when there's no class, no one ever comes here."

Kire wiped the sweat off his face. "And for a good reason. It's hot in here!"

"Let's go outside then!" Rose said.

"Did you find the booklet useful?" Kire asked. They made their way to a long concrete bench just outside the greenhouse that had rose bushes of various colors growing all around it.

"It's about flowers that were last seen some two hundred years ago."

"Tell me about it," Kire asked, trying to keep the conversation going to keep his mind occupied. Also, he wanted to hear Rose's soft voice some more. It calmed him down and made him feel more at peace.

"The author believes the energy spike detected earlier this week had some effect on our ecology and that those effects were last seen two hundred years ago after a similar energy spike occurred."

"Is he trying to say some plants require that energy to live?"

"Not just plants, but animals too," said Rose. "People actually reported seeing unreal animals in the forest where the five comets were projected to fall. Although there hasn't been any concrete evidence."

"And... you know this... how?" asked Kire.

Rose shrugged. "I came across something on the internet. It must have been a big deal, right?"

"Right."

"I'm going to wait until school is over and then try to see if I can't find one of these animals in the White Garden."

"White Forest," Kire corrected. "A forest is a dense uncultivated tract of trees and undergrowth, larger than woods, and that just about describes it."

"That must be exactly how 'forest' is defined in the dictionary," Rose said, laughing.

"Oh, I know," Kire said, "and I'm glad you know, too."

"A forest is just an overgrown garden."

"Just because it has plants?" Kire said. "It's dangerous, don't go."

Rose snorted. "It's you who's in danger," she said, "you've got some people who want to kill you."

Kire sighed. "Maybe I should've just listened to them; done what they wanted when they asked for it, pretended I didn't see through Kaos' attempt to hoodwink me."

"It doesn't matter now, does it? They'll never forgive you for standing up to Kaos."

"Looks like I'm trapped then."

Just then, the bell for the next class rang and Kire went to class alone, feeling calmer than he'd felt in days. He felt a lot safer in Rose's company than he felt in Andrew's.

The rest of the day drained away slowly like smooth grains of an hourglass sifting from one hold to another. There was an impromptu test that afternoon in biology, and Kire couldn't help thinking he was being set up for failure based on how the test was written.

Finally, the last bell of the day rang, and the students surged out of their classes as though trying to run away from a fire. Kire didn't bother looking back to see if his nemesis was leering at him from behind. He threw his books into his bag, including the test he took and somehow forgot to submit, and started slowly down the hall toward the exit, dreading the walk home. As he walked by Mrs. Goody's classroom, he heard someone bark his name. He stepped reluctantly into her classroom.

"Y-yes, ma'am?"

"How are you doing, kid?" she asked as she packed up her bag. "Seemed like Trace and Kaos were bugging you this morning."

Kire chuckled nervously and said, "Oh, that. You know... it's whatever."

Kire lingered in Mrs. Goody's classroom for a few moments before she said, "Is there something I can help you with?"

"No, ma'am," he said, looking down at the floor. "I just don't want to go home."

"So, you'd rather stay at school?"

He nodded quickly.

"Hmm, I've never heard a kid say they'd rather stay at *school*." She paused for a moment before saying, "How about you walk me home? I live close and we can chat some more if you'd like."

"Yes, please! I'd love to walk you home!" he said, perhaps a bit too enthusiastically.

Mrs. Goody looked at her student with a bit of suspicion but led him out of the classroom anyway.

Mrs. Goody's place wasn't at all far from school. Even at her slow pace, it was only a ten-minute walk. It was in the opposite direction from his home, however, defeating his plan of having someone escort him part of the way home.

"Are your folks at home treating you well?" Mrs. Goody asked.

Kire shrugged. "Mom is so nice to me; frankly, she's the only one who cares much about me. Dad is just the opposite. He doesn't care about what I want or like; he just wants me to join a sports team and go pro, even if I don't want to. Last semester, I found out I was at the top of my class. Dad told me that meant nothing unless I won an award or something."

Kire hadn't expected to say so much, but somehow his words spiraled out of his control, and he kept on talking. "I'm-I-I'm sorry," he muttered. "I'm just a lousy kid, I know. Dad tells me that every day..."

"Oh, come on, it's all right..." Mrs. Goody said. "Those words would've eaten you up from the inside if you didn't let them out."

"Yeah?"

"Of course, kid. Listen, you can always come to me if you

need to talk about something again. It sounds like you have a lot going on."

"Thanks, Mrs. Goody," said Kire.

"Now, you be sure to go directly home, you hear?"

While walking home, he successfully passed the front of the school without incident, but just as he reached the end of the school's property line, he saw someone running toward him at full speed.

10

K ire prepared himself to run in the opposite direction until he saw that it was just Andrew running toward him.

"Why are you running like there's an angry mob after you?" Kire asked as Andrew approached him.

"There's an angry mob coming after *you*!" Andrew said, pale and terrified.

Panic set into Kire's stomach and his brain was working so quickly it felt like it would shut down. Did Trace and Kaos go hire people to get him? What mob was Andrew talking about?

"Kaos and Trace were hot after me," Andrew panted. "They thought you sent me to see if they were lying in wait."

Kire's mind was racing, and his heart was pounding. He wished he could just go home and go to bed and pretend he was safe.

"You know what we've got to do now?" Andrew said.

"We? Who's 'we'?" Kire asked.

"Kire, there's no way I'm leaving you with those two bullies out there. They're waiting for you, and who knows what they'll do when they catch you."

"I'll cry out for help when they catch me," Kire said desperately.

"I doubt anyone would hear you; it's kind of deserted down here. Anyway, if anyone heard you, they'd probably think it was just kids playing around."

"Fine, what should I do then?"

"Oh!" exclaimed Andrew. "How about we hide in White Forest for a bit? They'll quit looking for you eventually."

Kire nodded his head quickly. "Sounds like a plan," he said, "and thank you so much; I don't know what I'd do without you."

Andrew just shrugged and kicked at a rock. Both boys then set off into the forest just behind the school together. Andrew led the way while Kire followed closely behind. They cut through bushes and briers, going deeper and deeper into the forest until dense foliage and huge trees surrounded them.

"Wait!" Kire called and paused to catch his breath. He leaned against a hemlock and sank slowly to the ground. How could he have forgotten Trace and Kaos had a shack for their misdeeds somewhere in the forest?

"Wh—what I—is it?" asked Andrew, leaning over with his hands on his knees.

Andrew wasn't leading him away from Trace and Kaos; he was leading him right up to them—right to their shack.

"Kire? Wh—what is it?"

Kire pushed himself back up. If he turned back now, he could be safe. Trace and Kaos were probably counting on Andrew to lure him to their covert base. He didn't bother trying to explain before turning around and preparing to run in the opposite direction. As he turned around, he saw Trace and Kaos standing right behind him.

"It's a little too late for an escape now, is it?" Kaos said, sniggering.

Kire shot an angry look at Andrew. "You're a coward

through and through, aren't you?" Kire spat at Andrew. "You licked their shoes, right? Wasn't that what you said to me? Tell me, Andrew, did you do their laundry as well?"

"Andrew did us a great service, Kire," said Trace, "and he'll be rewarded, all while you're stuck in a coma at the hospital for the next several weeks."

"You must think you scare me," Kire said, shoving away his fears and summoning all of his bravery.

"You can go, Andrew," Kaos said. "And remember, no one is to hear of this—*ever*." Trace and Kaos looked at Andrew menacingly before Andrew nodded his head nervously, turned around, and sprinted out of the forest.

Kaos and Trace walked toward Kire, who stood his ground, a scowl on his face.

"Look who we have here," someone said behind him.

He turned around to find Amberly looking as beautiful and terrifying as ever. She had her long blonde hair up in a tight ponytail and she held her arms out as if to tell Kire he was surrounded and shouldn't attempt to try anything funny.

"Oh, she came for the party, too?" Kire teased.

This angered Amberly, so she turned to Trace and hissed, "Get him to shut up! Go on and do something to him!"

"Shut up, Kire," Trace snapped.

"You should've brought the whip like I asked you to," she said grudgingly to Trace.

Trace walked over and kissed her. "Kaos wants to talk to him first; if that fails, I'll come in."

Amberly giggled.

Kaos looked irritated. "How many times do I have to tell you, Trace? If you come in, you'll put him in the hospital! How's he going to write our physics papers then?"

Trace glowered at Kaos. "Fine, but if you ask me, he doesn't look like he's gonna budge unless we break a few bones."

"I'll be the judge of that," Kaos snapped. He then faced Kire and flashed his evil grin. "It didn't have to come to this," he said, "and it doesn't have to go beyond this."

"If I wrote your paper, that would be cheating," Kire said through gritted teeth.

"Who cares? No one is going to know."

"Why can't you make Trace write it? He's kind of smart for a bully. Is he even trying to help you here at all?" Kire said, hoping Kaos would turn his anger toward Trace, and he would have a chance to escape.

"Trace is busy, Kire," Kaos said.

"Then you will have to retake the class," Kire said, shrugging. "Too bad."

"That, Kire, is where you come in. I don't want to retake the class."

"Why does it have to be me? Why not anyone else?"

Kaos laughed. "Because the whole school knows we asked you to write our term paper for us and you turned us down. In case you didn't know, we're kings at St. Bernard, and kings have an image to protect."

"That's why? Ego? That's why you're doing all of this?"

"Don't waste our time, Kire. What's your answer?"

Kire looked from Trace to Kaos and back. "How about I tell Trace my demands?" Kire said.

"Demands?" asked Trace in disbelief. "Who said you could make demands?"

"Oh, Kaos, let Trace step in. You've had your chance already," spat Amberly.

"Enough," Kaos barked. "Come on, Trace, I always back down when you ask me to. You should do the same for me. And, Amberly, *stop talking*."

Trace cracked his knuckles and approached Kire. "What do you want?" he asked.

"Come closer," Kire said, "take one more step."

Trace growled angrily but did as he was told.

"Now, take this!" Kire threw a punch straight at Trace and hit him squarely on the nose.

Kire tossed his backpack aside and bolted into the forest. It took Kaos and his unfriendly company a little while to recover from the shock Kire's sucker punch brought. Kire heard Trace roar about how he was going to kill him.

11

Kire ran past towering Sequoia trees with dense leaves that shaded the forest from the sun overhead, making the forest dark, humid, and uncomfortably cold. As he ran, he felt like his lungs were about to explode, but perhaps his body was waiting to fail him just as the thumping getting closer and closer finally closed in on him.

When the chase first started, taking in long breaths and then holding them in proved to be the best breathing strategy, but it no longer mattered whether he held his breath in his belly or exhaled until his soul escaped through his nostrils; every single breath of air he took in left a trail of fire burning in his throat down to his chest and belly.

He leaped over giant roots sticking up out of the ground and fallen branches the size of trees. The smell of rot and moisture hung thick in the air like fog on a misty morning. Somewhere in the distance, he could hear a gurgling sound of a stream merging with the river. The forest was treacherous territory—twice he slipped on rocks covered with moss, leaving him covered in mud.

Another fallen branch presented itself before Kire and he

leaped over it, landing on a carpet of dead leaves. This felt like a game of Temple Run or Danger Surf, except not fun and full of dread because if he died, he couldn't respawn. It was he himself, Kire Hunter, who would be killed. Kire's surname was Hunter, but today he ironically found himself as the prey fleeing with its tail between its legs.

St. Bernard High School's two apex predators, Kaos and Trace, were two of the beings chasing after Kire, and who could forget Trace's girlfriend Amberly McHenry, who was the special angel sent to Kire from the darkest pits of hell. Kire would never understand why she was always out to get him, just to make his life as miserable as can be.

Kire fell again after running into a clump of moss and ferns hanging from some hemlocks. "Ugh, how do I get out of here," moaned Kire. "Oh! I can call for help." He felt around all of his pockets, searching for his phone before groaning in disappointment. He then remembered when he punched Trace Henderson in the face earlier, he quickly threw his backpack aside and started running—the backpack, of course, had his phone in it.

A little too late, Kire noticed a very familiar girl bending over something. Before he could stop himself, he smashed into what looked like a pot, but pots don't break to pieces, do they?

He muttered hurried apologies and scurried to his feet just as Trace boomed out in that rich bass voice of his.

"There he is!" the tyrant called happily. "We have to get him! I can almost taste him!"

Trace's words "taste him" filled Kire's weary legs with adrenaline and he found himself picking up the speed he didn't know he had in him. How could Trace say, "I can almost taste him," as though Kire was a warthog being chased by a pack of coyotes?

The thumping of the trio's feet drummed a scary echo through the forest and Kire thought someone had joined;

when he risked a glance over his shoulder, he saw that someone *had* joined the pursuing party. He scoffed in disbelief.

"Kire, if you stop right now, I promise I won't lay a hand on you," someone called. It was Kaos.

"That's right, Kire," Trace bellowed behind him. "You'll only lose an eye for that sucker punch you threw at me!"

"Oh, stop talking," Kaos snapped at Trace. "You're good at using everything but your brain. Don't you think luring him over beats the chase?!" he exclaimed.

Kire scoffed; fat chance he would stop at Kaos' request. That kid was as sly as a snake and as cunning as a fox.

"I got him!"

Kire's eyes were bulging as Amberly came straight at him from out of nowhere.

"No!" Kire yelled as Amberly crashed into him, bringing them both down into the gorge. The last thing Kire thought of as the world of green leaves and black rotting wood swirled in his eyes was his mother smiling in the kitchen—then the day snapped into darkness.

KIRE COULD HEAR Trace yelling Amberly's name once they had landed at the bottom. He managed to gain his bearings and saw Amberly a couple of feet away from him, unconscious. Kire didn't understand how he was conscious, but he guessed that the unreal amount of adrenaline pumping through him had something to do with it. He staggered to his feet and trudged forward, wondering how long he had been in the forest so far—his mother must be worried by now.

If he could just escape before Trace and Kaos found him, then he—

His thoughts were interrupted as he heard leaves rustling.

When he looked up, he saw Trace and Kaos sliding down the gorge, headed straight for him.

"Do these guys ever give up?" Kire groaned. He started running again and then he felt someone grab him by the arm and pull him aside.

"Please don't hurt me," Kire said quickly, shutting his eyes tightly.

"I should kill you for cracking my flower pot!" the female voice said.

Kire looked up, and when he saw who it was, he brought her into a tight embrace without thinking. At first, he felt Rose stiffen her body in his embrace before relaxing and rubbing his back.

"It's all right," she said. "You're safe now. Let's get you out of here. Come with me."

"Kaos! Come here, I found him!"

"How do they keep finding me?" Kire said in panicked disbelief.

Rose groaned, grabbed him by the hand, and started sprinting.

"Where are we going?" Kire asked.

"Somewhere safe," Rose replied, brown hair flying behind her like a flag in the wind.

Kire didn't ask any more questions; rather, he couldn't help focusing on the pain in his chest. He was certain he broke a bone when he barreled down the gorge.

"Are you all right?" Rose asked, still running.

"No, how much further?"

"We're almost there," she said.

Kire glanced behind him and saw Trace and Kaos running at full speed, along with a somehow conscious Amberly.

"In here!" Rose cried, dragging him into an opening in the side of a rocky hill.

They walked into the darkness for a while in silence.

Though Kire couldn't see anything, he knew they were in one of the many caves that littered the White Forest. The inside was cold and reeked of mold, and he could hear water rushing, trickling, and dripping. After walking for a bit, his eyes were finally beginning to adjust to the darkness when he stepped into a hole.

"I'm falling!"

"No, you're not. That hole is only a foot deep; I measured it once."

He didn't fall as Rose had said, but his pant leg was now soaked up to the knee.

"How did you know about this place?" he asked after they resumed their walking.

"I grow ivy here."

"Doesn't ivy need sunlight to grow? I don't see any sun here, Rose."

"There's a part of the cave that has a small hole in the ceiling that allows enough sunlight in. That's where I'm taking you."

Suddenly, they heard footsteps behind them.

"How did they find us?" Rose whispered.

"We should hurry. I'm certain they came with their phones," replied Kire.

"There's no reception here."

"They don't need reception," Kire hissed. "They need lights. Don't you have your phone with you?"

"No, I left it with the flower pot."

"Really?" Kire said sarcastically. "I hope it's charged, so your flower can dial 911."

"Shut up."

They moved in silence for a while, and Kire strained his ears for any sound behind him.

"They're still following," Rose said flatly. "I hope we can lose them in one of these chambers."

The cave began to light up gradually. Littered all across the walls were tiny dots of green, red, and yellow lights of all sorts. It was as though they were looking up at the Milky Way, except they were inside of it, completely surrounded by thousands of colorful celestial bodies.

"Bioluminescent algae," Kire noted.

"Yeah," Rose said, "I brought them here to make it less dark."

"They're beautiful," Kire said, amazed.

The cave had many chambers; every time they passed by one, a cold waft of air would blow, sending shivers all through them.

"Come here," Rose held Kire's hand and led him into one of the chambers.

"Wow," he remarked when he saw it.

A small hole overhead allowed some sunlight into the chamber. Kire was certain Rose had to cut the branches of the trees above the cave to let this light in. How did she feel, hurting one plant for another? The sunlight fell on a table covered in flowers right in the middle of the chamber.

"Is this your project?" asked Kire, walking around the table.

"Yeah," she said. "I started it a year ago."

In the dimly lit chamber, Kire could see nettles, spider plants, snake plants, and other low-light plants in the cave.

"I'm sorry I have to ruin this sweet moment," an unmistakable baritone said sarcastically.

Kire and Rose swiveled immediately, finding Kaos, Trace, and Amberly standing at the mouth of the chamber.

"Hello, Kire," said Amberly. "I see you got yourself a girlfriend. Poor thing."

They walked slowly toward Kire and Rose, the latter taking a step back.

"Poor Rose? Poor Trace, having to have you as a girlfriend," said Kire.

"What did you say?!" Trace bellowed. His hands were already clenched in a fist.

"Calm down, Trace," said Kaos, standing before Trace to keep him from lunging at Kire. "Do you want to go to jail?"

"We're not *killing* him. Trace is just going to teach a certain kid not to run his mouth," Amberly said.

"Amberly, how about you quit running your mouth? You seem to be intent on—"

He was interrupted by Trace yelling, "It's caving in on us!"

"What is happening?!" Rose asked, panicking.

"THE CAVE IS CAVING IN!" Trace boomed at her.

They all threw themselves on the ground and covered their heads with their hands as the tremor became more violent.

"This isn't how I planned to die," whimpered Kaos, on the verge of tears.

The hole in the cave's ceiling somehow closed. They were left in complete darkness again. They all screamed as the quaking shook the cave with renewed intensity. Nobody could see anything, and the only sound anybody could hear were the screams of the person next to them and the low grumble of the Earth. The rocky ground they flattened themselves against moved under their bodies like waves in the ocean.

And then, just as suddenly as it started, the quaking stopped altogether, and a dark silence fell on them all. The hole overhead that had been shut off was opened again. Nothing in the cave showed any sign that an earthquake had just happened, save for the five frightened kids in the chamber. Kire tentatively raised his head off of the floor, looking around to see the rest still flattened against the floor like hostages in a bank robbery.

"Uh, do you guys mind if we kill each other outside? I don't want to get trapped in here," said Kire.

"Run!" Kaos yelled.

All at once, as though they were snapped out of hypnosis,

the five of them jumped to their feet and began scampering out of the cave. Trace turned on his phone's flashlight so they could see in the dark cave. His was the only source of light they had, as Amberly's phone had been lost during her tumble down the gorge and Kaos' phone broke in the chaos of the earthquake. As they stumbled their way around the cave, Amberly kept barking conflicting orders like, "Trace, wait for me!" and "Oh, hurry out of my way now!"

When they reached the spread of bioluminescent algae, Kire felt relief flood through him, knowing they were nearing the entrance. But when they reached the entrance, it was no longer there.

"Wait, the cave had an entrance, right?" asked Kaos when they arrived at a wall of rocks instead of an opening to the world outside. "Someone, please answer me. There was an opening wide enough for a full-grown elephant here. Where is it?!"

"Well, I guess this beats being crushed to death by rocks," Kire said.

"I'd choose getting crushed to death anytime," Amberly said darkly. "Beats dying of hunger or thirst."

"She has a point," Rose conceded. "Getting crushed is faster."

"Have you all gone mad?! I have to get back to my mother! I have to!" Trace yelled at them all. "She can't survive without me!

"Fine!" said Kire. "Let's try to push our way out. Since there was an earthquake, I figure the rocks must have just fallen over the entrance."

Trace brought his phone closer, so Kire could better examine the blockade before them.

"Oh my goodness..." Kire murmured when he saw what they were dealing with.

"What? What is it?" asked Kaos, nearing hysterics.

"What is it, Kire?" Rose asked.

"Whatever is blocking the entrance didn't crumble from the top; it grew over the entrance of the cave," Kire said breathlessly.

"Can you, like, restate what you just said?" Trace said. "Please don't say we're stuck in here forever."

"Well, we're eternally stuck in here unless Rose knows another way out."

"There's no other way out," she answered darkly.

"And how can you be so sure?" asked Amberly. The bravado had gone out of her voice; all that was left was the whimper of a girl realizing she was in her tomb, alive.

"Because I searched during my visits here, the other chambers are either too dark or too small," said Rose. "Many don't even allow air inside."

Kire thought about his mother. Would she have the strength to bear his loss? Not to mention that their bodies might never be found at all.

"I wish I came with extra bones," Rose said.

"Why? You would've dug your way out with one?" asked Trace.

"No, but I'd have loved to give the archeologists something to brood over."

"Ha!" Trace scoffed. "Very funny, but I'm not dying here. I've got to get out."

"And see your mom? We get it," Amberly snapped.

Trace's phone began to vibrate and the screen glitched like a TV without a signal. Kaos was the first to notice Trace struggling with his phone, their only source of light.

"Trace, why is your phone acting weird?" Kaos whimpered.

Trace held up the screen in response; it was flashing pink, green, blue, and yellow at once.

"That's creepy. I've never seen a phone act like that," Amberly remarked.

Then, the phone went black and wouldn't turn back on, leaving the five of them in abject darkness.

"Trace, what spirit possessed your phone?!" Amberly shrieked at him.

"I don't know... wait... did you hear that?" Trace said.

They all fell silent. They could hear the soft rustle of something approaching from the opposite end of the corridor.

12

"**D**on't you try to play a prank on me, Kire," Kaos said, eyes welling up with tears. "I'll kill you. I'll break your spine and crack your sku—"

"Wh-what is that?" Amberly whimpered. Emerging from the end of the dark corridor they were in was a pink glow of light.

"Hey, guys, that light is coming towards us," Trace said, pointing at the pink glow inching towards them. The glow lit up the darkness like a signal flare shot into the sky; though they couldn't see the source of the light, the glow grew more intense with each passing second.

"Hey, Kire, you're the smart one. What is it?" asked Trace.

"I don't know, you tell me," said Kire.

They all stood in panicked silence for a few moments before Kire said, "My candid advice to you all is to go headfirst."

The other four glanced at each other in the faint pink light.

"What do you mean, headfirst?" Amberly whimpered.

Kire chuckled. "Lava is usually pretty hot so—"

Amberly and Kaos interrupted him with screams and shrieks.

"Why are you guys screaming?" asked Kire, as though he didn't just tell everyone they were going to be burned to death by molten rocks.

"Kire, don't be insensitive," Rose murmured.

"Nothing I say to these three can be called insensitive. They were going to knock my teeth out just an hour ago."

"I told Trace, 'no tooth'!" Kaos cried out in his defense.

Kire scoffed. "How reassuring; break all his bones but spare his teeth."

Suddenly, the source of the light emerged from around the bend at the far end of the corridor; five dragon egg-like objects were burning with a fiery pink light.

"Oh, thank goodness." Rose exhaled softly. "That," she said, "isn't lava."

"No kidding, lava doesn't float in the air, and they certainly don't look like elephant eggs," Trace said.

"Elephants don't lay eggs," said Rose. "They're mammals."

"I know," Trace said hotly. "But if they did lay eggs, they would be that large. And why do they keep approaching us? Why are they moving toward us?"

"Relax, Trace," said Kire, "they'll be here soon enough; you can ask them then."

The eggs kept approaching slowly, floating midair like five comets stranded in space, only they had direction and seemed to be self-aware. They floated side-by-side a few feet above the ground and glowed a bright neon hot pink. By the time the five rock-eggs got within a few feet of them, Kire was pressed firmly against the sealed entrance behind him.

Trace was trying hard to push the rock out of his way. Amberly curled up like a ball against the wall. She was sobbing so violently it was almost as though the tremor from earlier had resumed in her body. Everyone was trying to stay as far away from the eggs as possible—who knows what would happen if they touched the eggs.

Would the eggs attack? Would a monster be born from an egg?

Suddenly, the eggs stopped moving forward and began descending to the floor. The dark pink glow around them increased to such blinding intensity—an almost white-pink. When the five eggs settled on the floor side-by-side in a straight line, the pink glow dimmed so that only the eggs themselves were barely glowing dark pink, but they weren't casting a halo around themselves like before.

"Okay, that's creepy," Trace said in the darkness.

"Maybe they ran out of battery?" Kire suggested.

"Eggs don't run out of battery, stupid," Amberly said between sobs.

"Eggs don't fly like space drones, *stupid*," Kire returned.

A loud hissing sound filled the air, and everyone went silent again. Then each of the eggs split in half and opened like jaws of some sort. Their insides shone a bright, cold blue light. Hovering above the blue light from each egg was a black object of no definite shape because it kept changing and flowing like water in a zero-gravity setting. The black walls of the cave and the five students in it were illuminated by the bright blue light shining from inside the eggs.

"I think," said Kaos, "that we have been sucked into a video game."

"What does it matter?" cried Amberly. "We're still going to die anyway."

Kire took a step forward toward the eggs.

"Kire, you really think you have an extra life?" asked Kaos.

Kire, however, wasn't listening to them anymore. He continued to approach the eggs, searching for any suspicious activity—anything more suspicious than what was currently happening.

"Kire, don't touch it!" Amberly warned. Kire had been reaching for the object hanging over the center egg.

He straightened up and turned around to face her. "Or what?" he asked.

"Fine, die if you want."

He rolled his eyes and resumed his investigation.

"Do you think he's going to vaporize?" Trace whispered to Rose.

Kire grabbed the shapeless, formless object and pulled it away from the egg; the blue light of the egg went out, but the remaining four eggs still glowed. It felt just like he imagined it would—very squishy and gooey but not sticky. It really didn't have any weight and was a bit warm to the touch. He closed his hand around the blob and then slowly opened it back up. Before his eyes, the blob transformed into a book. The book was as small as a diary and looked at least 200 years old. It had a smooth thick hazel-brown leather cover with symbols that looked like hieroglyphs on them. Two leather straps bound the book together.

"A... book?" murmured Kire.

Trace, Kaos, and Rose inched reluctantly towards Kire. Amberly remained curled up against the entrance. Rose put a hand on his shoulder and said, "Open it."

Kire nodded, undid the straps, and opened the book—it glowed a brilliant, cold white light and there were golden lines on the pages. The pages of the book were worn and torn around the edges—and also lacked any content.

"There's nothing written," Kire said, disappointed.

"Grab another egg," Kaos said. "Let's see if there's a pen or something."

"Or a pair of glasses to see the hidden words of the book," Trace said, snorting.

"Or a pencil," Amberly added quickly, but her response drew no laughter from the rest.

Kire stared at the luminous white pages of the book and turned to another page, but it was all the same bright blank white pages with thick golden lines. He went back to the first page again; maybe he had missed something like an instruction revealing how the book worked.

Upon going back to the first page, he found a note written over four lines and in a language similar to the one on the cover. The words burned like bright gold flames and a golden ray of light wove in and out of the underlying pages.

The book had come alive.

"Wait! It's... it's not blank," Kire announced.

The rest of the group, besides Amberly, rushed toward him.

"Wow," Trace said. The bright light from the book reflected itself in his pupils. "Is that Sumeric?"

"Or Akkadian," suggested Kaos. "Maybe it's Coptic."

Kire looked from Kaos to Trace with a look of perplexity on his face. He glanced at the open book in his hands and looked back at them. "What are you guys saying? Did a rock drop on your heads or something?" asked Kire. "This is English... maybe a little bit old-fashioned... but it's English."

Trace and Kaos frowned and looked at the book again.

"Fine," Trace snapped. "You tell us what's written in the book, know-it-all!"

Kire turned to face Rose. "You can read it, right?" he asked her.

He wasn't expecting to find the crestfallen look on her face. She didn't say anything; rather, she looked at him with furrowed eyebrows.

"How about you tell us what's written in the book?" said Rose.

"That's a brilliant idea, Charlie Rose, the invisible. I didn't think you could come up with one," Kaos said.

Kire was about to say something nasty to Kaos, but then Rose spoke for herself. "Let's face it, Kaos," she said calmly. "You haven't been thinking at all these days."

Kaos looked furious.

"I like a girl who can defend herself," Trace remarked. "Go on and read the book, Kire. Bury my friend's shame with your revelation."

Kire cleared his throat. "Okay, it says:

"He who finds me first shall I serve,
He shall be my master, and I, his sword,
Like my four brothers, even I have come,
To stop the enemy seeking to cut the world in half."

"And that's pretty much all of it," said Kire when he was done.

"A poem!" Trace boomed crazily. "Just what everybody needs when trapped and dying in a cave! Hey, Kaos, feel like Shakespeare yourself?"

"Yes, my noble friend, thou doth know what occupiest my soul," Kaos said with a bow.

Rose rolled her eyes. Kire ignored the duo and turned to the second page of the book finding something written there now that wasn't there before.

"There's more, guys," he announced, looking back at the group. "Wait... where's Amberly?"

Kaos snorted. "Right there," he said, pointing to where the entrance used to be before it got sealed up. "Oh, wait," he said when he noticed she wasn't there.

"There she is," said Rose, pointing to Amberly, who was reaching for the formless object hovering over one of the eggs like Kire had done when he found the book. Like Kire's egg, the blue light went out immediately when she grabbed the object. She closed her hand around the object and when she slowly opened it back up...

"A glove?" Trace said.

"No," said Rose, hurrying over to Amberly's side. "It's a gauntlet."

The gauntlet was made of tightly linked small brilliant silver metal rings forming a sort of mesh. It had silver nails on the outside and rings of white and silver on all the fingers except the thumb. A thin white plate covered the back of the gauntlet's hand and delicate silver branches decorated it all over.

"I wonder if she can punch her way through the rocks with it," Trace murmured.

Amberly put her hand into the gauntlet, which reached up to her elbow. Silver birds with their wings spread decorated the gauntlet from the wrist upwards. Amberly raised her covered hand with a glint of amusement in her eyes.

Kire began formulating a theory; if he was the only one who could see the writing on the book, then was Amberly the only one who could wear the gauntlet?

"Trace?" Kire called. "How about you take the gauntlet from Amberly and see if you can use it to get us out of here. Maybe it gives some sort of super strength or something."

"Fine idea," Trace said and turned to Amberly. "Bring it, honey, let me have a go at it."

"It's a woman's," Amberly whined as she pulled it off her hand.

"Just hope this does not give super strength, Kire," said Trace as he slid on the gauntlet. "I'll break every single bone in your body." As Trace flexed his fingers, the gauntlet slid off his hand and fell to the ground as though it were too big for him.

"But that thing was almost too tight for Amberly," Kaos noted, puzzled.

Trace picked up the gauntlet and held it up; it still looked small. He had expected it to be so tight that it would constrict blood flow.

"Hand it over to Kaos," he suggested. "Maybe your hands just aren't the right size."

Trace threw a venomous stare at Kire but didn't raise any objection. Kaos put his hand inside to see if it would fit, and as Kire expected, the gauntlet fell to the ground with a splattering sound.

"Ho-ho!" Kire chuckled, excited that he proved his theory to be true. "It looks like the objects can only be owned by one person. Amberly, can you put that on again?"

She did, and when she threw her hands downwards, the gauntlet didn't fall as it did with the others.

"She's the only one who can use the gauntlet, just like I'm the only one who can read the book," Kire explained. "And there are three more objects left. Rose." He smiled down at her. "Wanna pick one? Show these folks strength and bravery is beyond chasing innocent boys into forests."

Kire saw Trace and Kaos stiffen and take a step back. He smiled inwardly, satisfied the bullies had been pushed into a tight, cowardly corner.

Rose bent over an egg; only three were left now. The object hovering in its blue light kept changing shape like some alien, otherworldly substance. She reached and grabbed that form-less object, and like the first two times, the egg's blue light went out. In her hand, the blob transformed into a golden chain with a woven circular pendant with a tree growing inside of it.

Kire smiled. "Fitting," he said. "Here, I'll put it on for you."

"Thank you," she said and gave him the necklace. He then handed the book in his hand to Rose.

Kire stepped behind her and clasped the chain together.

"It's beautiful," he said, looking first at the pendant and then into Rose's eyes.

She nodded shyly and her cheeks flushed a hot pink.

Kire couldn't help noticing how pretty Rose's eyes were in

the dim lighting of the cave. He cleared his throat—much more important things to be worrying about right now.

"Okay, boys," Kire said aloud to Kaos and Trace. "Your turn."

Trace flexed his arms and went to the eggs, looking back and forth before settling for the left egg.

Kire sighed. He couldn't shake the feeling Trace was going to get something terribly destructive. So far, everyone received something that suited their personalities. Rose got a necklace tree pendant, Amberly got a gauntlet—being the strong woman that she was. He, unfortunately, got a book that only he could read and that, if his assumptions were correct, had the power to predict events—events that will happen in the future.

Kire saw Trace bend over the egg and pull the formless object out. And then, right before their eyes, he saw the dark mass in Trace's hand become longer and longer and then burst into bright yellow, orange, and red flames that reached up Trace's arms.

"Your hands are on fire, dude!" Kaos cried.

"I know," Trace replied with surprising calm. "But it doesn't hurt at all."

The object in his hand had transformed into a sword, a flaming sword about two and a half feet long.

"It doesn't burn?" Kaos asked, surprised.

Trace shook his head. He then put a hand on the flaming sheath of his sword. Kire expected him to yelp in pain, but he didn't.

"Can I touch it?" Kaos asked. His eyes were wide with wonder.

"I wouldn't do that if I were you," Kire said. "So far, the items have only worked with those that choose them."

Trace pulled the sword from its sheath. Like its handle, the scabbard was made of smooth wood the color of honey. It had a blade of dull steel that looked like a river snaking its way through a valley. A winged golden dragon sat on the rain guard and extended a wing up to the fuller. The scabbard had an elaborate locket and was covered with engravings.

"Kaos?" said Trace, motioning toward the last egg.

"Okay," Kaos exhaled, rubbing his palms together. "My turn."

"And please," Trace said in an undertone, "don't pull out something stupid."

He went over to the last egg shining blue light and pulled the shapeless object from the air above it. Finally, the last blue light went out, and now the only lights they had were the fire from Trace's sword and the white light from the pages of Kire's book.

Kaos held his object up in the yellow-white light. Slowly, the black mass began to give way to a shiny round object—a delicate gold diadem with a huge emerald embedded in the front.

"Look at that," Trace said, impressed. "You got the top jewel!"

Kire rolled his eyes, finding himself wishing his book was a little more spectacular; of course, Kaos and Trace would both receive something so flashy. Alas! The life of a scholar was cursed to only shine behind the scenes.

The diadem appeared to have been made of braided smooth gold bands with a deep, rich green band running through the braids. In the front, the braids frayed off to create branches that held the huge emerald, which was about three inches tall and an inch and a half wide.

"Of course," said Kaos to Trace. "Should I show them who's king?"

"Yeah!" Trace hollered.

Kaos put the crown on his head and—boom! A blinding flash filled the cave.

Kire covered his ears and fell to his knees; along with the

blinding white light that flashed with the suddenness and intensity of a lightning bolt striking right in front of them, a harsh ringing and screeching sound began to drum in his ears. He squeezed an eye open in that harsh white light and saw that everyone else was on their knees as well.

"Hello, conquerors of planet Earth," a majestic, booming male voice greeted cheerily. "My name is Albus Bridge, and I bridge the gap between Albus and Earth." He was quiet for a moment before saying, "Oh, my apologies. You may rise to your feet. Both the light and the sound are gone."

Kire staggered up and helped Rose, who was still testing the waters, by slowly letting one of the hands covering her ears drop.

"It's safe now, I think," Kire assured her.

"I find it surprising that none of you are applauding, or at least remarking how brilliant the light is. And the music, I had the engineer work on it. Said I wanted brilliant light and super sounds—he added 'sonic' to the music, whatever that meant."

Kire squinted his eyes and rubbed them in disbelief. "Music? That was just ringing and screeching!"

"What are you?!" Trace exclaimed.

"I'm not *what*," said Albus, in a voice of injured pride. He then raised his head haughtily and put a hand to his chest. "I'm a *who!* Albus Bridge at your service."

"No," said Kire stubbornly. "No! 'Whos' don't look like... that." He gestured up and down the visitor.

"Surely, there has got to be something normal about me," Albus said crossly. Floating before them was what looked like a poltergeist, a foggy blue figure of half a humanoid-type figure. He had completely white eyes, a long and narrow nose, and large pointed ears. He had a lot of hair; it was white, curly as a French wig, and nearly ran down to his waist. He was putting on a powdery-blue robe of some sort, but only the flaps of the robe up to his waist and his collar were visible. The rest simply ceased to exist.

"Where's the rest of you?" Trace asked, bewildered.

The lights in the five empty eggs that had gone out were burning bright white now. The jagged walls of the cave were lit better than they ever had been.

"Back home," Albus said in response to Trace's question. "The rest of me is happily at home. In fact, none of me is on planet earth right now. What you see right now is a projection of me. My engineer says it's called 'hologround' in your place. Although, this is more advanced witchcraft because I can touch, and your obsolete 'holograntz' cannot."

"Holo*gram*," Kire corrected and then said. "So, this is just a projection of you?"

"Yes," said Albus. "Now, I haven't come to discuss the mechanics of my planet with you. There is something far graver that you all must know about."

"You're going to tell us about these gifts then?" asked Rose.

"Yes, sweet dear," said Albus, beaming brightly. "I see..." He sailed to her and touched the pendant on her necklace. "You found the Pendantix. It's you who wields Earth elements then."

"Wields Earth elements?" Kire asked.

Albus floated around the space wildly like a punctured balloon. "Let me speak now," he said when he came to a halt. "That is the first warning I won't be here for much longer. Before I tell you what you lot have stumbled on, let me first tell you a story—"

"Wait, why do you say 'stumbled on'? It didn't choose us?" asked Kaos.

Albus chuckled and waved Kaos' words away.

"Kaos," he said. "None of you folks were chosen, and as I said, you all stumbled onto the quintet gifts. Humans have such a shrewd view of things about folks being special. We Albuses don't think so."

"You don't believe certain people are special?" asked Amberly, meekly.

Albus cooed and tutted thoughtfully.

"You punish yourself, my dear. There's no such thing as special. There are only people who choose to be proud of what they have and what they have become. Now, settle down, children; I don't want to be interrupted again," he said, eyeing everyone dangerously.

They fell silent and Albus began his story. "A long, long time ago," he said, "the Albuses and humans shared the same planet. We ate the same food as you, drank the same water, and shared the same culture. The only difference was that we had magic, and you had ingenuity. Humans learned to live without special powers of any sort, which further backs my point; special people are those who choose to be proud of what they have and who they have become.

"Everything was peaceful between us all. We even intermarried, though it didn't always turn out well. But everything was fine and dandy until 'Chaos' came. They sowed the seeds of discord in men, convinced roses to grow thorns, and told lions being vegetarian was boring.

"Chaos is a ship as large as planet Earth. They have one leader, Yash. Don't forget the name Yash. Now, as the 'ash' in his name might have suggested, Yash burned down every planet he ever visited, and now that he was on Earth, he planned to toast us all."

"But you guys had magic!" Kire said before he could stop himself. "Sorry..." he muttered.

"It's all right," said Albus, sighing. "We had magic, but so did Yash and his minions; horrible-looking creatures. An ape would win the beauty pageant against Yash's minions.

"After this came the Great War..."

"World War One?" ventured Trace.

Albus chuckled. "I don't mean to undermine the sacrifices

made by men during that war, but you all could've simply spoken with one another and stopped the war. But you all chose war like you usually do. With Yash, however, you don't choose war; war chooses you.

"Half the men were wiped out in that war, alongside a significant portion of the Albus population. But we managed to repel Yash. I certainly wouldn't say we won the war; we lost far too many people.

"But we knew it wasn't over. If Chaos was a ship, it was bound to return. So, we Albuses traveled to another planet through a small wormhole at the end of your solar system. We decided to stay between Earth and Chaos, so every time Chaos approached, we were able to keep him away from our cousins on Earth."

Trace cleared his throat. "Okay, so what's the essence of the quaintest gifts—"

"*Quintet*," Albus chipped.

"Whatever," Trace fumed. "What's the essence if you guys already beat Yash? You can always stop his ship from coming anyway."

Albus chuckled. "Mothers have babies," he said, "even Chaos has smaller ships the size of a house sufficient for five of Yash's minions."

"Why don't you guys just send soldiers over?" asked Kaos. "Save us all the trouble."

"That's probably because people hate what they don't understand. It would be hard convincing the world that the Albuses are not the enemy," Rose suggested.

Albus clapped his hands together excitedly. "I love it when I get to hear the ideas of women," he said. "Throughout much of history, the men have forced women out of all the conversations. And all the ideas men ever had involved brawn and that's a no-brainer. Men love violence, don't they, Trace?"

Trace snarled and clenched his fists.

"We believe Yash has sent his minions again, and please, do not be fooled when I call them minions. Each one has enough power to wipe out thousands—they're not to be underestimated. It has fallen on you now to save your home, your planet."

"What does Yash want with us?" whimpered Amberly. "Why can't he just leave us alone?"

Albus smiled sadly at her. "Some things don't need reasons to happen," he said. At this, Amberly looked away and seemed as though she might curl into a ball again.

"Yash is one of those things. What were you expecting of a fellow that names his ship Chaos? Were you expecting peace?

"Yash is trying to find another means of reaching Earth. And he has grown desperate enough to try twice in two hundred years, which has led us to believe there's something he specifically wants here. Whatever it is, it cannot be good, and we cannot let him have it."

Albus went berserk again, bouncing off the walls like a ping-pong ball. When he finally came to a halt, he was panting hard.

"That was your last warning," he said frantically. "Now about your gifts. The book," he pointed at the diary in Kire's hand. "Halo. She can predict the future, though I would like to warn you that it is not set in stone. She will also teach you to understand languages; our languages, an important skill in your journey. But most importantly, Halo can generate a force field that acts as a shield, and if the magic is too heavy, as a repellent. A boomerang kind of shield."

Albus smoothed his long white beard and pointed to Rose. "The Pendantix, as I said, allows you to speak to children of earth; plants that you so love, animals you should care for, and on days when darkness rules your heart, your fellow humans will crumble to your will. May that day never come."

"Amberly, you have Gomora in your hand, a gauntlet worth

thousands more than any ordinary pair. Telekinesis is your power, my dear. But I look forward to seeing you move things inside of you." He floated towards her and cupped the side of her face. "There's hate inside of you, Amberly. Move it and be free, don't let Yash's men sniff it out."

To Trace, he said, "You have with you Pentfire. She is a sword that spits fire. Your journey will be one of self-discovery. To control the fire outside, you must first learn to master the raging flame inside of you."

Finally, he turned to Kaos and said, "I hear it has always been your desire to be in charge. Well, good thing you now have a crown that lets you into the mind of others. But you will soon learn that this isn't always as much fun as it seems."

He stretched his arms out wide as though he was going to embrace them all. "The reason why the quintet gifts are here is that there is a contrary energy. The Albuses can help watch the front, but it'll be for nothing if Yash finds a way to go around us. You cannot use your gifts on each other. They do not allow that. As defenders of your world, you must seek unity like never before. Only all of you, not one or four, can face what is to come.

"And Kire? There's more to Halo than telling the future."

Then without warning, Albus went off again, rocketing wildly around like a drunk fly. However, he didn't come to a halt as before. Instead, he sped into oblivion.

Just then, the five rocks from which the quintet gifts had been taken shook before disappearing as well, and the rock that sealed the entrance of the cave crumbled into sand before their eyes and was gone. None of them were as eager to step outside as before; they feared that at any minute, one of the beasts Albus spoke of would pop out of the forest.

After exchanging glances, the five tentatively walked out. Kire exhaled when he stepped out into the fresh, cool, green forest. They heard the chirping of excited birds and busy insects, felt the gentle kiss of the afternoon zephyr wafting over their faces and noticed all the other small miracles they took for granted before. A moment in the cave proved to them how much of life they had missed.

Everyone parted without many words. Rose threw everyone a nervous wave and disappeared into the forest. Kaos went for his car with Trace following behind. "Amberly, don't you want a ride?" Trace asked.

"No," she said, "I want to walk home."

Trace just shrugged and kept walking with Kaos.

Turns out Kire and Amberly's houses were in the same direction, so they had a bit of walking to do together.

"Hey," Kire said softly. It was hard to say if Amberly had become more approachable after that ordeal—he hoped so.

"Yeah?" she replied.

Kire swallowed. He looked around as they exited the forest, noticing people doing normal people things. He spotted a child being taught by his dad how to ride a bike. He saw some teenagers smoking cigarettes in a parked car. Did they know there was a mad man called Yash or that he owned a ship as big as planet earth? Everything felt so surreal to Kire.

"Amberly, I just wanted to say... for whatever I did wrong... I'm sorry," Kire said. "I don't want to be the reason you're bitter anymore."

"I'm not bitter," she snapped.

"Okay, sorry," said Kire, raising his hands in defense. "But, can you not hate me as much? I mean, you were telling Trace and Kaos to break my legs during the tryouts. If that's not bitterness, I don't know what is."

"There's a bigger plot happening, and I don't think you don't know about it."

"Amberly, please, I don't know what you're talking about. Just spit it out already."

"I won't!" said Amberly suddenly. "All these years, I've had to endure the solitude and—and the rejection—and—and I've had to watch her suffer because of you! It's all because of you!"

She was crying now, leaving Kire with more questions than answers.

"Amberly, I swear I…"

"I've had to work since I was twelve, had to fight the feeling of incompetence you brought to me. And it's all your fault I had it so hard—it's all your fault!"

Amberly turned around and ran in the other direction.

Dumbfounded, Kire stood there for a moment, looking back at her before continuing his walk home. He'd had enough for that day and just wanted to sleep and then wake up to a world without quintet gifts. Kire had a strong feeling, though, that the book in his pocket wasn't a dream at all; he could sense the book pulsing in his pocket—it was alive. This meant that whatever Yash was sending to Earth was also alive and as he stood there with a hand in his pocket, he was probably bringing Earth closer to its demise.

13

The next morning when Kire woke up, he felt like he'd taken a beating in his sleep and was more tired than he'd ever been. For the first few moments he was awake, he didn't remember anything from the day before. But the memories of the preceding day quickly came rushing in like ice water over the skin in December—a very rude awakening.

So many things had been strange about the day before. For one, Kire was positive he must have spent at least three hours in that cave. And as a result, he was supposed to arrive home late to his mother's worried face and troubled nagging. However, Emma was the same Kire usually is when he gets home. He glanced at the wall clock on the wall after seeing how calm she was and was certain it had to be incorrect; not one minute had passed since he entered the cave. From his calculations, time must have stopped as soon as he entered the cave; that idea was ridiculous, though, right?

The book from the cave with its brown leather cover was on his desk. Kire didn't hurry over to open it, still wishing it was all a dream. It was difficult dealing with his father's expectations of him, let alone adding the burden of saving the world. He felt like he would collapse under the pressure.

Luckily it was Saturday, which meant he didn't have to see Trace, Kaos, or Amberly... but he wouldn't mind seeing Rose. He thought about her sweet honey brown eyes and the long, dark eyelashes that surrounded them. He thought of her gentle, kind smile and her rosy pink lips and cheeks. Kire caught himself grinning like an idiot and slapped the smirk off his own face. "Hormones on fire, no more," he assured himself. He got ready for the day, spending a large chunk of time trying to tame his hair.

"Good morning, Mom," he murmured, walking into the kitchen.

"Good morning, Kire," she said, taking one long look at him. "Have you considered combing your hair?" she asked just as she set a plate of fried eggs before him.

"What I've considered," he said, grabbing a fork, "is shaving it all off."

Emma chuckled. "I knew you had combed it, just wanted to rattle you."

"Good morning, my family," Gerald said as he stepped into the kitchen. He drew his usual chair at the head of the table and settled in it. He was still clad in his robe.

"Should I even bother asking you to wash your hands before eating anymore?" asked Emma, placing a plate of eggs in front of her husband.

"I brushed my teeth, Emma. That's all I need for eating," Gerald said, grabbing an egg from the plate with his hand.

"Then what did you just use to feed yourself with?"

Gerald grunted. "I don't know what you're talking about, Emma," he said and spooned eggs into his mouth. "I'm the man without masters or master. Why should I give in to your scruples?"

"What does he mean 'by masters or master'?" Kire said to his mother.

"'Masters' because I have two post-graduate degrees while he doesn't, and 'master' because he thinks he's lord of the house," Emma explained.

"I *am* the lord of the house," Gerald stated matter of factly.

"And who dares to dispute that?" Emma asked with a flourish.

Gerald just grunted again. "Have you decided on a sports team yet?" he asked Kire.

Kire nodded. "Yes," he said, "we had the tryouts earlier this week."

"What sport?"

"Soccer."

"Ah, perfect!" Mr. Gerald said, snapping his fingers excitedly. "There's more money to be made there than anywhere else."

Emma took her seat adjacent to her husband. "And you want our son to spend the rest of his life playing for money?" she asked.

"What? You want him to play for the love of the game?" asked Gerald, with a mocking smile.

"Yes," Emma said, "I believe it's possible to make a living doing the things we love."

"Like you're earning right now?" he asked again, with that mocking smile of his.

Emma poured herself some milk. "Yes," she said, "I love taking care of the home and my family. It's only right that I get paid for it, especially since it's a lot of work. The last time you tried toasting bread, you made us burnt offerings—"

"The machine was faulty," Gerald murmured.

"And the *one* time you did your laundry, you didn't get the right temperature for drying and shrank the shirts. Also, that one time when you—"

Gerald snapped. "I give you an allowance!"

Emma poked at the eggs on her plate. "Trust me, Gerald," she said, "you don't give me anywhere near as much as I deserve."

"I want more eggs," Gerald said.

After breakfast with his parents, Kire retreated to his room to study his book some more. He had barely settled in his chair when his phone rang; the call was from an unfamiliar number.

He slid his thumb across the screen. "Hello," he said.

"Hello, Kire, this is Kaos."

Kire sucked in a deep breath. "What do you want?"

"I had this really weird dream..." Kaos said.

Kire's heart sank to his stomach. This really proved what happened yesterday was real. "Why are you telling me your dreams?" he asked, hiding the fear in his voice.

"Kire... can you perhaps come over to my party? I think we need to talk," Kaos said, ignoring Kire's question.

"What? So you and Trace can chase me into a cave again?"

Kire heard Kaos gasp on the other end of the phone. "You know! It wasn't a dream!" Kaos exclaimed.

"No, it wasn't," Kire assured. "Have you tried reaching out to the rest?" he asked. "I think we all need to talk."

"Fine, maybe I should just cancel my party?"

"What? No," said Kire, "there's no need for that. We can still live normal lives."

"You think so? Okay, well, if you come tonight, wear a mask."

"What? Why?" Kire asked.

I have an image to maintain. I don't want all the poor folks tainting my reputation. But you should still come."

"I'm not poor," Kire said adamantly.

"I'm not arguing with you. Party is at nine. Be masked and come early." Kaos then hung up.

Kire scoffed in disbelief; did Kaos just call him poor? His father literally sells gold!

He threw his phone on the desk with a clatter and undid the strap that held the book shut. Upon opening it, he saw that the first page was blank. The poem from earlier was gone. Nothing else about the book looked different from the previous day, however. The pages still glowed white light, yet the pages looked tattered and worn.

Kire grabbed a pen, hesitated, and then wrote 'Hello' on the first page.

His words disappeared into the page before some new words appeared: 'Hi, Kire, pleased to meet you.' The words were golden and burning like they had been in the cave.

Kire's mouth fell open with shock. Did the book just reply to him? He put his pen gingerly to the book again and wrote. 'How did you know my name?'

Like the first time, the sentence faded into the page and a response was returned.

'The quintet gifts know everything about their owners. It was us who told Albus Bridge about you all.'

Kire gasped and jumped back. He hadn't even thought of that! Albus Bridge had been talking to them all as though he was an old family friend who had lived with them all their lives. He seemed to know everything about them—knew not only their pasts but what was in their hearts and souls. How did he know so much about them? Did that mean Albus Bridge could use all of the gifts? So many questions were racing through his mind as he picked up his pen and began to write eagerly.

'You see the future, don't you?' he wrote.

'Yes, but I'd like to iterate: the future isn't set in stone.'

'Tell me the future,' Kire then wrote. He quickly bit his lip in regret. Maybe he shouldn't have done that. The book took a while to reply.

Then: 'Mr. Burke is coming over in five minutes.'

Kire groaned. Mr. Burke? The neighbor next door? What was he supposed to do with the man? Learn to shoot guns or lead cowardly dogs to hunt?

'It's important that you talk to Mr. Burke,' the book wrote. 'He knows something.'

Kire rolled his eyes. He already knew everything Mr. Burke had to say. He heard his story when he and his mom went to visit him that evening.

'Tell me another prediction,' Kire wrote and added. 'Something interesting and relevant, please.'

'I can't until my energy is restored. I can't make any more predictions.'

Kire banged his fist onto his desk in frustration. What sort of magical book ran out of juice?

'You just gave me a prediction of eight words. How can you be tired from that?'

This time, the words didn't sink in. The light on the pages flickered and went out. The book no longer looked special.

"What sort of charger do you need?" Kire asked aloud. He slammed the book shut and shoved it away. Just then, he heard his mother call him.

"Kire! We have a guest!"

He sighed.

14

____

W hen Kire arrived downstairs, his mother was saying, "I'm so glad you came over, Mr. Burke. I just figured you might like to get out of the house. How are you today?"

"Fine," Mr. Burke grunted.

"Good," Emma said. "Well, you can have a seat if you'd like, and Kire can keep you company while I make our coffee."

Mr. Burke shuffled over to a couch in the living room and fell onto it with a heavy groan. Kire perched on the cushion on the opposite side of the same couch Mr. Burke was on.

"How are you today, Mr. Burke?" Kire asked once his mother disappeared into the kitchen.

Mr. Burke screwed up his wrinkled face. "She's asked me that already, your mother," he said, "and you were right here when she did. So, you know the answer to that."

Kire swallowed; though he knew Mr. Burke wasn't the most agreeable person, the man's razor-sharp words still got to him.

What was Halo, his book, saying about the man knowing something?

"I wanted to ask you some more questions about what happened to you in the White Forest," he said. "Your bravery, even when Murphy ran away, still amazes me."

Mr. Burke grunted and scowled darkly. "Don't be patronizing me, boy," said he, "I know you think it was cowardice. I'm not an old fool, you know!"

"I know," Kire said before sinking back into his seat. How was he going to have a productive conversation with this man?

Kire then perked up when he realized, given Mr. Burke's personality type, maybe attacking his ego could do the trick.

"I agree with you, Mr. Burke," he said. "It was absolutely cowardice. Yesterday I was at the site where you were found, and the only thing displaced in the forest was your *mind*. There was never an earthquake!"

Mr. Burke looked ashen and pale. Kire could see the man's hands tremble, and he felt his own heartbeat falter behind his ribs.

"I saw the five pink objects you claimed to have seen," Kire tried again, maintaining the look of absolute aloofness on his face.

Mr. Burke snorted. "Yeah, right," he said. "And what did they look like?"

Kire went on to describe the five eggs he had seen in the cave, leaving out the part where they landed on the ground and started handing out gifts. He enjoyed the change that took over Mr. Burke's face with each word he said, from embarrassment to shock.

"That's it!" Mr. Burke cried. "You saw it!"

"Of course, I did," Kire affirmed, "but one thing still baffles me: Was it just the earthquake that was so frightening to you, or did you see something else? I think there might be a part of the story you're keeping to yourself."

Even if Mr. Burke denied it, Kire knew he was right; Mr.

Burke did see something else. Halo insisted Mr. Burke knew something, and this must be what it was.

The old man broke into a sweat and the trembling of his hands worsened. He took a dirty handkerchief out of his pocket and shakily dabbed his forehead with it before returning it to his pocket.

"Well," said Mr. Burke, clearing his throat uncomfortably, "you're right. I might as well tell you since you saw those glowing rock eggs—you'll believe me, I'm sure. You can't tell anyone what I'm about to tell you."

"Your secret is safe with me," Kire said.

"Not that anyone would believe you if you told them," Mr. Burke added with a sad smile. He looked around to make sure he and Kire were alone before beginning. "Here's what happened in the forest that fateful day. When I saw those rock eggs approaching and tried to touch them, that's when the earthquake happened, and then Murphy disappeared into the forest.

"I don't know if it was a stupid thing to do, but I laid flat against the ground during the quake. It lasted about two to three minutes. When it ended, those rock eggs were still there, hovering right above the ground. I stood up and began approaching them again when I heard a noise coming up from behind me. I thought it was the forest service, so I ducked behind a bush so they wouldn't kick me out for hunting illegally and take my gun. And the rock eggs, all five of them, just flickered like—like static on a TV before disappearing into thin air. That's when I saw the strangest thing I ever saw in my whole life."

Mr. Burke spaced out at this as if Kire wasn't there and he wasn't just in the middle of telling a story. Kire couldn't help wondering what was going through this man's head.

"Mr. Burke?" he said quietly. "Are you all right?"

Mr. Burke jolted in his seat and came to reality. "Ah," he said, chuckling nervously and wiping the sweat off his face again. "Uh, so, three of the ugliest creatures I ever saw popped out of the forest. They were really thin and were much taller than me, but still shaped like a human. Their skins were pitch black—I've never seen something so... dark.

"They had vivid purple cracks all over them, no nose, and three eyes on each of them. And the strangest bit of it all... they looked around themselves and right before my eyes, these-these spirits transformed into humans! There were just three regular men standing there in front of me! That's when I lost it. They grabbed me by the neck and lifted me up off the ground like I weighed nothing. They were going to kill me or something when I heard another set of footsteps approaching. That's when the forest service showed up.

"Before they dropped me and left, one of them said in English—they somehow knew English, 'Now isn't the time. Wait for Yash.' Whatever that meant."

Kire felt his stomach drop to the ground. "Did you say they said, 'Wait for Yash'?"

Mr. Burke nodded once. "It's hard to forget details when demons grab you by the neck."

KIRE DIDN'T ATTEND KAOS' party that evening; his mind was far too troubled by what Mr. Burke told him. He desperately wanted to believe that what Mr. Burke told him was just a product of the man's hyperactive imagination; there's no way things like what his neighbor claimed to have seen in the White Forest existed. Right? But the idea of a book predicting the future was equally ridiculous. Yet, there was one sitting right on his desk.

He was yet to see the other quintet gifts in action. He could only imagine what they were capable of. Trace's sword was on fire, and the fire didn't do as much as warm his hands or burn a hole in his pants. How to explain that, he had absolutely no idea. He spent the rest of the night tossing and turning restlessly.

15

Kire rose before the sun did that following Monday morning. He stared groggily at Halo sitting on his desk for a long moment before pulling himself out of bed and into the shower.

Kire took a 'manly' shower this morning, as his father calls it. Gerald claimed that it builds the strength of a boy, and makes him less of a woman. He stood in his freezing shower no longer than he had to before jumping out and attempting to conquer his hair.

It was three minutes to seven when he got downstairs, and the table was already set for breakfast. His mother turned around at the sight of her son and flashed a grin. She was beautiful.

And it wasn't in the loud, extravagant way—there was a peaceful beauty about her. Maybe that was why her marriage to Gerald somehow managed to last; if Gerald was the hurricane, Emma was the peaceful eye of the storm. Though Kire didn't know how much longer his parents could last. He could only guess that his calm and composed mother was on her last leg with his rude and inconsiderate father.

"You have changed so much just in these three days or so," she said, pouring Kire a cup of tea. "You wake up earlier and seem to have grown... older."

It scared Kire how easy it was for his mother to read him.

"Pancake?" Emma asked.

Kire nodded as Emma placed a small stack of pancakes on his plate.

He ate his warm, fluffy pancakes and savored his tea, and before he knew it, he found himself at school again. Everybody must have known about the chase in the White Forest the prior Friday with Trace and Kaos because everybody was staring at him in shock that he got out of that fight alive.

"Hey," he heard Kaos' voice behind him while he sat alone in the cafeteria at lunch. "We waited for you at my party, and you never showed up."

"We need to talk," Kire said simply.

Trace, Kaos, and Amberly took a seat on the other side of the table. Amberly looked absolutely miserable. Only Rose was absent from their meeting and he decided it would be best if she was there; also, he just wanted to see her.

"I'll send Rose a text," Kire said to them, fishing out his phone. "There's something I need to tell you all."

Trace sighed. "There's something we need to tell you first," he said in a voice that welcomed no argument.

Kire's shoulders dropped and he said, "All right, what?"

Kaos glanced all around them, and sure enough, every pair of eyes in there were fixed on them. Kire was sitting with Trace, Kaos, and Amberly? And there was no yelling going on?

"Are you certain these gifts are not there to kill us?" Trace asked in a low voice.

"Why do you say that?" asked Kire. "They're supposed to help us beat Yash, not kill us."

"Between Friday and today, we've had absolutely terrible luck," Trace continued, agitated. "Just last night, I was trying to get the fire to come on again. You know the stupid sword has fire, right?"

Kire nodded.

"It wouldn't come on until the neighbor's bearded collie was in range!"

Everyone gasped, including Kaos and Amberly, who had heard the story already but were still shocked by it.

"Please, don't tell me you set fire to a dog," Kire groaned.

"No, but I almost got his tail," Trace admitted. "It was really close."

Kire turned to Kaos. "What about you?"

"I enchanted someone," Kaos said flatly.

"Someone at your party?"

"No, his grandmother," Amberly said. "And she's like two hundred years old."

"She's sixty-seven," Kaos snapped. "And I didn't mean to! It was my cousin I was trying to enchant. Wanted to see if I could get her to make a fool of herself."

"Amberly? What happened to you this weekend?"

She shrugged. "Nothing. The glove is still home. I haven't looked at it since Friday."

Just then, Rose joined them quietly, pulling a seat over from another table. "Did I miss anything?" she asked.

"Trace and Kaos here have been sharing their war stories from the weekend," Kire said. "What about you? Did you figure your gift out?"

"I tried. Didn't make much headway, though, I'm sorry," Rose said.

"You're sorry?" asked Kire in disbelief. "At least you didn't almost set a dog on fire or make a fool of your grandmother."

Rose scowled at Trace and Kaos.

"Anyway, I've got some news for you all," Kire said. He then went on to explain what Mr. Burke had told him. He didn't, however, tell them Halo predicted Mr. Burke was coming over to make it all seem as though he acted on instinct rather than a tipoff.

"Are you sure Mr. Burke isn't senile?" asked Trace. "My sixty-year-old neighbor thinks his dog is a cat! The dog who... I almost set on fire..."

"Mr. Burke saw the five eggs long before we did," Kire added. "That's why I think he might be onto something here."

"Then Yash is already here?" asked Kaos in a trembling voice.

"No, I don't think so," said Kire. "Do you remember what Albus Bridge said? Yash is captain of Chaos; he won't want to leave his ship. So, I figure he sent spies first to see if there is a way around the Albuses."

"Or if there's something he needs here," Rose said.

Everyone turned to look at her.

"I mean," she began. "If there's going to be another way in, we might be looking at something that allows Yash to abandon the need for a ship to invade the planet."

"Albus clearly said Yash could send smaller ships," said Amberly.

"He would need an army of them to launch a successful attack," said Kire. "And if that's the case, NASA will pick it up; Earth will be ready. We have fighter jets, atomic weapons, war drones, and all that. Even Yash will have a hard time fighting us."

"That doesn't explain why Yash isn't attacking, and he'd probably still beat us. I'm sure he's been perfecting his own weapons during the last two hundred years," said Kaos.

"Maybe Yash hasn't tried attacking the Albuses because he doesn't want any of his soldiers to die," suggested Rose.

The five stopped talking when Andrew approached the table.

"Hello, Judas," Kire said coldly. "Feeling good about yourself?"

Andrew looked around distractedly; his eyes were frightened, darting around as though he was seeing something the rest of them weren't.

His shirt wasn't buttoned properly, and his hair looked like it hadn't been washed in days.

"Easy now, Kire," said Kaos, laughing. "This kid *wanted* to work with us, something you never had the *bravery* to do."

"Yeah," said Trace, putting an elbow on the table and leaning forward threateningly. "You were saved by happenstance. And let me warn you, we're not friends yet."

"What do you want, Andrew?" Kaos asked proudly.

With the same abruptness he had appeared, Andrew turned around like a soldier given orders and marched off. Kire could see surprise written all over Kaos and Trace's faces; both looked like they had been slapped. And to them, to be ignored may as well have been a slap in the face.

"What's wrong with that kid?" asked Kaos.

Trace clenched his hands into a fist. "Nothing that can't be corrected," he said.

"You always think in terms of blood and bones, don't you?" Rose asked with disdain.

"What's wrong with that?" Amberly retorted.

"I think we've talked enough," Kaos said, rising to his feet. "I don't want people thinking I joined the weirdo band."

"You *did* join the weirdo band," Kire stated bluntly.

Trace, Kaos, and Amberly glared at Kire and glanced around to see if anyone else was watching them.

Everyone in the cafeteria was watching them.

"I'm sure they all agree," Kire added, motioning around the cafeteria.

"Do you think they'll ever like you?" asked Rose after Trace, Kaos, and Amberly left the cafeteria.

Kire waved his hand. "Probably not," he said, "but at least

our goals are temporarily aligned, which means I'm safe for a while."

"So, I didn't want to say this when everyone was here, but you won't believe what happened to me this weekend!" Rose said excitedly.

Kire leaned forward eagerly. "What's it, Rose?" he asked.

"Last night, I spoke with a new friend," she announced gleefully. "He told me his name was Ramoni, although I think he's lying. Ramoni is from Japan. He's a climbing hydrangea."

"Okay, so. Ramoni is a... flower?"

"Yes!" Rose replied cheerily. She looked like she was putting in a huge effort to keep herself from clapping and jumping around.

"You said he told you his name," he said.

Rose nodded.

"And you said it was... a 'he'?"

She nodded again.

"And you think he's lying about his name?"

"Yes, Kire," said Rose, clearly excited.

"What?" Kire laughed. "Plants can't tell you their names, let alone tell lies! They don't have names anyway! They're not supposed to do anything at all; they're plants!" Kire felt a deep disappointment in his chest. He certainly knew he was developing a crush on Rose, but when she spoke nonsense like this, it made him doubt his feelings for her. Was she crazy? Maybe she was just plain weird. That's what makes her unique, though, right?

Rose shrugged. "Yeah... but... but this one did. I invited him into my room through the window. In fact, all the plants in the garden out my window have names, but they're not all as friendly as Ramoni."

"These quintet gifts are going to drive me insane," Kire said.

Just then, the bell rang, and everyone rose from their tables and began the slow, grudging walk of a sentenced criminal to their various classes. It occurred to Kire then that the sound of the school bell had become more than a sign for the students to march back to their respective classes. To some, the school bell had become a rapture trumpet of some sort, ominous and heavy like the hand of judgment on a convict. His eyes searched the faces of the students passing through the hallway, and he saw a common denominator in their eyes—gloom.

Maybe school bells should be banned, he thought.

THE TWO CLASSES Kire had left for the day were as dull and boring as ever, so it was a huge relief when they were let out of their last class early to go to an assembly. This was exciting for two reasons: One, the last class of the day got out early. Two, the school rarely held assemblies, which meant something special was happening.

In the gym, the principal, Mr. Schaefer, was standing on an elevated platform. Standing behind him on the left was Mr. Donnie, looking somber. Mrs. Goody occupied the right; her face pulled tight with her black and white ponytail.

"Good afternoon, students of St. Bernard High," Mr. Schaefer said in a booming voice. He had thick, black hair that stuck to his scalp like carpet and donned a black suit, black tie, and a navy blue shirt.

"Good afternoon Mr. Schaefer," the students drawled in reply.

"Your teachers and I have a very exciting announcement to make," he began with the energy of an aspiring senator. "Just yesterday, I was in my office when two distinguished gentlemen came knocking on or... or calling at my door. These guests are some of the founding members of our school, you see. And they told me that there's a certain secret no one here, not even I know about."

"There are many things we know about that you don't, sir," Trace said behind Kire.

"Keep your mouth shut, Trace, before you get us all in trouble," Kire hissed.

Trace just snorted.

"It would happen that there's more to Marilyn Moe kneeling outside the school."

Marilyn Moe was a statue of a seated woman in Victorian dress behind the school building.

"Fifty years ago, when the school was founded, someone locked a capsule inside the statue, and it was his desire that the capsule shouldn't be opened until after fifty years. The gentlemen that came to visit me in my office came to tell me that next week will mark exactly fifty years since the capsule was locked up."

An excited chatter broke out among the assembled students at the last part of Mr. Schaefer's announcement. A satisfied smile flitted across the principal's face and Kire thought he saw him nod proudly at Mrs. Goody. They had probably had a debate earlier about whether the students would find a fifty-year-old capsule interesting.

"So every day next week, come looking sharp and smart," Mr. Schaefer resumed. "We'll have some events planned each day. The mayor and his wife will be present, and I want you all to dress—" He pinned his eyes on Trace. "— and act to impress."

"Yes, Mr. Schaefer," the students chorused at once. Even Trace murmured a response and Kire saw it was because the principal's eyes were still glued on him.

"And there's one last piece of information," Mr. Schaefer said, turning to Mrs. Goody. "Would you be so kind and tell them the irregularity you informed me of earlier?"

Mrs. Goody nodded once and stepped forward. A sudden hush fell on the assembly as her stern eyes roamed over the young before her. "Just this morning," she said. "I found my office an absolute shipwreck compared to what I left behind on Friday. And the same thing goes for the other teachers, including Mr. Loch. The only office that wasn't torn apart like a crime scene was Mr. Schaefer's office, but even his iron door had scratches and dents on it. If any of you know anything about this—" She narrowed her eyes. "—come forward for your own sake. The police are involved in this investigation, and they *will* find out who did this."

Mr. Schaefer resumed his spot at the center. "And that will be all for now. You can go home now."

16

Halo didn't at all react to Kire for the next two days. Every time he wrote, his letters simply faded into the old pages before disappearing altogether. It wasn't until Wednesday evening before it started working again.

Kire left his mom sitting at the dinner table while she lectured her husband on the advantages of eating without breaking a dish. This time, it had been the sugar pot that cracked under his grip.

He sat at his desk and switched his lamp on. The cold white light illuminated the table and scattered light throughout the rest of the room. Though Halo said its battery was low and had to recharge, Kire found that line hard to believe. He felt Halo was deliberately avoiding him and that there was no battery to restore. He picked the book and absent-mindedly traced the hieroglyphics on the brown leather cover with a finger.

After a moment of just looking at the cover, he figured he might as well try to get Halo to work again. The pages were frustratingly blank. Though Kire expected this, it was still disappointing all the same.

Kire took his pen and wrote, 'Hello.'

As had happened during the previous few days, the 'hello' faded into the pages of the book like a torpedoed ship sinking slowly into the cold sea. He sighed and was about to close the book when the pages came to life. They beamed with golden light like there was some sort of flashlight behind them, but Kire knew this was just magic, pure magic.

'Hello, Kire,' the book wrote in gold letters. 'Did you learn anything from Mr. Burke?'

Kire was excited to see the book finally quit giving him the silent treatment. He replied, 'Yes.' He then hesitated for a moment before writing, 'But you already knew that, didn't you?'

'Yes. Something more is happening soon, but I don't know what it will be. Yash has already sent his spies to Earth.'

'Yes, I know that. Mr. Burke told me.'

'Then you know that you have met?'

'Yeah,' Kire wrote, and then it struck him. 'What do you mean "met"?'

'Oh, your paths have crossed once and they will again,' said Halo. 'But it's Trace that I fear for.'

Kire scowled. 'You should care for me and me only. What's your business caring for Trace? That dude is the reason I've got to become an alien hunter.'

Halo replied, 'Haha.'

Kire sat up straight in his seat, rubbed his eyes, and stared at the book again. 'Ha ha'?

'Why are you laughing?'

'You are not yet an alien hunter. In fact, none of you are alien hunters. You are all like distractions before the Albuses send in someone to save the planet.'

'No,' Kire wrote and shook his head. 'We were chosen.'

'Again, you were not chosen. Albus Bridge told you that.'

Kire sighed. 'So, the Albuses don't believe we can stop Yash's men from doing whatever it is they came for here?'

Halo took its time to reply, but eventually, it did send those two disappointing letters.

'No,' then it went on. 'You are all young, even by Earth's standard. Yash is more than five thousand years old, and many of these minions have been with him since then. Did we really think a band of high school kids have the strength to stop ancient evils like that?'

Kire felt something grip his chest tight. It was as though his father was seated before him now, reminding him how good-for-nothing his top grades were. And this time, his mother wasn't there to stick up for him. He blinked to push back the tears that threatened to fall. He thought he finally had a purpose, a quest to save the world. Well, bad news, the world didn't believe in him.

'Why did you come then? Why did you ask us to risk our lives when you don't believe we stand a chance?'

The golden light on Halo's pages flickered for a minute.

'To defeat the ancient, you need something equally as ancient. And you don't have the ancient weapon.'

Kire scoffed. 'We have the quintet gifts. You're one of them.'

'Haha!'

Kire fumed at this. 'Don't you dare laugh at me again.'

Halo's lights flickered again.

'The quintet gifts were formed after Yash. You need something older.'

'And what is that?' Kire wrote.

'Love and Unity.'

'You,' Kire began furiously. 'Are the most comical book I've ever seen in my life.'

'You all cannot even beat the animosity between yourselves. How can you face an enemy as strong as Yash or any of his minions?' And then the lights went out.

"Stupid, worthless, old rotten book," Kire spat. "Love? Great! All I need to do is walk to the nearest convenience store and buy a truckload of Love. And Unity—dozens of unity." He rose from his seat angrily and threw himself on the bed. There was nothing to think about, the book had gone clean crazy—if books went nuts, that is.

What did it matter if all five of them were not exactly friends? At least they all agreed they were joined together by a common goal. In the meantime, what more could any of them ask for? By their standards, sitting down at one table to talk about anything without throwing punches was a great success. Trace was still a complete jerk who saw violence as the answer to everything—the guy almost set fire to a dog's tail. Kaos was still as manipulative as ever.

What did he do first after he had a little idea of how his powers worked? He controlled somebody's mind! Amberly didn't care to figure out her stuff at all, but he was certain if it was a method to break his bones, she would've mastered it already by now. Rose put in a good effort, but Kire wondered what good talking to plants was. And he, of course, was stuck with a senile self-sufficient talking book.

Kire groaned and kicked the air with his feet. The clock on the wall said it was a few minutes past midnight. Trace and the rest were probably sound asleep, and here he was worrying himself silly over them. Kire got out of bed and out of his room. He descended the stairs and walked to the kitchen.

"Having trouble sleeping?" he heard his mom say behind him, just as he opened the refrigerator.

Kire looked out from behind the open door. "I guess," he said with a shrug. His eyes roamed over the foods and drinks in the refrigerator and eventually, he settled for yogurt.

"Care to join me?" he said as he opened the lid of the small bowl.

"I'll sit with you," Emma said and pulled out a chair. "What's keeping you up?"

"Homework," Kire lied.

"You're a terrible liar, just like your father."

Kire rolled his eyes. "I'm nothing like my father."

"I don't see why you should be ashamed," she said, putting her elbow on the table. "He's your father, no matter what you say or think."

"He doesn't know how to treat people. See how he treats you?"

Emma sighed. "Listen, Kire, let me tell you a story my father used to tell me. Once upon a time," Emma began, "a sheep and a goat had to cross a bridge from opposite ends. Now, this bridge was so narrow it only allowed one animal to pass at a time.

"The sheep got to the bridge before the goat did and was already walking across when the goat arrived. However, rather than wait for the sheep to cross, the goat set out at the same time and hurried so that he could meet the sheep in the middle of the bridge.

"Then the goat said to the sheep, 'go back and let me pass, for I am older than you are.' But the sheep couldn't turn back, and the goat knew this before he set out on the bridge. That bridge was too narrow to even turn on. Under the bridge was a raging river, dark and full of rocks and strong currents. If one fell from the bridge, they were never to be seen again.

"So, the sheep knelt and told the goat, 'Walk over me. I can't turn, and neither can you.'

"And so, the goat crossed over the sheep, and both animals went on their way. Now, the real champion here is the sheep, who was smart enough to find a way to keep them both from drowning. But it turns out goats think differently; the goat saw walking over the sheep as a form of dominance.

"Now, the very next day, the same goat had to cross the bridge again. And this time, it wasn't a sheep that stood on the other side. It was another goat, and as expected, both galloped onto the bridge and met at the center. 'Out of my way,' our old goat said. But the new one merely laughed and said, 'Over my dead body.' And you can guess what happened after that. They both locked horns and fell off the bridge into the river, never to be seen again."

"I know you want me to be like the sheep, but really? Sheep are kinda stupid," said Kire.

Emma chuckled.

"No, Kire," she said and reached for his hand. "I'm just saying sometimes it's better to be the one that makes life easy for everyone, even if it means you have to subject yourself to the things others might consider lowly. I'm saying you should be the person that doesn't fall into the river because someone else is being stubborn. If you want change, then be it, no matter what anyone does to you."

"It's hard, Mom. People can be frustrating at times," he said.

"Like your hair?"

"Mom," Kire groaned.

"What?" Emma giggled. "I'm just saying you complain about your hair, but in the end, you do nothing about it."

"Well, I can't comb people," Kire said.

Emma rose. "You would be surprised to see how people mirror your actions, Kire. That's how you comb them. Be the good you want others to see." She leaned over and kissed him on the forehead.

"If Dad sees that," Kire muttered, "he'll say you're making a pansy of me."

"Better a pansy sheep than a proud dead goat. And one more thing, Kire," she said. "The things people go through tend to shape them in ways they sometimes have no control over. You might want to consider that too."

Kire nodded his head grimly and watched his mom disappear up the stairs. He took one more spoon from his bowl of yogurt and put it back in the fridge before going back upstairs too.

17

Kire woke up the next morning full of energy. He quickly dressed and scarfed down his breakfast, making it to school ten minutes early. The next morning met an energized Kire doing his push-ups and was ready to change the world. His first-class that morning was physics with Mr. Loch.

"Good morning, Earthlings," Mr. Loch boomed with a grin.

"Good morning, Mr. Loch," the class responded, still half asleep.

"There's another interesting news story on the subject of outer space. Do any of you know what I'm talking about?" Mr. Loch asked.

He was met with silence, as usual, when he asked such a question.

"Kaos," Mr. Loch called. "I'm sure you know what I'm talking about. Would you mind sharing the latest science news with us?"

Kaos rose to his feet and cleared his throat. When he began speaking, Kire thought he heard a bit of fear in Kaos' voice.

"Although it has been dismissed by NASA, a group of hikers

exploring the mountains north of the White Forest claimed they saw what looked like the remains of a blown-up plane or something. They claimed the debris didn't in any way resemble any of the aircraft seen on Earth, but NASA said this is false, that the debris was actually the remains of a plane from the World War II era. The general consensus in the scientific community is that they believe NASA. However, many fear that NASA might be trying to cover up something."

"Very good, Kaos. Thank you for sharing that," said Mr. Loch.

The class was silent; Kaos seemed to have transferred his fear to everybody during his speech. "Well, now," Mr. Loch said after a moment, clapping his hands together to get the class focused again. "What do you all think about this?" Kire immediately raised his hand. "Ah, Kire, let's hear from you."

He could hear his heartbeat pounding in his ears. This was his chance to let everyone know they were all in danger—if only he had evidence to prove it. Would saying he believed the alien theory not make him a target for minions already here? Kire looked at Trace and Kaos sitting in the last row of the class. Was Trace nodding at him to... speak? Tell the class he believed in aliens? Kaos just stared directly forward.

"I—I think that NASA is right," said Kire. "There are no such things as aliens. The hikers probably said what they said to rile everyone up."

"There are such things as aliens, Kire, and you know it!" Trace broke in.

"Yeah, and why wouldn't they have discovered some World War II-era plane a long time ago?" Ventured another student. "And wouldn't we have heard about that from somebody other than NASA? A crash like that should've been on the news!"

"This is interesting," said Mr. Loch. "Trace, is there something you would like to share with the class? An alienware you all found by chance, perhaps?"

"There are no such things as aliens," a blond boy sitting in the front row said. "They're only concepts designed by excited minds to give storytellers and Hollywood something to earn from."

Mr. Loch smiled. "Interesting, ah, pardon my manners. We do have a new kid in class. You all know that, but he hasn't been introduced yet."

"Good morning, everyone," the blond boy in the front row said. "My name is Stephan Krause." Stephan Krause was tall and had a build as solid as Trace, and he wore a white shirt, black tie, and a gray coat with black pants.

Kire suddenly had a gut feeling that there was trouble lurking when Stephan's eyes flashed over to Kire. He felt an odd shiver down his spine when the kid grinned.

From the corner of his eye, he saw another one of Halo's predictions coming true—Trace was getting heated up in his seat. Kire hoped the boys would never need to cross paths; Kire had a bad feeling about them having one-on-one time.

"I know it's unusual to have new students midyear, but Stephan joined under special circumstances; his family moved from Blueberry Ridge down here to Montgomery. So, you should all make sure he feels welcome," Mr. Loch said with a warm grin. "Well then, everyone, I advise you all to listen to the news more often. It's good to be informed, you know."

"Yes, sir," said Stephan, "but some find ignorance convenient. They have built a world of lies around themselves, and as you probably know, ignorance is bliss, and bliss is ignorance."

"This, my dear Stephan, isn't a philosophy class. Let's leave such complex matters for philosophers to handle."

Stephan opened his mouth to argue but changed his mind. Instead, he smiled. "That's correct, sir," he said, and Mr. Loch began the lesson for the day.

AT LUNCH THAT DAY, Kire approached Trace and Kaos at their table amidst all the stares and whispers from the other students. Oh, if only they knew.

"Hey," he greeted. The boys glanced at him in response and looked away. Kire took this as an invitation to join them.

"Trace, we need to talk," Kire said.

"And what if I said I don't want to talk to you?" said Trace lazily.

Kire sighed. "It's about the new kid."

At the mention of Stephan, Trace's expression grew cold.

"What about the new kid?" he asked, in a voice that warned Kire to be careful.

Kire glanced around and then lowered his voice. "So, Halo told me yesterday..."

"Hold it right there," Kaos said, raising a hand. "Who's Halo?"

"That... that's my quintet gift, Halo," Kire mumbled. "But that isn't the point right now. You need to lay low, Trace, or else—"

Trace frowned. "Or else what? Are you asking me to let that kid think he's the smart one?"

"Yes," Kire said, excited that Trace was cooperating. "You'll know it was you who let him win. He's the goat and you're the sheep."

Trace and Kaos scoffed.

"What?" asked Kire.

"What you said right now makes zero sense," Kaos said. "Where'd you get this sheep and goats stuff from?

"And besides, sheep are like the most stupid thing on the planet. At least goats have charisma and attitude," said Trace.

"Trace, you need to listen to me. Don't go looking for trouble this one time. We've got trouble coming our way."

Trace snorted. "You shouldn't be talking! You missed your

one chance to let everyone know what we're dealing with. We could've recruited some people."

Kire sighed. "Halo said we have met them already." His voice dropped. "Yash's men."

"They're not *men*; they're *aliens*," Trace said. "Do you think Stephan here is one of them?"

"Mr. Burke said they turned to men, and Halo says we have met them."

"We didn't meet him until today," Kaos argued.

"Yes, I know, but—" Kire started.

"Listen, Kire," said Trace, stabbing the steel table with a finger. "Even if this guy is an alien, I'm going to be the one that smacks that smirk off his face."

"Trace, don't," said Kire.

"Trace, I agree with you," said Kaos, winking mischievously at Kire. "Are we supposed to listen to some book? Besides, what if he's just saying it to stop you from showing Stephan who's the boss?"

Kire covered his face with his hands. "Oh my goodness, Kaos," he muttered.

The bell rang and the students headed to their respective sports teams for the first practice of the semester. He went to the boys' soccer team locker room and got changed. When he stepped out into the field, he saw Stephan Krause wearing a soccer uniform, talking with Coach Turner.

Coach's shrill whistle brought the twenty-two boys out onto the field wearing the black and white St. Bernard soccer uniforms. Trace came up behind Kire and whispered in his ear.

"Your boy came here after all," he said before joining the rest of the team on the field. The boys arranged themselves in two rows, with eleven boys in each row. Stephan Krause was standing beside Coach, with a faintly sly smile on his face.

"Good afternoon, St. Bernard," said Coach Turner. The harsh sun was making a heavy statement on his smooth head.

"Good afternoon, Coach," everyone boomed in response.

Coach put a hand on Stephan's shoulder.

"I'm sure most of you have met Stephan here," he said. "And if you haven't, you are now. This is Stephan Krause, and he wants to join the team."

Trace guffawed at this. "Yeah, right! He's a little too late," Trace said. "Tryouts ended last week."

"You're partially right, Trace," Coach began, and Kire couldn't help but shiver under the cold blanket of dread that covered him. The tone in which Coach spoke suggested he had made an exception for Stephan. "But," he continued, "Stephan here is exceptional, and I believe we'll need his service on the field."

"Yeah, we need more ball boys," Kaos suggested.

Everyone laughed at this, except for Kire. He just couldn't help feeling something awful was about to happen.

"On the team, he's a forward, a supporting forward, and an attacking midfielder. I'd watch out if I were you, Trace. This kid *knows* how to use his left leg."

A murmur began among the students, but it soon stopped after Coach clapped his thick hands together for training drills to begin. What Coach's announcement meant for Trace was that he had new competition. Trace was a brilliant forward, and his size made him almost unstoppable. But he was the only left-footed forward the school had, which meant he wasn't as indispensable as he had been before. Kire wondered what Stephan showed Coach to make him change his mind.

The team was jogging around the field when the coach walked up to Kire. "Where's your shin guard?" he asked sternly.

"I don't have one," Kire replied. "We're only jogging. Do I need one?"

"If you don't get one in five minutes, you're off of the team," Coach said through clenched teeth. "There should be a spare pair in the locker room."

Kire sighed and trudged off, but when he heard Coach yell, "You have four minutes left!" he broke into a jog. He burst into the door and found Andrew searching through all the lockers and making a mess of the room.

"What are you doing?" Kire asked, bewildered.

Andrew's head was behind a locker door when Kire spoke. He took a step backward and pulled his head back to see who it was. A mechanical smile stretched across his face.

"Hello, Kire," he said in a thick baritone.

Kire felt anger and confusion bubbling up inside of him. "Keep your greetings to yourself, Andrew," he said coldly. "Why are you destroying the locker room?" he asked, motioning to all of the clothes and equipment scattered throughout the room.

Andrew looked around with surprise written all over his face, and for a moment, Kire thought he was going to deny making the mess.

"I'll pack it," Andrew replied dully.

Kire found a shin guard lying on the floor and picked it up.

"You better be quick about it," he said as he left the room. "Coach may see this."

When training ended about an hour later, there was absolutely no sign it had been absolutely torn apart just an hour prior.

18

Kire was grateful when the weekend arrived. It was nice to take a break from having to see Trace and Kaos, especially Trace, who had become obsessed with Stephan. He wouldn't stop talking about the kid, worried that he was going to be dethroned as the top dog of the school. That morning, Kire woke up to the sound of his parents walking in the front door. What were they doing out so early?

Upon going downstairs to see what was wrong, he learned that his father drunkenly went into the neighbor's house, the one opposite Mr. Burke, thinking it was his. He tried drinking water from a glass and, as expected, broke the cup. The alarmed neighbors called the police and Gerald was taken to the station. Emma had just picked up her husband and they walked into the house arguing with one another.

After Kire was filled in, he decided to skip breakfast so he didn't have to listen to his parents scream at one another and went back to his room. Halo hadn't responded for the last few days, and like the first time, he felt it was deliberately refusing to talk to him. In his frustration at his family, school, and the world, he decided to take a long walk to clear his mind.

He went down the street, up to the point where he and Amberly had parted the day they walked together. His mind went to her automatically. Kire wondered what she was up to at that moment. She was probably drafting a new plan on how to make his life even more miserable. The thought barely formed in his head when she turned the corner and nearly ran into Kire.

Amberly held two bags full of groceries in one hand and held the hand of an older woman with the other. Amberly's bright blue eyes were devoid of the hate they were usually filled with; rather, they were clear and cheery.

Kire's first instinct was to turn around and run as fast as his legs could carry him, but he decided he'd rather bring an end to all of this. Not just because they were now on the same hopeless world-saving team, but he was sincerely tired of the pain she brought to the pit of his stomach every time she looked at him.

Time to be the stupid sheep, he thought wistfully.

"Hey, Amberly." He waved nervously.

The small smile on Amberly's face dissolved and in its place, her usual scowl returned.

"What are you doing here?" she asked coldly.

"This is my neighborhood!" Kire said. "You know that."

Amberly scoffed.

"Who is he?" croaked the woman Amberly was with. "There's something familiar about him."

Kire moved closer, despite the warning glare from Amberly. He was determined to make things right.

"Mom," he heard Amberly say. "Everything about him is familiar," she quietly hissed to her mother.

Amberly's mom gasped. "Oh, is that so?" she said softly.

Amberly nodded vehemently as though she had just reported Kire to a teacher for doing something terrible.

"Then he must come with us," her mother said.

The anger on Amberly's face transformed to surprise at that instant. Kire could only assume her mother was acting contrary to Amberly's expectations. He seized the chance and hurried over to take one of the plastic bags from Amberly, but she refused, as expected. He then turned to Amberly's mother, and the latter put her hand in his. Her hand was tiny and warm.

"You're Kire?" she asked.

"Yes, ma'am."

"I'm Elizabeth McHenry, Amber's mother," she said with a warm smile.

"It's a pleasure meeting you, Mrs. McHenry," said Kire.

"Now, Kire," she said, "I hope that you can come over for a visit? Your—Amber has told me a lot about you. I want to see what's true."

Kire chuckled and glanced at Amberly. Had she been talking about him at home? Kire seriously wanted to know what she said about him.

"I don't have anything important to do this morning, so—" started Kire

Mrs. McHenry laughed heartily and began coughing.

The walk to Amberly's was about the same distance as to Kire's house. Only it was in the opposite direction. They arrived at the bungalow about twenty minutes later, making frequent stops for Mrs. McHenry to catch her breath.

The house was tall and had a poorly tended front lawn. Two flights of wooden stairs led up to the front porch. Inside, the house was warm and smelled like a hospital. The walls were bare except for one framed picture of who Kire could only guess was Mrs. McHenry holding a baby Amberly.

Mrs. McHenry settled onto a chair in the living room and motioned for Kire to take a seat.

"This is where we call home," she said. "Amber, would you get Kire something to drink?"

Amberly frowned, and Kire would've died before he

allowed Amberly to serve him anything. What if she had spit in his juice or something?

He quickly said, "I'm not thirsty. That's okay."

Mrs. McHenry shrugged. "Very well. Amber, go put the groceries away then. Your—your—" Mrs. McHenry looked as though the next words were fish bones stuck in her throat. "—your shift starts soon."

Amberly grabbed the grocery bags and stormed into the kitchen. Kire could hear her banging things noisily back in there.

"She can be quite a handful at times," Mrs. McHenry said, putting a hand to her mouth just in time to stifle a cough. "My condition is a side effect of the kind of past I had. It's always one disease after another with me. I recently battled emphysema."

Kire was sorry he had come. How on earth was he going to sleep without seeing Mrs. McHenry's gaunt face in his dreams?

She looked like she could be reaching her elderly years but judging by the photo where she was holding Amberly, Mrs. McHenry was likely in her forties. Amberly had her mother's blonde hair, blue eyes, and oval face.

Mrs. McHenry was hauntingly thin, drowning in the green sweater with a canary she wore. Kire wondered if she worked— she looked far too weak to leave the house on her own, let alone hold a job. When he saw Amberly emerge in a furniture shop sales shirt, the question answered itself—Amberly must provide for herself and her mother.

"I'm off to work, or do you want me to stay?" Amberly asked. She knelt before her mother, and the latter planted a delicate kiss on her forehead.

"I want you to never have to work," she said. "I'm sorry."

Amberly rose to her feet. Her long hair was done in two long braids. She threw Kire her customary angry look. "If you do *anything* to her, I'll find you and I'll kill you."

Kire gulped.

"Amber," Mrs. McHenry scolded. "Don't be paranoid now. Go on and be on your way."

Amberly turned around wordlessly and left, closing the front door gently behind her.

"She hates me," Kire said as soon as he heard Amberly lock the door from the outside. "I don't know what I ever did to her, but she loathes me."

"Don't join Amber in her paranoia," Mrs. McHenry said. "I wonder if you kids know what it means to truly hate someone."

Kire didn't raise any argument, but he couldn't shake off the feeling Mrs. McHenry knew just what he was talking about. When he said her daughter hated him, she didn't do as much as flinch or gasp in surprise; it was as though she was expecting him to say just that.

"Amber is such a tough girl," said Mrs. McHenry, smiling. "She used to be such a little angel."

Kire shifted in his seat. "Then what happened?" he asked. "How did she grow up to be so different? Mrs. McHenry, I know Amberly is your daughter but... maybe I just find her hard to understand."

"I don't find her hard to understand. Ever since she was ten and realized she had no father to look up to, it sort of changed something in her."

"Her father died?" asked Kire.

Mrs. McHenry shook her head. "That's what we wished happened. No Kire, he didn't die. He walked away at her birth when he found out she was a girl."

Kire frowned and shook his head in disbelief.

"That's insane," he said. "Why would he leave his daughter? It's his child! And what if he never gets a son? Girls or boys, there's really not a difference—a person is a person," he said, exasperated.

"Such a sweet boy," she said to Kire, reclining into her seat.

"But you see, Kire, life does not happen the way we always plan it. When I was pregnant with Amber, her father was cheating on me and ended up getting another woman pregnant, too. She delivered a boy just a month after I had Amber. I still don't know if he would've stayed with me even if I had a boy. He loved that other woman."

"That doesn't make any sense," Kire said hotly. "It isn't up to anyone to judge others because they were born a boy or a girl. Every child deserves to be loved."

"Amber's father does not understand any of that, Kire," Mrs. McHenry said. "And you would probably understand that if you ever walked in her shoes."

Kire fell silent. "I think I should leave now," he said after a moment.

"Kire, I shouldn't have said that. I'm sorry."

"No," he said, "there's nothing to be sorry about, you're right, you know. I've never walked in her shoes. I've never walked in Amberly's shoes, but she has never walked in mine either. Have a good day, Mrs. McHenry. See you around some-time soon."

Once outside the house, Kire broke into a run and only stopped when his lungs threatened to explode. He sat against a tree and tried to catch his breath. He didn't understand why Amberly and her mom assumed he had an easier childhood just because his father didn't run off.

"Never walked in her shoes," he spat furiously.

His mind was filled with all the words he wanted to say but refrained from. Amberly assumed he had a sweet and loving childhood, and it would seem the same went for her mother. He wondered if Amberly and her mother discussed him over dinner at night, telling each other tales of a life he never had. Did either of them know his father was—and still kind of is—a terrible drunk? Or that there were times when he would leave for months and all he ever did over the phone was ask if he joined a sports team yet?

Kire realized as he grew up that all his father saw in him was just a boy to fulfill his dreams and meet his expectations. When he realized this as a young boy, his relationship with his father was never the same again.

19

Gerald returned home late that night in the same condition he often did when Kire was a little boy; drunk, angry, and argumentative. Emma was surprisingly calm, given the condition in which her husband arrived home and the whole ordeal with him getting arrested the previous night.

Kire and Emma were eating dinner when Gerald returned home. The way he slammed both hands into the door before coming in like a caged bear trying to maul a deer told Emma and Kire that Gerald was home—and drunk. He staggered inside, stumbling over a chair, then hitting his leg against a small stool. He howled in pain and hobbled over to the dining area.

"Welcome home," Emma said. She was smiling with such impossible ease, while Kire had an extreme opposite expression on his face.

Gerald grunted and fell into his seat at the head of the table. "You should've picked me up from the police station earlier, Emma, instead of making me stay there all night," he boomed and then belched aloud without covering his mouth.

"But what did you do instead? You waited until this morning to pick me up like you had something better to do in the meantime."

"We've already discussed this, Gerald. I was called in the middle of the night, and I knew it would wake Kire if I brought you home from the station at such a late hour. I figured it would be best for myself and Kire to wait until morning," she said before taking a small sip of water.

Kire sighed.

Gerald grunted. "I'm hungry," he said. "Gimme something to eat."

"Right after you shower," Emma replied.

Gerald cast a hateful look at her before rising to his feet reluctantly. "Never mind, I lost my appetite," he said, staggering away from the dining area. A loud crash sound came next, and Kire jolted, but Emma didn't do as much as wince.

"Don't ask anything, Kire," she said, smiling at him. "I can barely hold it in. If I let this anger out, we'll all fall into rivers of blackness and guilt."

Kire nodded and finished his food silently before kissing her goodnight and going away to his bedroom. In the warm comfort of his room, he changed into his pajamas, climbed into bed, and curled up like a ball. Yeah, this was the life everyone assumed was perfect, his life, eh? Absolutely lovely childhood. He heard a small noise coming somewhere and he sat up. Kire glanced around; his phone was on the bed beside him—silent and still, alongside his headphones and as expected, the small clock alarm he never listened to.

The sound came again and this time, it sounded more like a voice, almost like a little boy's.

"Kire..." it said.

He got out of bed and moved slowly around his room, trying to locate the sound. His heart beat fiercely and he was flooded with fear, fear that Yash had finally sent some of his minions to Kire and all he had to protect him was a drunk father and a talking book.

"Kire..." the voice called again, soft, whispering and urging.

Kire took one uncertain step toward his desk, where he gathered it had been coming from. Could it be.... Halo? He swallowed and reached out for the book on the desk. Maybe it was his eyes playing tricks on him, but the old writing on the thick brown leather back was glowing a golden light that appeared to be shaking.

He slowly undid the strap binding the book together and took a quick step back to put a safe distance between himself and the book. The book threw itself open and the pages came alive, glowing like smoldering embers.

Kire's heartbeat quickened even more as he craned his neck to see what was written in the book while staying as far away from it as possible. He frowned; the writing on the book was strange and ancient-looking. He couldn't recognize anything it said anymore.

"What the..." Kire gasped. Could it be that he had lost his powers? He remembered Trace, Kaos, and Rose being unable to read the book back in the cave. Had he been booted out of his own book?

'Kire,' the book wrote.

Kire gave the room a quick sweep with his eyes and found a pen lying on the floor close to the bed. He snatched it up and jumped over to his desk chair.

'Hello, Halo,' Kire wrote. 'What is happening?'

His words had barely sunk in when Halo replied.

'Yash is coming.'

Kire felt his heart seize for a moment and his breath quickened. Then without thinking, he jumped to his feet and ran out of the room straight downstairs. His mother was in the living room watching TV when he ran to the front door and pulled at the handle to make sure it was locked. He peered through the blinds, scanning the dark and empty street. Save for the assembly of yellow lights suspended from poles curved over the road. There was no life to be seen outside the Hunter household. He breathed a small sigh of relief.

Next, he began to close all the windows one after the other and pulled the curtains together.

"Kire, have you been bewitched?" Emma asked. "And why are you panting like that?"

"No," Kire replied, breathless. "It's nothing. I just wanted to make sure we were security-conscious."

His mother eyed him suspiciously.

"I wonder what is up with you these past few days," she said. "You should go back to bed and get some sleep. I think you're very sleep-deprived."

Kire simply nodded and ran back up the stairs. He locked his door behind him and returned to a glowing Halo.

'You could've waited for me to finish before running out like that,' Kire read.

'What did you expect me to do?' replied Kire.

'Yash's minions are on their way,' was all Halo said in response.

Kire's eyes grew wide in panic.

'Should I call the police? And the rest of—' Kire paused. What exactly was he supposed to call Trace, Kaos, Amberly, and Rose as a group? Guardians? No. Classmates? Too vague. Since they were not all exactly friends, he didn't know if he could use that term as well.

Eventually, he squeezed his eyes shut and wrote, 'friends?'

'What would you tell the police?' asked Halo.

Kire scoffed. 'That a mad alien is trying to attack my home.'

'Read what you wrote, as a cop.'

Kire was going to hurl the book against the wall when he realized he sounded crazy.

'Maybe I should replace 'mad' with 'dangerous' and 'alien' with 'extraterrestrial war criminal?' wrote Kire.

Halo didn't have a mouth, but Kire swore he heard it sigh as though it was dealing with a really stupid kid.

'He is not coming here, Kire. He is going to school, your school.'

All the built-up tension in Kire seeped out like water in a sieve at that.

'If he isn't coming here, then what's the problem?'

'He is going to your school, Kire,' Halo replied. 'There is something inside of the Marylin Moe statue that they want. But they don't know for sure it is there, and all they know is that it is something within St. Bernard's, not the precise location.'

'It's probably safe there then. The school is a big place to search.'

'Only one of Yash's three main men is coming right now. Call the rest so you all can destroy him; they are unstoppable together.'

Kire put the end of his pen in his mouth and heaved.

'Who's unstoppable together?' he wrote.

Halo took time to respond. 'Any group of people who care to work together.'

The corner of Kire's mouth lifted in scorn; he knew just what Halo was insinuating, that he should be friends with the rest.

'Kire, there is an alien heading for your school. Call the rest, wait for him at school and destroy him.'

'You said he was looking for something, right? What if he never finds it?'

'Oh, he does not have to.'

Kire's frowned. 'What do you mean?' he wrote.

'Your principal will bring out the Djigi from its hiding place in three days. Yash's men will find the Djigi, which is why you have to destroy them one after the other as quickly as possible.'

It all made sense to Kire then. All the offices that were reported to have been ransacked were done by Yash's men. And they had been looking for the Djigi.

'What is a Djigi?'

'I will tell you when you return; call the rest now.' Halo's lights went out.

Kire closed the book and pinned it shut. He changed out of his pajamas into some clothes fit for battle. What exactly should he wear to fight an alien? He settled on workout clothes and a hoodie. He then grabbed his phone and began to type a message. He shook his head as he typed, hardly believing he was texting Trace, Kaos, Rose, and *Amberly* in the middle of the night to go meet him at school to fight an *alien*.

He finished the message and hit the 'send' button. Two marked signs indicated the messages had been sent and delivered to the appropriate quarters.

Kire put a flashlight and Halo in his backpack before silently making his way down the stairs. He found his mother asleep on the couch with a half-knitted sweater on her lap and a bamboo knitting needle in her open hand. The TV was still on, which meant she had only just fallen asleep. But if there was one thing he knew for sure, it was that there was no way he was going to sneak past his mother without waking her. Unlike his father, his mother had the ears of a true hunter. His father's snore would've been sufficient to drown his footsteps and scare any wildlife within a mile radius.

But his mother...

Kire groaned internally. He glanced at the watch on his wrist and pushed the lights button. Seven minutes before midnight. His mother would never let him get out of the house, even if it meant the end of the world.

He heard heavy footsteps from upstairs and ducked behind a curtain at the window about the same second Emma woke up and Gerald appeared at the foot of the stairs. Kire tried to hold his breath but found himself on the verge of hyperventilating instead.

"Where's the plane?" he heard his father ask in a drawl.

Kire rolled his eyes. Plane? Since when did the family own a plane? They didn't even have a picture of a plane.

"What plane are you talking about, Gerald?"

"What? I parked my plane right on the table. Has the pilot taken it out?"

"Yes, Gerald," Kire heard his mom say sternly. "If you didn't drink so much of that aviation gin, you would've known better than to park your plane in the living room."

"Oh..." Gerald said absentmindedly. "My plane."

"Come here now," said Emma.

Kire peeped out through the curtain and saw his mom put Gerald's arm over her shoulders; she was going to take him back upstairs. He chuckled behind the curtain, finding it hard to believe his luck.

"Who's there?" Emma asked, looking around.

Kire bit his tongue; *why* did he have to chuckle aloud? It wasn't that funny. He could see his mother's eyes boring a hole through the curtain, but because of her husband, she couldn't concentrate long enough to make out his silhouette behind the material.

There was a moment of silence, and then his father mumbled something about a singing plane. That returned Emma's attention to her husband, and she led him up the stairs. For a moment, he feared his parents were going to topple down the stairs, at which point Kire would have to come out of hiding and call off his alien hunt; or perhaps that would be the perfect distraction for him to leave?

They didn't end up falling, so the minute he heard the sound of a door upstairs closing, Kire slid out of his hiding spot and made a beeline for the door. Once outside, he broke into a sprint before stopping, realizing he shouldn't rouse suspicion among the residents of Gabby Drive, who didn't take kindly to eccentricities and quirks or anything remotely out of the ordinary. He jumped behind a tree when he saw a police car flashing its blue and red lights in his direction. He held his breath until he saw them turn down another road.

Why am I hiding? Kire asked himself. *I'm not doing anything illegal—I'm saving the world!*

Once the police car was out of sight, he continued his brisk walk down the empty street toward his school.

20

———

Kire waited at the school's front door for ten minutes before the first member of the team arrived, glancing at his watch every five seconds or so. To Kire's greatest pleasure, it was Rose who arrived first, clad in a dark green corduroy dress with leaf prints and green stockings.

"Hey," he said to her, smiling.

"Hey," she replied. She clasped her hands together tightly in front of her and blushed a gentle pink, avoiding eye contact.

"I'm sorry I had to call you out like this..." Kire said. "You probably had to sneak out of your house."

She chuckled. "Not probably, Kire," Rose replied. "It's midnight already. What parent would let their child leave the house for a mission like ours?"

"Yeah, right."

An uncomfortable silence lingered between them for a while.

"I—I didn't mean this isn't important," said Rose. "I'm just saying—"

"It's all right, Rose," Kire said with a reassuring smile. "Even if there's an alien here, nobody is going to believe us." He scoffed. "I mean, I don't believe myself either."

Rose laughed quietly.

The sound of music approaching made Kire and Rose reflexively jump behind a pillar to hide. They watched as a red car peeled into the parking lot and screeched to a halt. Then much to Kire's chagrin, Trace and Kaos just sat there in the car listening to their music as though they had just driven there for fun.

Kire jumped out of hiding and marched toward them with clenched teeth.

"Turn off the music, you idiots!" Kire strained. The veins on his neck stood out like snakes under his skin.

Kaos poked his head through the truck window and turned off the music.

"What is wrong with you?! We don't even know what we're dealing with, and you come here blaring music and all. And what are you clowns wearing?"

Trace and Kaos wore identical white jackets with a silver zip that ran from bottom to neck instead of buttons. They wore white, skin-tight pants of the same material and huge white sneakers that flashed red and blue when they walked. Kaos was wearing his quintet gift on his head like a Julius Caesar right before he became a knife salad, and Trace was holding on to his sword like a gladiator ready to impress a hungry crowd.

Kire heard Rose snort at the sight of them.

"What's up, Kire?" said Trace, grinning. "You like our outfits?"

"I bet he's jealous," Kaos said to Trace.

"Oh, look who we have here," said Trace, motioning toward Rose. "If it isn't the flower girl. Kire, did you raise your voice at her too when she came, or did you like her outfit better than ours?"

"She put on a dark green material which will blend her in

with the darkness while you two are dressed in clothes that scream, 'Hey, alien, I'm here! Come get me!'" said Kire, with the same energy one would use when dealing with a stubborn child.

"What? Don't you like it?" asked Kaos.

Kire put his hands on his hips.

"Why not? Shiny white? It blends right with the general color of the night. And... cool shoes with flashing red and blue lights? Just what we need for an encounter with an alien!" Kire hissed sarcastically.

"Don't be a sore loser, Kire," said Kaos. "We know you're just jealous. Our outfits fit the mission. As defenders of Earth and enemies of the darkness that doth beset us," Kaos said before bursting into a roar of laughter with Trace.

"More like the Unlikely Defenders," Kire muttered.

"That actually has a nice ring to it," Kaos said while pumping a fist in the air. "I like it! The Unlikely Defenders!"

"We're doomed," Kire groaned to himself. "Where's Amber?

Trace and Kaos glanced at each other and then back at Kire.

"Since when did you call her 'Amber'?" asked Trace, glowering.

Kire winced; the name stuck because Mrs. McHenry kept calling her that. But if he even dared mention he was at Amberly's house, all hell would break loose. He didn't trust the pair to remember they were here to stop an enemy they knew nothing about.

"It just felt right," he said. "Amber is short for Amberly. And if you think I have a thing for your girl, you can let that thought perish. Now, where is she?"

"She's busy and won't be able to make it," said Trace. "Now, where's the monster of yours?" He grabbed his sword by the hilt and pulled it out of its scabbard, and the sword burst into bright yellow flames in his hand.

"Just look at that," Kaos mooned over the burning sword in Trace's hand. "I bet Kire wished he had something as hot."

Kire did indeed, but there was no way he was going to admit that to either of the two boys before him. "Thank you, but I'll pass," he said. "Don't want to set the neighbor's dog on fire."

Trace growled.

"Where's this alien friend of yours, Kire?" asked Kaos impatiently. "My folks let me off the hook for everything except mass on Sunday morning. And I still have to get my beauty sleep tonight, so please, let's get started already."

Kire cleared his throat and took off his backpack. He unzipped it and brought out Halo and the flashlight.

"I don't suppose any of you came with a flashlight?"

Rose patted her bag while Kaos turned to face Trace.

"Who needs a torch when you have this?" Trace lifted his sword again, and it burst into flames.

"Does it ever run out of gas or anything?" Kire asked.

"Dear Kire, these things are magical. Have you ever seen a magic element that needs to be refilled?"

So, he was the only one who managed to end up with a sick book that ran out of gas after every prophecy. He wanted to slam Halo against the floor and stamp it to pieces, but he knew that would be the stupidest thing he could possibly do right now. Instead, Kire opened the book. Nothing happened. Halo looked no different than an old blank diary and nothing more.

"What's wrong with your book?" asked Trace, "I thought it had a backlight or something. I mean—wait—does *yours* run out of gas?"

The boys roared with laughter.

Meanwhile, Kire was beating Halo at the back surreptitiously like it was a broken TV in need of encouragement. The book flickered and its letters came on; Kire breathed a sigh of relief at this. The light on Halo's pages flickered on and off like the faulty lights of an old subway train.

"I think you got a fake," said Kaos, chortling.

Kire tried to shut out the voices of both boys so he could focus on rickety old Halo. Oh, he was *so* going to burn that book for sure when he was done with this whole ordeal. He retrieved a pen from his bag and wrote.

'Hello, good for nothing, Halo.'

The words sank in, as usual, though much slower than usual, taking nearly half a minute to get in. Then he had to bite his nails to keep from tearing at his hair after the book took the same amount of time to respond.

'He is here. Protect Marilyn,' Halo replied.

Kire snapped the book shut and threw it into his bag.

"He's behind the school," he announced to the rest and started running.

"Come on, boys, we've got a job to do." Trace imitated the walk of a bouncer with oversized arms and Kaos followed suit.

They made their way around the school in the darkness. Kire wanted the group to be discreet and crouched low, but it was unbelievably difficult to achieve stealth with Trace and Kaos blaring lights behind him. With every step they took, the blue and red lights on their sneakers would flash with the intensity of an ambulance's emergency light. And so, everywhere the group went, the light from their shoes painted the walls red and blue. Eventually, Kire gave up and straightened himself.

"Why are you walking like that?" asked Kaos, still crouched. "What if someone sees you?"

"Oh!" said Kire, feigning surprise. "Yeah, they'll notice me wearing all black, but no one will see the lights from your shoes. In fact, I wouldn't be surprised if *Yash* saw two pairs of sneakers flashing red and blue lights."

"Yash is in space," said Trace.

"Exactly!" Kire said, exasperated. He was torn between telling them to just go home so he could do it alone and the fact that he definitely couldn't do this alone. "Everyone can see the lights from your stupid shoes," he said through gritted teeth.

"Duh, he's just jealous," Kaos said to Trace.

Kire was about to say something nasty to Kaos when Rose touched him on the shoulder.

"Yeah, what is it?" he said harshly. And then, when he saw who it was, his temper subsided. "I'm sorry," he said in a much softer voice. "What is it?"

"I think I saw something," Rose whispered.

The way Rose said 'something' filled his chest with doom and made the hair on the back of his neck stand up. The grins dropped from Trace and Kaos' faces.

While there's no difference between the word 'something' seen in a meadow in broad daylight and the 'something' seen in the middle of the night on an alien hunt, the word had a significantly different effect on the feelings associated with it.

Trace and Kaos crouched beneath a classroom window; it suddenly struck them to act with more sense and stealth than they had all their lives.

"Where did you see 'something' Charlie?" asked Trace.

"It's Rose," she snapped at him.

"This is unbelievable," said Trace, "We're about to be killed by aliens and you care about what name you're called?"

Rose scoffed.

"You both look like clowns here to entertain the alien while he fights Kire and me," she hissed.

"Drop it already, Trace," Kire snapped when he saw the big dude stand up. "Where did you find this thing? What did it look like?"

Rose shook her head. "It was too dark to see, all I saw was purple lines moving, and then I remembered your neighbor. It has to be one of Yash's men, right?"

Kire nodded. "Where did you see it?"

Rose pointed to the small gate that led into the school building.

The team formed a single line and made a crouched beeline for the gate ahead. Red and blue lights flashed against the walls and Kire groaned internally.

"The door is locked," Kaos hissed. "The tension must have gotten to you, Char—" she glared. "—Rose. What's *wrong* with women?" he muttered aside.

Trace simply put his head against the iron door with the air of a man tired of life.

"Wait," said Kire, "I think she was right. Look at this." He waved toward a hole no more than two inches in diameter. What was strange about the hole was the smoke issuing from the edges. It was almost as though...

"Something burned its way through that? Laser technology, maybe?" said Trace, observing the smoking hole. "But last time you told us your neighbor's story, you said they were almost nine feet? Even if your neighbor added five feet to their true height, they still wouldn't fit in through this hole."

Kire rubbed the back of his neck, thinking hard. There was something he was forgetting about what Mr. Burke said about Yash's men. Something about them—

"Oh!" he gasped. "I get it now. They don't have to fit in when they can just shrink to whatever size they want."

"You want to make these aliens more powerful than they already sound, Kire," said Kaos, "They can lift a man clean off the floor with one hand, they can take anybody's form, and now, they're shape shifters. You know what? I think I'm terribly under-armed for this sort of expedition."

"Why?" asked Rose quietly. "You have this lovely crown sitting in your head."

"Yes," Kaos retorted hotly. "What am I supposed to do with it? Tell an alien nine feet tall to bow down to my will?"

"I'd have appreciated a flaming gun as well," Trace said suddenly. "It would at least spare me the need of getting too close to our alien friend. Instead, I get a thousand-year-old sword with fancy pyrotechnics."

Kire was losing his wits at this point. As much as he wanted to tell the two bullies off, he knew the mission would become a lot more impossible than it already was if they backed out now. And besides, the fear building up in him had been more bearable with them there. Kire didn't want to admit it, but it was true their presence made him a lot safer. He had to keep them all together—whatever was ahead would be easier to face if they didn't split up.

"What if there's nothing inside there?" Kaos started. "What if—"

A loud crashing sound erupted from inside the school, and everyone froze in their tracks, eyes bulging.

"Keep the 'what ifs' to yourself, Kaos," Trace hissed. "There's something in there."

"We have to open this door," Kire said desperately. "We can't let this...thing... leave."

"Why?" asked Trace. "I think we should all just go peacefully back to our homes and go to bed. It'll probably notice and appreciate that we're not trying to attack it and return home like a good puppy."

"No, it won't," Kire said breathlessly. "There's three of them. If we can't bring them down one after the other, they'll stand as one and beat the flashing sneakers out of us."

"Kaos has the key," Trace said.

"What key?" asked Rose.

"The door key," Trace replied drily.

"Perks of having a father who donates *generously* to the school," Kaos said proudly.

"Does he know you took it?" asked Kire.

Kaos snorted and took out a key from his breast pocket. "Of

course not, and meanwhile, why are you not crooning about how smart I was to remember to take the key with me? If it weren't for me, we'd all have to give up now."

The door unlocked, and Kaos pushed it open. A cool breeze and a strange putrid smell wafted out into their faces when they opened the door, welcoming them into the wide white corridor of St. Bernard's. Come Monday morning, the same corridor would be filled with students who didn't have to worry one bit about a mad man in a ship named after the mother of troubles.

"Can you hear that?" Rose whispered. There was the sound of chairs scratching against the floor; someone or something was pushing the chairs around.

"Yeah, can you smell that?" Kire replied, turning on a flashlight. "You may have remembered your key, but did you remember to bring a flashlight, Kaos? Didn't think so."

"That's why we wore these sneakers," Kaos replied hotly.

"I hope you can see well enough with them," Kire mocked.

They continued walking in silence until they arrived at the end of the corridor. From here, the corridor led into another one that went sideways.

"You know what?" Kaos said ominously. "I think Trace and I will just go on our own. If you need help, you and Char—Rose —Rose here can scream."

"Wait, I don't think we should split—" started Kire

They had already started running away. Trace and Kaos went right, while Kire and Rose went left. He glanced at her and saw her necklace, the Pendantix, sitting elegantly around her smooth neck.

Her hand went to her neck when she saw him staring, and Kire had to look away, flushed.

"How is it coming up?" he asked. "You know... your stuff."

Rose sighed softly.

Despite the strange smell that hung in the air, he could still make out Rose's scent; the girl literally smelled of roses.

"I'm worried," she said.

Kire frowned. "Are you scared?"

"Yes—no—I mean, yes, I'm scared, but that isn't what I'm worried about."

Kire shone his flashlight on the wall. There was the doodle drawn with a green marker that got Trace in trouble one time. When the cretin was apprehended, he claimed explicitly that he was trying to immortalize Mr. Schaefer. But the round head, round teddy bear ears, four lines of teeth nonsense he drew on the wall didn't look human, let alone the principal, so he got detention for a week.

"What bothers you then?"

She shrugged. "My power is to use plants for defense and attack."

"That's true," said Kire, "and a significant advantage is that you don't need to be within reach to use your powers; the plant can always go where you want it."

"Yes, but—"

"Ha! I wish Trace was here. It would've been nice seeing the look of shame on his face with that sword and all."

"Kire!" Rose called quietly but in a firm voice. "There are no plants in here; just chairs and tables and books and I can't wield them. I'm useless."

"Well," said Kire when it finally sank into his head. "Thank goodness Trace isn't here."

A loud noise that sounded like a man groaning underwater reverberated through the entire building.

"Kire!"

It was Kaos' voice, with unmistakable terror in it.

21

"Kire!"

The call came again, and this time it was closer than before. Kire handed his flashlight over to Rose and brought Halo out from his backpack. He remembered Albus Bridge saying something about Halo forming a shield, but he hadn't tried that trick out yet. And he didn't know if the book had the strength for a shield deployment right now anyway.

The sound of approaching footsteps echoed through the empty corridor. The skidding sound of more than one pair of shoes beat against the tiled floor; Trace and Kaos, or either one and an attacker? Kire didn't have to wait long for his answer. Two people with shoes flashing red and blue emerged from around a bend at the far end of the corridor.

"What is it? Why are you both running like that?" asked Kire.

"Your friend, he's here. Look at my hand!" Kaos held out his hand for Kire to see.

There were three distinct red circles around his wrist, about the same kind of bruise an octopus tentacle would leave on its victim.

"How did this happen?" asked Rose.

A loud unearthly groan filled the whole place. It was almost the same as the one Kire heard the first time, only this one was filled with anger.

"What is that?" asked Kire.

Trace and Kaos were, however, bounding out of the building already. They pushed through the gate they came in through earlier and burst into the school compound.

"Let's go to the greenhouse," Rose suggested.

"I'm not going anywhere else here," Kaos replied. "I'm going home."

Rose snorted. "You really want whatever that is to go into town? Will you be able to live with whatever damage it causes out there?"

Kaos bit his lower lip. "If that thing gets either of us, we won't live long enough to have any regrets."

"Which I think is far better," Rose said, running toward the greenhouse. Kaos looked from Kire to Trace. It was Trace who made after her first.

"She's right," said Trace. "We can't be the reason anyone out there gets killed."

Kire looked at Trace, surprised, before running after Trace and Rose. He heard Kaos hiss and curse bitterly before making after him.

Upon entering the greenhouse, the four of them bundled themselves in a corner under a concrete table with eyes darting around like those of a frightened rabbit.

"Now, tell me what you saw back there," Kire demanded.

But it would seem that whatever it was they saw didn't want to be discussed, for Kaos had hardly opened his mouth to talk when the lights hanging overhead in the greenhouse came on.

"That isn't supposed to happen," said Kaos shakily. "That isn't supposed to happen."

"We know! You didn't have to say it twice," Kire snapped.

A loud creak announced the greenhouse door was being opened.

"Kaos, did you not lock that door?" asked Trace.

Kaos held his knees to his chest under the table. He had taken the diadem off his head and held it in his shaking hands.

"It's hard to think straight when you've got a walking octopus on your tail. Trace cut one of the tentacles with his sword. That's why our alien friend is angry."

Kire gulped. He had to know just what they were dealing with, and it didn't seem like a horribly frightened Kaos would be able to help much in that regard.

"Hey," he whispered to Rose. "You can do stuff here, right? We have got plants everywhere."

"Yeah, I can try," she replied.

"Are you scared?" he asked.

She fixed her honey brown eyes on Kire and nodded. "Yeah," she said.

"Good, that makes two of us."

He crawled out from under the slab and looked toward the door for any sign of their pursuant. And, he found him... or rather, they found each other.

What Trace and Kaos called an octopus was no octopus at all, though it did share some traits with one. The upper part looked like a man but was not; there were two human-like arms, one long flat head with three eyes. It was the lower half that looked like an octopus. Rather than legs, it had at least ten tentacles squirming like the snakes on Medusa's head. The monstrosity had a skin of a wet-looking jet black, with bright purple cracks all over it. Kire could see one of the tentacles was a bit shorter than the rest, and it seemed to be dripping a purplish liquid of the sort.

He retreated into the corner with a face as pale as death itself.

"What the heck is that?" Kire whimpered with bulging eyes.

A loud screech erupted from the end of the greenhouse, followed by a flapping sound.

Kire jumped out of his hiding place. "It found us!"

The other three jumped out from under the slab in time to escape being crushed under a powerful tentacle.

"Whoa!" Kaos exclaimed, starting toward the exit.

But their attacker was equally fast and intelligent.

"Get down!" Kire yelled when he looked behind him.

Trace didn't get down soon enough and got scratched by the slab the monster threw their way. The slab then fell against the wall, breaking a window. The greenhouse looked as though a tornado had swept through it; there were pots of plants scattered all over the place. Soils of varying colors covered the once sparkly floor. Even the Edax Animae were snapping their jaws open and shut at the commotion.

The four of them went to the wall and tried to lift the slab. Another loud screech told them it was safer that they didn't turn their back to what was coming from behind. The creature was no longer running, Kire even thought he saw it smile, but he must have been imagining things. Monstrosities like the one pirouetting towards them don't smile, do they?

"I'm very disappointed," he heard the creature say in a smooth baritone that seemed to be coming from all around them. The proud creature wrapped a tentacle around a flowerpot, brought the plant to its nose, and sniffed. It then threw the pot away with a disgusted look on what wasn't entirely a face.

"It can talk!" Kaos said to the rest. It was almost like the time at the cave when they were all flattened against the stone walls: different scenery, same dilemma, more fear.

"Yes, I can talk nitwit. I can also hear," said the creature.

"My name is Jago, but that doesn't matter since the four of you will be dead in a minute."

"What do you want?" Trace boomed, holding his sword out before him. The fire wasn't as proud and bright as it had been when he was showing off earlier in the night.

"I'm here for the Djigi," said Jago.

"What's that?" cried Kaos.

Jago purred and crawled closer to them. "I would've believed you, saying you don't know about the Djigi," he said, "but you do have the quintet gifts, which discredits whatever it is you say."

"We... we just stumbled on them," said Kaos. "We can give them to you if you want."

"Is that so? Well, I thought as much," Jago said. "All the last heroes have been..." he eyed the four frightened students with disdain. "... matured, sensible and worthy. You all shame me. It'll be a massacre, not a fight."

"You fought with others before us?" asked Rose.

Jago laughed in delight. "Of course I did! And if I'm still standing before you, I assume you understand why that is?"

"You beat them?" ventured Kire.

Jago turned to face Kire with all three of his sinister black eyes.

"It's you who holds Halo?"

Kire swallowed and held the book even more tightly.

"I will have you know that Halo is about the most useless of all the quintet gifts I have seen."

Kire's eyes stung and he wanted to just run away and cry about all of this instead of face it. He felt Jago's words cut right into his heart like a double-edged saber.

"Wait, hold it right there," said Rose with fire in her eyes. "It was his 'useless gift' that told us where to find you, and I'm certain you were not expecting company."

Kaos nodded his head thoughtfully. "She does have a point there, you know?"

Jago's eyes swam a bit closer together on his face. The purple stripes that ran against his jet-black skin glowed and shimmered like a liquid.

"I killed your predecessors, and I will do the same to you," he growled.

"Do you regenerate?" asked Trace.

"No," Jago barked. "Why do you ask?"

Trace turned to his three other companions with the flourish of a magician about to give his best act. "I think we were the first to chop one of Jago's wormy legs."

"Fools," Jago growled. "Let me kill you and put your parents out of their misery."

Kire felt hot anger boil inside of him like lava. He clenched his fists, and he could feel his face grow impossibly hot.

"What did you say?" Kire heard Trace say. He was surprised to see that Trace wore the same look of unbridled anger on his face.

Jago seemed amused by the change in tone.

"Looks like I pushed a button," he said, laughing bitterly. "And what can *you* do to stop *me*? You're nothing but a bunch of little children who had to sneak from their parent's homes to come and die for nothing. I have been alive for more than two hundred years, and you think you can stop me? There's nothing, absolutely nothing special about any of you little children."

"I'd rather be a foolish child than be an ancient evil!" Trace roared and charged.

Kire's eyes went to a hand trowel lying on the floor and he immediately ran for it. He didn't know what happened, but he heard a loud groan escape from Jago, and it was similar to the unnatural sound that erupted back in the school building. It sounded so far away, yet so close, and seemed to be coming from all around them. When he came back to his senses, he saw that Trace had chopped a tentacle in half.

Kire jumped to his feet and charged at Jago with the trowel in his hand. He saw Trace sail past him like a ragdoll after Jago landed a blow on him. But rather than fear, he was even more emboldened to do something about their situation. Kire hurled the trowel at Jago and the monster caught it a half-inch from his face.

"Putting up a fight now, are you?" asked Jago, snarling.

"We'll be your end, Jago," Kire said hotly.

Jago chortled. "Oh well," he said. "We'll see about that." He then clapped his hands together and closed his eyes for a moment. When they opened, each hand was glowing with red intensity. Jago began separating his hands, but his movement was strained. It was almost as though his hands had become magnetic all of a sudden and wanted to stick to each other.

"What's he doing?" asked Kaos in shock.

The space between Jago's hands was no longer empty. Instead, there was a ball of purple lightning forming in that space.

Kire's eyes widened at the sight before him. Something snaked past him; it was the stem of a crawling plant. He glanced at Rose and saw her muttering something and watching the stem. The stem rose high and was soon joined by several others. Then, like an army given the charging order, all the stems headed straight at Jago and wrapped themselves tightly around his hands.

When Kire saw that Jago was incapacitated, he looked around for Trace. "Trace! Come and finish him before he breaks free!"

Kire looked at Rose and didn't think she would be able to hold on much longer. She was straining and looked as though she was in pain.

"Trace?" Kire yelled angrily, looking around for him. He

found Trace sprawled on the floor, unconscious. "Trace!" Kire yelled again, shaking Trace, but there was no response.

Kaos bounded over the broken flower pots and slabs and was at Trace's side immediately. "Hey, buddy," he said, shaking him, but again, there was no response.

Kire felt sweat break out across his forehead. He had called innocent kids together to die in the most gruesome and unbelievable way possible. Something then snapped behind him and he turned to look. Jago had broken the leash Rose put on him and the ball of purple lightning between his hands was growing bigger.

What sent shock waves down Kire's spine was the fact that Jago was facing Rose directly; he was going to throw the ball of lightning at her!

"Rose!"

She looked at him, still pressed against the sealed door of the greenhouse. The fear in her eyes made Kire sick to his stomach and his head pound.

"Kire! Kire!!" It was Kaos standing beside him with bravery Kire had never seen in him before; Trace's injury seemed to have changed something within him. He was wearing his diadem again, and his eyes burned with the fires of vengeance.

"Can you use the shield?" Kaos asked.

"What shield?" Kire replied.

"Albus said something about your book having a shield that can deflect attacks. Can you bring that shield up?"

"I don't know, Kaos," said Kire. "I've never tried it before. I don't know how it works."

"Well, you have the next twenty seconds to figure it out," Kaos said hoarsely.

"Wait, what do you mean?"

Kaos just flashed Kire a smile that sent chills down his spine.

Kire swallowed. How was he supposed to set up a shield he

had never summoned before? What if it was too weak to repel whatever Jago was going to throw at it?

"Hey, you ugly thing," Kaos called at Jago. The latter groaned and turned his cone-shaped head to face the insolent teenager.

"I see you're trying to distract me from her," Jago announced.

"You want to fight a harmless girl first? I challenge you, Jago, fight me," he barked at the monster and then said to Kire. "Are you ready yet?"

Kire clutched his book tightly. "I'm not ready, Kaos. I don't think I'll ever be."

"Good," said Kaos, "because that thing is going to hit us with all its got—"

"What?" whimpered Kire.

"—and you have to be able to get that shield up in time to deflect its power and send it back. I don't think it'll let any of us near it again. Our only chance is to use whatever it is conjuring against it."

"What if that thing does not kill it? What if it makes it stronger?"

"Really, Kire? Do you think our friend here *wants* to make any of us stronger? He wants to kill us! Do you have any more stupid questions?"

Kire shook his head nervously.

"Good," Kaos said and turned to Jago. "Come on, Jago, give it your best shot."

Jago scoffed. "For a young boy, you're certainly eager to die. Well, so be it."

He continued to open his hands slowly and as he did, the size of the ball in his hands increased. White lightning flashed through the purple ball of energy like webs of electricity.

"You're not going to like this," Jago bellowed.

Kaos smiled and said, "Speak for yourself, alien."

Jago growled loudly and threw the ball of purple energy at them. Kire's eyes widened at the basketball-sized ball of energy heading their way.

"Kire, now!"

Kire squeezed his eyes shut and threw the hand that held the book forward.

"Shieeeeeeld!" he yelled as loud as he could with as much faith in the book as he could muster. Kire felt so powerful at the moment that he could swear he felt the earth shaking below his feet. Kire's eyes widened in shock when he didn't see anything pop up in front of them. There was no shield! And the ball was approaching with the speed of a comet!

He was paralyzed with fear and couldn't peel his eyes off the ball of destruction approaching him. Then, when it was just inches from making contact with Kire and Kaos, the ball slowed as though it hit an elastic wall, then rebounded in the exact direction it had come from. All he heard before Jago was blown into oblivion was that unearthly, haunting, horrifying scream again. Jago had disappeared completely and there was a hole wide enough for a small car to pass through on the other wall.

It was over.

Rose burst into tears and slid her back down against the wall until she was sitting on the floor. Kaos returned mournfully to Trace, who was still sprawled on the floor.

"I'm sorry, buddy," said Kaos, tears streaming down his cheeks. "I'm really sorry."

Kire put a hand on Kaos' shoulder and gave him a gentle squeeze.

Someone snorted.

"Trace?" called Kaos doubtfully.

"I've always wanted to see you cry, idiot," Trace said, shoving Kaos good-naturedly.

"Trace!" said Kaos excitedly. "You're alive!"

"What? Were you expecting me to die at the hands of a psychotic, overgrown octopus?"

Kaos pulled Trace into a tight hug that made him wince.

"Easy there now," Trace groaned painfully. "I think I broke a rib or two."

Just when they were starting to relax, a white light flashed in the greenhouse.

"Tell me it's not another one," Rose whimpered.

"Oh, well," said Trace. "If we're expecting another alien, then I'd better die again." He relaxed back on the floor and closed his eyes.

"Move over, Trace. I want to die, too," Kaos said, lying down beside Trace.

"What for?" Trace asked. "You're still alive!"

"So are you!" Kaos hissed.

"Guys, it's Albus," Kire announced excitedly.

Kaos and Trace sprang up from their pretense at once.

"Albus? The floating guy from the cave?"

"You are as right as rain, young heroes," said Albus. "You do not know how happy I am to see you all alive."

"I'm happy to be alive," said Trace.

"Back home, I placed a bet that at least one of you would die."

"What?!" they chorused at once.

Albus chuckled. "It is a stupid trick I learned from a human friend. Reverse psychology is what he calls it. He said to always expect the worst and you will never be disappointed. The next time you fight another of Yash's stooges, you keep that in mind."

"What do you mean 'another'?" asked Kaos angrily. "There are still more of them?"

"My dear boy—" Albus started.

"I'm not your dear boy! I'm not your son!" Kaos snapped.

Albus smoothed his long soft beard. "Indeed, you are not my son; he died two hundred years ago."

Trace cleared his throat. "Why don't you have another son?"

Albus laughed heartily and darted around like a balloon. "Albuses undergo fission to have children, and it is unfortunate that you can only split yourself into two halves. But cheer up, you all. The whole population of Albuses is celebrating because of you. And that is some bravery on your part, Trace, no one has ever done as much as touched Jago, and you cut him!"

Trace shrugged. "It was easy when he was distracted."

"Downplaying your praises, I see. Humble. I like it," Albus said and clapped like a five-year-old again. "You folks should not worry about anything here in the greenhouse in terms of cleaning up. We will take care of it."

"And Jago?" asked Rose.

"He is gone, a victim of his own obliterating powers; you won't find a body."

Kire thought Albus looked more gaunt than usual.

"Albus, I have a question," Rose said, stepping forward. "Were you guys just watching us the whole time? And didn't try coming to help?"

Albus scratched his right cheek with an index finger. "We did not try because we cannot help," he said.

"I think I've had enough of your gift," she said angrily, taking off the Pendantix. "You can have it back."

"I cannot take it," he said. "The gift leaves on its own when the dark hour has passed. If you do not want it, you can dump it in your wardrobe, as the last of you had."

Kire knew Albus was talking about Amberly.

"I want you to imagine for a second that you had to deal with two Jagos at once," said Albus, "or five or ten. If one shook you this badly, imagine what an army of them would do."

"If we can beat them, then the *actual* army can," Kaos opined.

Albus shook his head. "Jago underestimated you and that is

why he fell. Did you hear when I said no one had laid hands on him in forever? He is sly and dangerous and evil. We do not know how he plans to do it, but Yash is trying to bypass Albus to the Earth realm."

Kire blinked heavily. "I—I don't understand," he said, stepping forward. "You mean he's going to find another way to Earth?"

"Precisely," Albus said. "And he is launching a barrage of attacks on Albus, so we cannot help you here. Every man counts in the Albus defense... so you see, you are Earth's only hope."

"He nearly died!" Rose pointed at Trace. A glassy wall of tears threatening to fall had gathered in her brown eyes.

"I know, Rose," said Albus, "and you do not know how much it hurts that all I and every other Albus back on Albus can do is watch you and your friends fight for your lives. We watched you battle an enemy a hundred times as old and a thousand times as cunning."

Rose sniffed and wiped her nose with the back of her hand.

Albus' flickering projection came down to Rose and caressed her cheek. "We ask you to die, that all might live... because that is exactly what we are doing ourselves..."

He vanished slowly into the air like dissipating smoke.

"That went well," Kaos murmured, starting towards the exit.

Together, they pushed the slab away from the door and left. The air outside was chilly and piercing. Gray clouds had scattered themselves all over the black sky.

"It's nice to see a world without tentacle people again," Kaos acknowledged when they arrived at the car. "Hop in. I don't think anybody can make it home on foot after what happened tonight."

Kire didn't raise any objection. Kaos drove, Trace rode shotgun, while Kire and Rose shared the backseat.

"And by the way, Kire," said Trace, "I won't be available when the next alien comes. I have a family commitment."

"We don't even know when he's going to show up," Kire croaked.

"Yeah? I won't be around whenever he does, so please don't call me at all."

Kire heaved.

"Me, too, Kire," said Kaos, "I think I'm going to have a broken leg that day. A hero with a broken leg is a liability in battle, so don't call me either."

The drive was mostly silent after that. First, they drove over to Rose's house and dropped her off, then Kire.

He watched the car zoom off into the distance, tail lights flashing as they went. Halo was right. After all, they would need all their strength to face what was coming their way—all of it. Today, every single one of them had played a role in bringing down Jago, their first villain. And if Albus was to be believed, the first of many to come.

Kire considered asking Halo if there was a future where his mother didn't catch him sneaking inside at three in the morning. Fortunately for him, there was such a possibility, and he was able to sneak in without any trouble. The door was still unlocked when he got there too; Kire hoped he didn't put his parents in danger by leaving the door open like that.

Once Kire was inside his room, he locked the door behind him and put Halo on the desk.

'Thank you,' he wrote. His words sank into the glowing golden page.

'The pleasure is all mine,' Halo replied. 'And you don't have to yell next time you need a shield, just hold me in the direction and will it.'

Kire snorted. 'You should've given me training on that before.'

'There is something I have to show you immediately,' Halo wrote.

What is it?' Kire wrote with a frown.

'The past, and it's inside me. Put your palms on both open pages.'

Kire did as he was told.

'Are you ready?' Halo wrote. This time the words were hanging in the air in front of him.

"For what?" Kire said aloud.

The world shut down.

22

When Kire was seven years old, his mother took him to Prince Edward Island for a family wedding. While the party was going on, he wandered off and went toward the apple orchard nearby, where he had seen a well when he first arrived at the island three days before. The well had a shed above it, and a wall of rough stones surrounded it up to his knees. There was a blue cup hanging from a cord tied to the shed. The cup had a red rose with one green leaf on its side and a small dent on the rim.

Seven-year-old Kire, wearing a black suit, starched white shirt with a collar that covered his neck entirely, and a red bow tie that was definitely too big, leaned forward and peered into the black waters of the well. The inside of the well was as rough as the outside; the stones used looked as though they were stacked together in a hurry.

Little Kire leaned in closer to the well, which seemed to be calling him.

"Who are you?" someone said behind him.

Kire startled and nearly tripped over the small wall around the well. His heart picked up speed immediately and began to pound furiously behind his ribs. He turned to face the inquirer and saw it was a kid with a fat square face, eyes nearly covered by a chin, and thick red hair. The boy was larger and probably older, although Kire was just an inch or two taller than him. The kid was clad in a black suit, too, only his fit a bit better and was of better quality.

"You don't need to know," Kire said before turning back around. The kid walked up beside Kire, so they were both looking into the depths of the well.

"It's not so deep," the kid said, bending far over the well. He dug his fat white hands into his trouser pockets and smiled at Kire. He relaxed at the boy's smile and looked back into the well. Both boys were standing with the tips of their shoes up against the stone wall of the well. Their images were reflected in the black water.

"It's nearly twenty feet deep," Kire said. "That's more than five times your height."

"That's the entire depth of the well," the boy said. "The water is only five-to-six feet away. I know my math, too, you see."

Kire swallowed. "Oh." He felt outsmarted.

"I'm too big to jump into the well."

"Why would you want to jump into the well? There's a pool somewhere around the house," Kire said innocently.

The red-haired kid laughed and said, "How about you jump inside the well!'

"What?" Kire gasped. He glanced down at the ominous abyss again; it called him, reaching for him like the voice of a siren at sea. But he could drown, and nobody would be able to hear him struggling.

"Looks like you need a little help getting in," the boy said.

He felt a pair of surprisingly strong hands wrap around his ankles and pull him off his feet and into the well.

Traveling through Halo—or getting sucked into it—felt

exactly like falling into the well felt. There was only darkness and the cold feeling of helplessness like the ground had just been pulled out from under him. His hands felt too small and weak to reach the walls of this vacuum.

Kire held his eyes shut as he fell further into the black hole, and he drew his legs up to his chest and wrapped his arms around them. How long would he spend in the well? Would he endure the night?

Kire didn't know exactly when he stopped falling, but it wasn't until a hand touched him on the shoulder that he realized he had landed. He lifted his head from between his legs and squinted as bright light hit him square in the face.

"Where am I?" he muttered.

"You look just as I imagined you would look," someone with the voice of a prepubescent boy said beside him.

He turned to see who it was and wasn't prepared for what he saw. The person had the shape of a human but had powder-blue flurry fur like a rabbit's and was only about three or four feet tall.

"What are you?" asked Kire in wonderment.

"Ha," the figure exclaimed in apparent relief. "At least you are not screaming," he said and then added, "Although I wished you were screaming; I have just authored a book called 'How to Handle a Meeting with your Quintet Spirit,' but it looks like I will have to wait until the next holder. Hopefully, he will not be as brave, so I can put some more interesting memoirs in the book."

Kire's cheeks grew hot pink. "Who are you?" he asked.

The small figure chuckled. He had four large front teeth—two on the top and two on the bottom. His big bright blue eyes were round and wide with excitement, and he had ears like a rabbit's.

"I am Halo," he said.

"Halo?" he repeated in disbelief. "You're... Halo? My book?"

"That's me!" Halo said.

"Am I—did I—where am I?"

Around Kire was the most boundless land he ever saw. The landscape was dreamlike in a sense where everything was serene and perfect, yet... off. There was absolutely nothing around him except the landscape. The ground was covered with plush dark green grass that reached to just below the knees. On the horizon, he could see a dreamy periwinkle sky with the softest pink clouds kissing the field below. There was nothing or no one else—just grass, clouds, and this bunny-book-boy.

"Where is this?" Kire asked again, looking around. "And you're *Halo*?"

"You are in my mind, Kire," said Halo proudly. "And it is true; I'm Halo. But we do not have all day long to babble and chatter. Grab my hand. There is something I must show you."

Halo held out a hand; it was small with three nailless fingers. "Put your hand in mine, Kire," he repeated. "There is somewhere we have to go together."

Kire knitted his eyebrows together in worry. "Where— where are you taking me?"

Halo sighed impatiently. "Quintet past, Kire. Now grab my hand."

Kire didn't really see what choice he had here; he couldn't turn around and go back to his room if he wanted to. He looked all around him once again to see if there was any way to escape —there wasn't. He figured it was best if he just did what Halo told him to do.

"The past is always a hard place to visit, is it not?" said Halo.

Kire looked away from the pair of piercing eyes and slid his hand into Halo's outstretched hand. Then...

Lights out.

The darkness that Kire was tumbling down into was quite similar to the one he fell into when he rolled down the gorge in

White Forest. And the horrifying, uneasy feeling of the earth parting ways with his feet was very much like the time back at Prince Edwards Island with the well. He squeezed his eyes shut and tried not to think of the speed at which he was falling through nothingness like a rocket shooting through the endless darkness of outer space. Before he knew it, he felt ground suddenly beneath his feet, though he didn't necessarily feel himself land—it was almost like the ground simply had just reappeared, or his feet lost all feeling and then regained it.

"Open your eyes, Kire," Halo's voice broke through. "We are here."

It was night on a corn farm. The stars were vast and expansive—Kire had never seen so many. The corn seemed to stretch out all around him for miles, and there was a gentle, mild breeze that gently caused the corn to sway. Kire saw a short man with lines deeply creasing his face who wore an old brown hat and held a rake in his hand.

Aside from the man, the only thing Kire could spot that wasn't a corn stalk was the rather ominous-looking scarecrow. They were in the middle of the corn field in a sort of clearing. No barn or buildings to be seen. The man was looking up at the night sky. Kire looked up at the sky again and noticed five astonishingly bright comets gliding across the heavens. The comets were faintly pink, just like the comet-rock-eggs he saw in the cave, except the colors were fainter since they were much farther away.

"Those five comets up there are the quintet gifts, right?" asked Kire.

Halo nodded. "Yes," he said. "This was two hundred years ago, the tenth time the quintet gifts showed up."

"Did—were they... successful?" asked Kire, trying to avoid asking if everyone with the gifts died.

"No," said Halo frankly. "The first ones with the gifts were hopeful but were killed off by Jago. The second was killed by

Heno, but Rezin has never had to touch anyone. In fact, no one has seen him in action before. He is the last resort of the last resort. And basically, for the last couple thousand years, Jago and Heno have taken turns demolishing anyone who tries to fight them."

"So Jago, Heno, and Rezin—are those the three aliens Mr. Burke saw back at the forest?" asked Kire.

"They are," Halo replied.

"And Jago is the alien we just defeated, right?"

"That is correct," Halo said. "Neither Heno nor Rezin have ever been defeated, though."

Kire rolled his eyes, thinking back to earlier that night at the school. "Why does that not surprise me?"

"Sounds like you have a bone to pick," Halo said, "but you don't know the whole story, do you? The first people to wield the quintet gifts were not only chosen but were also trained by an Albus we sent to them."

"You sent an Albus to them?" asked Kire in disbelief.

"Yes," Halo answered. "And Jago took them out like they were nothing.

"Jago has been around for two thousand years? Didn't you kill his men during the first invasion?"

Halo chuckled and then smiled sadly. "Yes," he said. "We thought we did. It turns out Yash was a more slippery creature than we gave him credit for. He was prepared for a reality where he lost the fight against Earth."

"I don't understand," said Kire.

"Think of the possible outcomes of the war as contingencies. And for each contingency, he prepared a plan."

"And you guys didn't?"

"There is a reason Albus is no longer merged with Earth, Kire," said Halo. "We prepared for them to never come again, but what we didn't plan for was the possibility that he was already on Earth."

"How could he have prepared so well for every possible outcome?"

"In war, there are only two outcomes: a win or a loss. There are, however, many ways to end up at both outcomes. Yash left Jago, Heno, and Rezin behind as a contingency plan; he wanted to give himself another go at Earth in case he lost."

"Why didn't you see that?" asked Kire. "If you could see the future, how didn't you see that Yash was going to leave sleeper agents on Earth? All those people who died fighting Jago and Heno would never have been killed if you saw it. And we almost lost our lives fighting the same monster! What good are you if you can't do the one thing you were created to do?"

Kire was breathing heavily by the time he was done talking. He slightly regretted being so harsh, but it's true—they could've died! Trace looked like he may as well have been dead—it's a miracle the guy survived at all. And all of that could've been avoided?

He didn't want to meet Halo's eyes, so he pretended to be looking at the waving corn stalks and the ears of corn with golden hairs hanging from them.

"You are right, Kire," said Halo. "I should have seen Yash was going to leave three powerful monsters behind. But I can only see the things revealed to me by nature."

"Really?" Kire scoffed. "And nature thought it was cool to be hiding stuff from you? Even if you're the good guy?"

"It's called balance, Kire. There is no good without evil, no light without darkness. In the darkness, you will find light, and in light, darkness."

"What does that even mea—" Kire was interrupted by a tremor that shook the entire farm and he had to throw his arms out for balance. Then, just as soon as it started, the tremor ended abruptly.

Kire looked around, curious. "What just happened?" he asked.

"The timeline is not stable, so we cannot stay here too long. Let us go somewhere else."

Halo held out his small blue hand again for Kire to hold on to. Kire hesitated; he didn't enjoy the ride at all. Maybe Halo was right; the past is always a hard place to visit.

He groaned and grabbed the blue hand stretched out to him. The world went black, and Kire felt the Earth under him fall away. He was falling fast and hard through void and darkness.

"Where are we now?" Kire asked when he opened his eyes. They were standing on the peak of a mountain and the dark sky was littered with an unfathomable number of stars.

"This is more than six thousand years ago," said Halo, "just before the war started."

Kire heard the sound of footsteps approaching from behind and he turned around to see who it was. Two hooded figures, far taller than any human, in large black flowing cloaks, were climbing up to the peak where Kire and Halo stood. They were carrying a large, cylindrical package.

"Don't we have to hide?" asked Kire. Unlike the farmer he had seen staring at the comets, these men had a cloud of dread hovering around them that was so powerful even visitors to the realm could feel the ruthless grip on their souls.

"There is no need for that," said Halo. "This time has already passed. We are in its shadow."

Halo's words didn't put Kire's troubled mind at ease. A bitter cold washed over him as the men drew nearer.

"I'm scared, Halo," he said. "I'm scared."

"Stay behind me," said Halo.

Kire snorted. "You're far smaller than I am. What good will staying behind you do?"

The cloaked men were nearly where Halo and Kire stood at the edge of the peak.

"Is that Yash?" Kire whispered.

"Yes," Halo replied in a normal voice. He didn't seem afraid at all.

Just as they passed by, Kire swore he'd just seen Yash's eyes, or what seemed like eyes. The rest of Yash's face was covered by the hood and a black shadow.

"What is he?"

"No one knows. Yash was not born; he just... *is*. He is probably one of the oldest beings in the universe. Even if this event happened thousands of years ago, you could still feel his dark power. Do you want to know what it feels like to be around him in person?"

Kire shook his head no.

The cloaked men came to a halt and opened the cylinders, bringing out two similar objects from the cylinders. The men spoke in a tongue so old and powerful; the sound of it alone sent a wave of dizziness through Kire's body. The language had a lot of hissing yet was somehow dark, deep, and groaning. It seemed to be coming from all around him, just like how Jago's voice was when he spoke in the greenhouse. They unrolled the objects, stood up the cylinders, and pulled legs from them, so they became a sort of tripod. Then they hung the two unrolled objects on the cylinders.

"Is that the Djigi?" asked Kire, pointing at the enormous mirrors that hung from the cylinders.

"Yes," said Halo. "The Djigi is a twin element. It can work only as long the twin is still functional. Like Jago, Heno, and Rezin, the Djigis perish when they lose purpose."

"What does it do?" Kire asked.

Halo simply silently pointed at the hooded figures.

Now, the cylinders were set opposite each other so that the mirrors were facing each other. They began to glow bright purple light around the borders. Yash stepped into the first mirror like it was a door and then emerged through the second mirror. He returned through the second mirror and stepped back through the first.

Kire's eyes widened. "Is that what I think it is?"

Halo nodded. "The Djigi is a portal," he said. "Yash has always had the first one with him."

Yash bent over the floor and burned a line into the rock with his finger across the spot where the mirrors stood. The line his finger drew was bright red and melted to lava.

"What *is* this thing?" asked Kire about Yash again. He shook his head in disbelief and stared at the creature with wide eyes.

"Take my hand," said Halo, stretching his small blue hand toward Kire again.

Kire groaned. "Can't you just say everything with your mouth? Why do you have to show me everything?"

"It'll be easier to convince the rest if you see things for yourself."

Kire sighed, resigned to what was coming. He snapped his eyes shut and put a shivering hand in Halo's firm and warm grip.

Blackness and free fall.

When Kire opened his eyes again, he was somewhere vaguely familiar. The air smelled wet and damp and the woods around looked like he had seen them before. Three men in long coats and flat caps were huddled around the statue of Marilyn Moe.

"When is this?" asked Kire. If this was Marilyn Moe, then they were back at St. Bernard. But there were no buildings, no soccer field, no grass. Everywhere was just trees.

"A little over fifty years ago, two years before the construction of the school. What's left of the five came to bury their half of the Djigi. They're probably the most successful of all the quintets to have ever existed."

Kire's face was pale with dread and fear. "Only three of them survived?" he asked.

"Two of them survived; the third man was the then-mayor of Montgomery," said Halo. "They hid the second pair of the Djigi in that statue. But it would've been weird to leave the statue in the middle of nowhere, so St. Bernard was built around it to douse suspicion."

Kire was violently shaking with fear. "Only two survived?"

"Yes," said Halo, "and they were thoroughly trained and well-prepared."

"But didn't the comet shoot one hundred and fifty years ago?" asked Kire when he noticed the farmer from the first time travel. "How come he's still alive?"

"The quintet gifts give life to its holders until the time is past."

"What time?" asked Kire.

"For the Djigi to work, it has to be parallel with its twin mirror. No matter what distance is between them or what obstruction is between them, they will connect, but they *have* to be exactly opposite each other."

Kire sighed in relief. "That's good then," he said. "Since Albus is between Yash and Earth, he'll never be able to accurately set the mirrors across from each other."

"Yash is far too cunning, Kire," said Halo. "He is wicked and sly. Underestimate him and you will not live long enough to regret it. Did you see him on the mountain peak last time? What do you think he was doing?"

Kire pursed his lips. "I don't know... testing the mirrors?"

"Taking measurements," Halo declared. "He knows the location of the peak and will set the mirror with him in such a way that..."

"... when the second mirror is on the mountain peak, it'll connect with its twin back on his ship," finished Kire.

"Exactly," Halo said and opened his small blue hands. "And the sacrifices made by all those quintet holders who have had to come every two hundred years or so will be wasted. The

Albuses got tired of training the people who had the gifts because Jago and Heno always won anyway. That's why you were not chosen; we just left the gifts lying around for whoever stumbled upon them. And by the strangest stroke of luck, all five gifts were picked by a single band at the same time."

"You want nature to decide who won this time around?"

"Yes," said Halo. "Nature had to see that we had tried enough times and were tired. Life gives breaks, you know. The mirrors must be used in ten days, so you should expect an attack from Heno soon."

"Why ten days?" asked Kire. Halo's words and revelations so far had done nothing to convince him they stood the tiniest chance against Heno.

"After ten days, the Earth would have revolved away from the known position. Since he cannot get to Earth or communicate with his underlings, he won't be able to calculate the next position to align with."

"Makes sense," said Kire, who still didn't understand a whole lot of what Halo had said.

Halo pulled Kire around so they were facing each other.

"Kire, I know this is a lot. Heck! People far more valiant have tried and failed, but you beat Jago, and that is our hope. Now that Heno knows the mirror is somewhere around the school, he will want to come for it. You cannot let him have it. Destroy the Djigi if you must. See you next time, Kire."

"What? Wait, Halo! Wait!"

Kire found himself sitting in his desk chair, panting and dripping with sweat like he'd just run a marathon. The faint light of the encroaching morning pushed away the darkness of the night. Kire winced and staggered to his feet. He went to the bathroom, where he freshened up before collapsing onto his bed.

His mind was racing so fast, going over the events that occurred over the last six hours or so, that it was all a blur, and he could hardly focus on one thought. Somehow, however, he managed to doze off for just a moment.

His mother knocked on the door thirty minutes later to remind him they had to make the early morning mass.

Throughout the sermon, his head kept bobbing low in drowsiness and before jerking back awake. After what felt like an eternity, he was back home again and didn't waste a minute before hurrying to bed.

He didn't wake up until dinner time and his head felt like there was concrete hardening inside it.

"You look terrible," his mother said when he came downstairs.

"Don't do drugs, kid," his father said. "Once you get started on that road, you're going to lose a whole lot before you find yourself again."

"Yeah, all right, *Dad*," Kire said, shooting a glare at Gerald.

23

Kire woke up early the next morning after having a restless sleep full of odd dreams filled with blue rabbits, pink comets, and flaming swords. After lying in bed for a while, he trudged downstairs for breakfast. He mumbled a good morning to his mother.

"Good morning, Kire," she said. "Sweetheart, are you *sure* everything is okay?"

He mustered up the most genuine smile he could, kissed her on the cheek, and said, "Of course. I promise I'd let you know if there was something wrong."

Emma smiled reluctantly and tentatively said, "Okay."

After finishing his breakfast of oatmeal and chatting with his mother a bit, trying to reassure her and get her to quit worrying about him, Kire left for school. When he arrived, he had flashbacks of the events that took place over the weekend and felt his heart racing as he broke into a cold sweat.

It's okay, he reassured himself. *Jago is dead; it's all over for now.*

He was shocked to see how well Albus Bridge cleaned up after the fight; there was no sign that there had been an extraterrestrial at school shooting lightning and breaking things. He hurried to the greenhouse for any sign of damage; surely, there must be some sign of the events that took place Friday night. However, there was nothing. Not a single flower was displaced. Kire was filled with feelings of awe and resentment, awe at the speed and efficiency the Albuses cleaned with, and resentment at the fact that every sign of their victory had been swept off like a page ripped from a book.

"Do you believe this?" Kaos said bitterly. "There isn't a single scratch on the school grounds. It makes no sense! I had to call Trace just to confirm it wasn't a dream."

"My ribs still hurt," Trace admitted. "That's a reality check I could live without."

"If the Albuses can clean up after us, why can't they get rid of Yash's men themselves?" groaned Amberly.

"*Us?*" Kire shot Amberly a dirty look for being absent from the fight on Friday.

"That's a question we'll ask the next time Albus Bridge shows up," Rose said to Amberly, ignoring Kire.

"No!" Kaos said, shaking his head adamantly. "I don't want to ever see that weirdo again. Every time he shows up, it's because there's trouble. If we don't fall into any trouble, we'll be just fine."

"Trouble is going to come and find us anyway," said Kire darkly.

Amberly narrowed her eyes suspiciously. "Is there something you're not telling us?"

"There are a whole lot of things I haven't told you yet," Kire said coldly.

"Easy now," said Trace. "Need I remind you we're *not* friends? Once this is over, I'm beating you out of this school."

"Suit yourself," Kire replied harshly. "While we were fighting for our lives, your girlfriend was hiding at home."

"Shut up, Kire," Trace growled.

"Or what? I don't like you any more than you like me."

"I don't like you at all," said Amberly, glowering at Kire.

"Even better!" Kire said. "I don't like you at all, and I wish I didn't have to talk with you every day about this mess we've found ourselves in."

"Maybe he would be more sympathetic if he knew Amberly's mother was battling for her life that night," Trace said coldly. "And here I was thinking we were the bullies."

Trace, Kaos, and Amberly rose from the table and sauntered off without another word. Rose and Kire were left to battle the awkward silence that occupied the empty seats.

"I shouldn't have said all that," said Kire. "I'm supposed to be trying to keep the team together, but here I am being what breaks us all apart. I'm so insensitive. It's not Yash that's tearing us apart now; it's me."

"Stop beating yourself up, Kire," Rose said. "You didn't know Amberly was taking care of her mother."

"Yeah, but I could've asked."

"She wouldn't have answered, and you know that," said Rose. "It's just her way of getting back at you."

Kire just sighed and the two sat in silence as they ate their lunch.

"Tomorrow is the unveiling of the capsule of Marilyn Moe," said Kire. "And there's something you need to hear before then. It's important."

He was staring into Rose's eyes with all the fear that had piled up inside of him these past three days.

"Kire, what is it?" asked Rose.

"I'd appreciate it if you could convince them to gather for a meeting after school," Kire said. "I—I have to get this burden off my shoulders."

The bell rang and Kire returned to class with a doleful expression on his face.

"Kire, why do you look like you just had a date with Mr. Schaefer?" Andrew scoffed.

"Mr. Loch will soon be in class, Andrew," Kire warned. "It would be terrible if you lost a tooth or two before he arrived."

Andrew simply scoffed again.

Kire still had trouble figuring out Andrew. Ever since he had tricked him into going into the White Forest, he had been a different breed altogether. He spaced out a lot, was always looking for a fight, and had been standing up to Trace and Kaos regularly.

"There is something I want to ask you, Kire," Andrew said. There was no fear in his eyes, no cowardice. Instead, there was reckless pride spread as a smirk in the corners of his lips.

"What do you want?" Kire asked coldly.

"Did you notice anything happening at the school over the weekend?"

Kire blinked. "I—I don't understand. What are you talking about?"

Andrew straightened up. "Never mind," he said, "you don't seem to know anything about it. What I need is someone who does, someone to pay."

Kire watched on in bewilderment as Andrew turned around to face Mr. Loch, who had just stepped into the class.

"Hello, ladies and gentlemen," Mr. Loch said.

The remainder of the day passed in a blur as Kire thought and worried about everything that was going on. He was relieved when the last bell of the day rang. While packing up his backpack, a boy with sleek, golden hair appeared in front of him with an unsettling grin on his face.

"Hello, Kire, I'm Stephan Krause," he said.

"I know who you are," Kire shot back. "Can I go now?"

"Do you mind sparing a few minutes of your time?" Stephan pressed.

"Yes, I do. I have to leave now," Kire said and tried to walk around Stephan, who just kept blocking his way.

"Not so fast, Kire," Stephan insisted. "We have some business to take care of."

Kire sighed. "What is it?" he asked.

"I've heard that if there is a new tough guy at school, he can challenge the top dog and the loser can never show his face at St. Bernard again."

"I—I don't know what you're talking about," said Kire.

Stephan laughed coldly and slapped a hand on Kire's shoulder; his cool façade was replaced by a devilish demeanor.

"You know very well what I'm talking about, Kire," he said. "Surely you must know Alfred, the kid Trace beat to become the top dog in this school."

Kire twitched a brow. "I might have heard of him," he said. Stephan didn't seem at all pleased by the reply, so Kire added. "What about him?"

"That kid hasn't been the same ever since," said Stephan. "And you can guess why."

"Uh, what's wrong with him?"

Stephan cocked his head. "No one knows."

"You do realize that Alfred hurt many people before Trace beat him, right?"

Stephan gritted his teeth. "None of them are as badly affected as my cousin, though. That's right—Alfred is my *cousin*. He refuses to speak to anyone or come out of the house because that's the only way he can cope with the situation he's in now."

"Look, I'm sorry for what happened to Alfred," Kire said, "but he created the system of 'top dogs' himself. He would beat kids until they couldn't stand up anymore. Trace was just a tougher kid who brought an end to Alfred's reign, and I daresay he's the better man here."

Stephan's face grew red. "Oh, is that so? You're gonna stick with Trace now, huh? Correct me if I'm wrong, but didn't he try to kill you just a couple of weeks ago?"

"Yes, he did," said Kire stubbornly. "But I'm still standing. That wouldn't have happened if Alfred was still the top dog. I'm sorry for what happened to him, but it was his choice. He created the top dog system, and he brought down lots of kids before he was dethroned himself."

Stephan eyed Kire menacingly. "You might want to watch your back from now on," he said before turning around and leaving.

"I see you're standing up for Trace," said Kaos. "I would've never believed Kire the righteous would ever defend a bully."

"Did you send him as a test of some sort?" asked Kire.

"Dude, we don't even talk. I think he genuinely hates Trace, and at least now we know he has a reason to."

"I hope you see how you create more monsters with your bullying," Kire breathed harshly. "C'mon. We have a meeting to get to."

Kire and Kaos walked silently to the back of the school where Trace, Rose, and Amberly were waiting.

"What is this?" said Amberly coldly. "You call for a meeting and arrive late."

"Sorry, I had to deal with something," Kire apologized.

"I can vouch for him," Kaos said. "I know a perfect spot where we can sit and talk for a while."

"I have to get home on time for my shift," said Amberly.

"I'll pay for the hour spent," Kaos offered.

"I don't want your money," Amberly fired back. She looked like she wanted to hit Kaos, but Trace grabbed her arm before she did.

"See, Kire," Kaos said. "You're not the only one she tries to fight; only you get it in more frequent doses. Follow me, guys, let me take you to Aunt Marg's."

The quintet crew arrived at Aunt Marg's a little over ten

minutes later. It was a grocery store in the front, but there was a door that led to a large room in the back. There was a large wall clock with teacups for numbers on the wall. On the wall, there was also a shelf of painted ceramic teapots with colorful knitted covers around each pot. The clothed tables were round and had four chairs surrounding each.

They found a quiet table in a corner and pulled up a fifth chair.

"All right, Kire, what is it you wanted to say so badly?" Kaos said.

Kire cleared his throat and regaled them with his encounter with Halo. With each scene that he told, each word that he said, he saw the corresponding reaction on their faces—reactions reading exactly how he was feeling as he went through this himself. They were especially disturbed when he mentioned the part where Halo said that only two survived of the most successful quintet group to date.

"And," Kire concluded, "that's all I have to say."

For what seemed like an eternity, nobody said a word. Kire watched the horrified expressions on their faces.

"Looks like everyone is afraid of dying," Kire said and chuckled sadly.

"What? Are you okay with losing your life?" asked Trace. He picked up the jar of cream and poured it into his steaming cup of tea.

"I don't know if my death will be worth anything," said Kire, "but I can't bear to think about the pain my mother will go through if I die. I can't do that to her."

"We're not going to die," said Amberly. "I wish you all could act like men."

"Me, too," said Trace.

"Oh, come on," Rose groaned.

"What? Boys aren't made of stone, you know?" Kaos insisted. "I don't know where you all get that idea that men are stronger than women. My dad can just walk into the room and start crying when things aren't fine, while I've never once seen my mom cry."

"Sounds like my dad," said Rose.

Kire knew his father would probably do the same under the guise of being drunk.

"The Djigi will be unraveled tomorrow. I'm sure Heno will be a happy spectator among the crowd," said Trace abruptly.

"He'll know Jago is gone, and he'll suspect the mirror is in school," said Rose, readjusting her ponytail. "You know, I can't help thinking he's among the students already. They can change forms, right Kire?"

"Yeah, what about that new guy?" Amberly suggested. "He seems to have something going on. He doesn't seem right."

"Definitely not him," said Kaos. "He does hate Trace, though, and has a good reason for it." He took a big slurp of his tea.

Trace leaned back into his seat. "We should organize a fight back in the White Forest. I'd like to knock some sense into that kid."

Kaos beamed and punched Trace on the shoulder. "Yeah... that's more like it, man. And—" He put his tea cup in the saucer. "—we should hype it up a little before the fight then make people pay to witness it."

"You guys are worse than I thought," said Kire, rolling his eyes. "We have a mad alien on the loose and it's some stupid *top dog* you'll be dropping in a year or so you're worried about?"

"I don't know what you want him to do, Kire," said Amberly. "Should he sit and mourn for his impending death?"

"*Nobody is going to die*," Rose asserted. "But we have to focus on the task at hand."

"Tell that to your boyfriend; did you not hear his story?" asked Amberly, snorting.

"I heard Kire say we're the only ones to ever lay a hand on Jago, let alone kill him. And we did that with *one of us* absent."

"I was absent because my mom was sick," Amberly snarled.

"And no one is blaming you for that," said Rose, "but stop gaslighting everyone."

Amberly's eyes flew open at this. "Oh, you think I'm gaslighting?"

"Stop making everyone feel guilty for the things that happen to you. We all have family issues to deal with as much as you do," Rose replied hotly.

"What? How dare—" Amberly started.

"Enough!" said Kire, slamming a hand down on the table. "How about we just enjoy some scones, hmm?"

"Oh, Kire, you really know how to warm up a man's appetite," Kaos said, licking his lips appreciatively. "Aunt Marg! We need some scones and jam here."

"This week is going to be very busy," said Trace. "We have a friendly soccer match with Bowell High School this Friday."

"Now, that's something we can all discuss," said Kire appreciatively.

Rose groaned.

They ate up and exited Aunt Marg's place a few minutes later.

"Today wasn't so bad," Kire said to his mom later that night as they ate dinner. "And something exciting at school is happening tomorrow—they're opening the time capsule from fifty years ago."

Emma brightened up at this. "That's cool. What's in the capsule?"

Kire shrugged. "I don't know," he said. "It's a relic of some sort."

"I should come and see," Emma said brightly.

"What?" Kire said, nearly choking on his water. "No way, no. Don't come and see. It's for students' eyes only, no moms or dads. I'll take a picture so you can see."

"Okay…" she said, eyeing her son suspiciously. "Okay, I'll stay home then."

"It's for students only, no parents, don't you come."

Kire tried to study a bit that night. He wondered if his father would be proud of him now with all that alien-fighting and soccer he's been spending his time on. He didn't bother rousing Halo that night. He dreaded hearing another story of ugly truths and hopeless pasts.

Kire found himself on that mountain peak in the White Forest thousands of years before it had all of the trees he knew today, where he'd first seen Yash. The sky was a deep blue and there was a river of purple rays spread across it, taking on a similar shape and look to the northern lights. The ground was as rough and jagged as it had been when he and Halo first made the trip. This time, however, Halo was nowhere to be found. Save for the jutting peaks of rising mountains as far as the eye could see. There was nothing else to see in that place.

"Halo!" Kire yelled at the top of his voice. All he could hear in response was his own voice echoing back. Kire shivered and wiped his nose with the back of his hand. He was in his pajamas, barefooted, and cold.

"Halo!" he yelled again, folding his arms across his chest to keep warm.

He heard steps slowly approaching from behind. Something, however, told him that these were not Halo's footsteps he heard. Heart pounding, he slowly turned around and saw two cloaked men carrying a tall cylinder approaching the peak he stood on. He had seen this before; this was Yash and some other horrible unknown figure. He sighed, relieved that he at least knew what was going to happen next. Yash would pass by him, no harm would be done, and he would just have to wait to be thrown back into reality, like when he was here with Halo.

They kept walking closer and closer, so Kire stepped to let them pass him by. Even though he was certain Yash couldn't see him, he didn't want to take any avoidable risk. When they were right beside him, one of the cloaked figures stopped while the other continued onwards. Kire shook his head.

"No, no," he muttered. "That isn't how it went the last time."

The cloaked figure's face was covered with the hood, but Kire could tell that this figure was very thin and at least seven feet tall. Kire knew this was Yash. Suddenly, he lifted his head and stared into Kire's eyes with those two red slits of his.

"Kire," Yash whispered sharply.

Kire broke into a cold sweat and whimpered, "No, you can't see me. This is the past. This isn't real."

Yash let out a disturbing noise that sounded like a laugh, but it was much closer to a growl than anything. "This is real. I can see you. This is right now." Yash then raised a foot in the air and kicked him in the chest. Kire staggered backward, lost his footing, and fell off the mountain, screaming.

When he woke up, he was still screaming. His mother was by his side, holding him, while his father leaned against the door with a disgruntled look on his face.

"Sweetheart, it's all right. Mommy is here," Emma said and held him tight in an embrace.

"You're spoiling him, Emma," Gerald grunted. "How's he going to handle things on his own if you're always treating him like a child? He needs to be a man!"

"I don't know where you got your idea of masculinity from, Gerald, but I assure you it's as wrong as two left shoes. And he'll always be my child."

"Suit yourself," Gerald grumbled before going out the door.

Emma pulled away and cupped her son's face. "Are you all right?" she asked.

Kire nodded. "Just... It was a bad dream."

"Oh, I know that very well," she said. "You were screaming for more than two minutes. It was almost like you were trapped in your dream. Do you want to talk about it?"

"No," he murmured. "I think I'd rather try and get some sleep. Tomorrow is going to be a busy day."

"Okay, darling." His mother rose from the bed and said, "Come wake me if you need anything."

"Thanks, Mom," said Kire.

Emma blew him a kiss and disappeared through the door.

Kire wasn't able to fall back asleep that night, afraid he was going to fall back into that nightmare. He spent the rest of the night reading and studying. When morning came, Kire was thankful that his mom didn't mention the dream and his dad wasn't there.

He decided to take Halo to school; the last thing he wanted was to be caught by an alien, unprepared and unwarned. Trace and Kaos were already in their seats when Kire got to school, both looking tense and on edge.

Mrs. Goody's voice announced over the PA that an assembly would be held in the gym that morning.

"Do you think Heno is going to try attacking today?" asked Kaos as they made their way to the gym. "It's broad daylight and there are hundreds of people around."

"I'm not sure Heno cares about that," said Kire.

"But he must be stealthy about whatever it is he's doing," said Trace.

"He's desperate," Kire added. "He has eight days until Earth revolves past the position Yash knows about. I suspect those things don't like failing their masters."

They pushed through the gym's double doors and met up with Amberly and Rose.

"Nervous about what may happen next?" Rose asked Kire.

"Yeah," he said.

They all took their seats while the rest of the school settled in.

"Attention, boys and girls," Mr. Schaefer began. He had on a black suit and a red tie with white polka dots. "Today, we'll unearth a treasure long-buried at this school. Today, we unravel the mystery of Marilyn Moe. Now please join me in welcoming a very special guest we have with us today, the mayor of Montgomery!"

The students all clapped politely as the mayor approached the stage. Kire and the group found themselves sitting frozen with fear and dread.

The mayor walked in long brisk strides. He wore a white suit that didn't fit him quite right and a white hat to compliment his rough tanned face and dirty blond handlebar mustache.

"Hello, boys and girls of St. Bernard," the mayor began in a shockingly high voice. The man was short and bore the resemblance of a teapot. "Today is a historic day for St. Bernard, and I daresay you're all lucky to be a part of this important moment."

Kire zoned out while the mayor spoke. His eyes roamed over the heads of the students as he tried to find any suspicious movement. Everything looked suspicious to the on-edge Kire today.

"... And now, we'll all move to the back of the school where we'll gather around the Marilyn Moe statue to unearth the capsule."

"If Heno is going to attack, now is probably the best time," Amberly suggested.

Trace shook his head. "I think he would wait until he was

certain the mirror is what's coming out of the capsule before he attacks."

"And he has to be disguised!" said Kire, "I just wish I knew what he was disguised *as*."

The hundreds of students poured through the gym doors while the teachers, staff, and mayor went around to a different door to avoid the chaotic crowd of kids. Kire looked back and saw Kaos running after the mayor. "What is he doing?" he asked Trace and nodded in Kaos' direction.

Trace scoffed. "He's trying to avoid the crowd, I guess."

After an unreasonable amount of time, everyone had finally gathered in the backyard around the statue. Marilyn Moe stood there, a statue that had witnessed the passing of time, witnessing events people would never believe happened. She sat with one of her legs crossed over the other and her hands resting gently on her lap. Two men with hammers and drilling tools stood by the statue, waiting to dig up the one thing Kire wished never existed.

"And now," the mayor announced. "We'll watch as these gentlemen dig this fifty-year-old treasure from out of here. Gentlemen, please begin. Does anyone have questions to ask?"

Several hands shot up that instant. The mayor tutted. "That's a lot of hands," he said, "Ah, let me begin with the gentleman over there, yes, you. What's your name?"

"Trace Henderson, sir," the voice boomed.

"Mr. Henderson, you're welcome to fire your question."

"Thank you, sir," Trace said. "Mr. Mayor, I just wanted to know *why* we're digging this out?"

Kire noticed a dark scowl had replaced the plain smile on Mr. Schaefer's face. The mayor chuckled and scratched his head as though trying to remember something he had forgotten. "I—I don't understand what you're saying," he said. "Are you not happy we're about to witness a fifty-year-old secret?"

"If it had to be buried then, why should it be unraveled

now?" asked Trace. "If you don't mind, sir, how did you know there was a time capsule here?"

The mayor furrowed his eyebrows and exchanged a puzzled glance with Mr. Schaefer. "How do I know there's a treasure here? Someone told me, two men. They said there was a treasure in school, and later on, Mr. Schaefer called to inform me there was a capsule inside of this statue."

"Trace, that's enough. Others have questions to ask," said Mr. Schaefer, scowling. "Any more questions?" he asked half-heartedly. Several hands shot into the air again. "Good, no more questions. Now let's begin."

Kire stared at the mayor, who still seemed a bit lost. He still looked as though he was trying hard to remember something important.

The areas around the concrete title slate were broken and the lid was lifted off the roughly 18-inch hole. A metal handle was peeping out from inside the hole. Everyone fell silent with anticipation. The curiosity and tension in the air were so thick, that it was almost palpable.

"Gentlemen," said Mr. Schaefer to the diggers. "Would you be so kind as to bring out the capsule?"

The men grunted as though Mr. Schaefer had just insulted their fragile honor. "Did you bring us over here? Why do you think you can order us around?" one of them growled his displeasure.

Mr. Schaefer frowned and looked like he was about to start yelling.

"Let me help, sir," Andrew said, stepping forward and smiling.

Mr. Schaefer was pleased by this turn of events. "But of course, my boy," he said proudly. "I know I can always rely on you. But don't you need a partner? The capsule might be tight and heavy in that place—well, it seems like you pulled it out fine yourself. It turns out we didn't need to hire *men* for this after all."

The capsule Andrew pulled out of the hole looked like a submarine pumping machine. It was four feet long and a foot in diameter.

"Let me open it, Mr. Schaefer."

Mr. Schaefer cleared his throat. "Ah, okay. I guess we didn't need to hire anyone for that either."

Kire knew Andrew was strong, so he opened it up with ease. The lid on the steel capsule was rusty, but the capsule itself appeared to be unscathed and new. It shimmered in the bright morning sun.

"Let me see what's in it. Bring it out, Andrew, and be careful with it."

Andrew threw the lid with such force it landed with a startling 'bang.' Kire scoffed. "Show off."

"You see that?" said Mr. Schaefer, grinning. "A man doesn't have to be a hired hand to have such power in his arms."

Kire puckered his brows when he saw Andrew bringing the Djigi out from the capsule. The Djigi was folded like a mat; the outer skin was black and glossy.

Andrew unfurled the Djigi from its fold and smiled greedily at it.

"What's wrong with your friend?" asked Trace. "He looks like he wants to eat it."

Mr. Schaefer, along with everyone present, gasped in amazement. The front of the Djigi was exactly like a mirror. Surprisingly, the mirror straightened itself out when Andrew unfolded it as though it was never bent.

The mayor's eyes were wide with amazement. He trudged over to Andrew. "Give that to me," he said, approaching to collect it. Kire might have been mistaken, but he saw Andrew hesitate. Frown at the mayor, maybe?

"Andrew, boy, give that to the mayor," Mr. Schaefer ordered when he noticed Andrew's reluctance.

Precious seconds passed with the mayor's hands hanging in the air, and the mirror unfurled to its full length in Andrew's raised hand.

"Well, boy?" the mayor repeated, this time with a hint of warning in his voice.

Andrew didn't flinch at the mayor's warning; his eyes still had a strange glint in them. His face was sinister and full of mischief. If Stephan smiled like a demon, then Andrew smiled like the devil. Kire found it odd Andrew had changed so much since he sold him out.

"Sorry, Mayor," said Andrew, smiling. "I got enthralled by the beauty of it."

The mayor cleared his throat and snatched the mirror from Andrew. "Don't get enthralled by the beauty of state-owned property, son," said the mayor coldly.

"That might not be state property," said Stephan aloud. "The state didn't bury it there, did they?"

Mr. Schaefer seemed appalled. "What insolence!" he said through gritted teeth. "Mayor, he's simply being childish. Do well to pardon him, will you?"

The mayor held the Djigi up for all to see; it was basically a standing mirror that could be rolled like a mat. But the quintet team knew that mirror could spell doom for the world.

"This will be kept in the town museum for everyone to see," the mayor said, "but congratulations to you all; you're the first to witness the unearthing of this wondrous treasure. I wonder how old this is."

Six thousand, thought Kire.

"When we have learned more about this, I'll have the information compiled and sent to your principal. Where's the photographer?"

A flushed man with round glasses ran forward with a

camera. Mr. Schaefer and the mayor stood side by side with the mirror between them.

"Have you taken the picture?" the mayor asked when he saw the photographer stare at the camera's viewfinder with a bewildered expression on his face.

"Well?" the mayor growled.

The photographer seemed flustered. "The thing is," he began shakily, "you both are in the picture..." He glanced from principal to mayor.

"*And*?" said the mayor impatiently.

"The mirror isn't," the photographer said.

A loud and excited chatter broke out among the students at this new and impossible revelation. Everyone fished out their phones to see if they could see what the photographer was talking about, including Kire, who had forgotten he promised his mother pictures of the capsule ceremony.

"It's true!" one of the students yelled, waving his phone in the air in excitement. "The mirror isn't showing on camera!"

Everybody started looking at each other's phones, comparing pictures, and chatting excitedly in disbelief.

"How's that even possible?" Kire muttered to himself, putting up his phone camera again. He tried to zoom in on the mirror, but there was nothing. It just appeared as though the principal and the mayor were holding onto air.

"All right, everyone," said the mayor, chuckling nervously. "Seems like we got ourselves a real gem this time around. We'll be taking this for further investigation and research purposes." He turned to the principal. "Congratulations, Mr. Schaefer, you just brought your school into the limelight."

The principal bowed happily at the mayor's words as the mirror was carefully returned to the capsule. Mr. Schaefer then dismissed the students back to their respective classes while he, the mayor, and some staff stayed behind for a quick discussion. Kire, Trace, and Kaos took their time going back to class and tried to see what was going on with that discussion with the mayor and principal. The mayor seemed angry and frightened, and the principal looked like he was trying to subdue his excitement for all of the attention this would bring his school.

"Have you ever seen anything like that?" asked Trace during soccer practice later that day. "It was as though the light just went through the mirror! Like it wasn't there!"

"My favorite part of the whole matter was the incredulous look on the principal and mayor's face," said Kaos, chortling. "I took lots of photos and will be spreading them *all* over the internet."

25

"All right, boys! Gather round now," said Coach Turner.

Kire, Trace, Kaos, and the rest of the soccer team jogged over to Coach and gathered in a semicircle around him.

"In three days, we'll be having our first soccer match with real opposition. The first match of the term for the veterans of the team," said Coach. He clasped his hands behind him and paced back and forth before the students.

"This is my style of play," he continued. "Attack is the best form of defense. All eleven players are to start marking right from the opposition half. Choke them, squeeze them, compress them, disorient them, knock them senseless, leave them crying for an escape."

"Why does the coach sound like he wants the other team dead?" Kire asked Trace in a whisper.

"I do want them dead, Kire," said Coach menacingly. "On the scoreboards. Now boys! My game plan is all about transition and shifts. You get the ball and push it to the best option forward, even if that's yourself. So, you know what we're going to be doing today?"

"Sounds like something terrible is coming our way," Trace said in a low tone.

"You will run all day long. Tired boys will be removed like weeds and thrown off the team. Every day is a tryout with Coach Turner, do you understand that?!"

"Yes, sir!" the boys chorused with military alertness.

"I said, do you understand that?!" Coach Turner yelled with bulging eyes.

"Yes, sir!"

"Now get to work!"

Kire felt like his muscles were on fire after he'd been running for a while, but he saw that he wasn't alone—the veterans of the team looked like they were ready to pass out too. Was Coach really going to kick people off the team today?

Well, he didn't have to—many weeded themselves out on their own. After running around obstacles for ten minutes, two boys had to be taken to the school nurse. By the time the zigzag runs were over, another boy simply walked off the field. By the end of practice, six people had quit the team.

Kire found himself on the bus home that afternoon. He didn't trust his jelly-like legs to take him all the way home. The school bus was filled with tired, worn boys who reeked of sweat. When he arrived home, Kire mumbled greetings to his mother, went upstairs to wash the sweat off him, and passed out for a deep nap in bed.

The sun was just falling below the horizon when Emma's voice roused him from his slumber.

"Yes, Mom?" he said when he got downstairs.

"You have guests in the living room," she said. "I didn't know you had such nice friends!"

Kire frowned; what friends was his mother talking about?

He didn't have any friends. Upon entering the living room, Kire was shocked to find...

"Trace? Kaos?"

Both Trace and Kaos were seated in the living room.

"Hey, Kire," Trace said.

"Hi, Kire," said Kaos. "We're visiting old friends and thought you would like to come along."

Something was wrong—Kire could feel it in his bones. When a member of the quintet showed up at his doorstep, he knew it was probably because there was trouble to tackle. He couldn't imagine any other reason why Trace and Kaos would pay him a visit.

"Okay..." said Kire tentatively.

Trace and Kaos stood up and started for the door.

"I'll be back later mom!" called Kire.

"Will you be home for dinner?" she asked.

"I-I don't know," Kire said in return. "I hope so."

Once they were settled in Kaos' car, Kire asked, "What's going on?"

"Oh, you'll find out soon enough," Kaos said as he peeled out of the driveway.

Kire relaxed into the back seat while Trace and Kaos tortured him with metal music blaring from the speakers. They drove into the school lot and parked.

"What are we doing here?" asked Kire impatiently.

"We're parking the car," said Kaos as he stepped out.

"I'm glad you drove all the way from your house to pick me up, just so we could sit in the parking lot at school," Kire said sarcastically.

"Easy now, Kire," said Trace. "We're only keeping the car here because we can't drive where we're headed."

"Where are we headed? Why can't a car—Wait. Are we going to the White Forest?"

Kaos groaned. "I told you not to give him too many clues," he said.

Kire's heart galloped in his chest, and he widened his eyes. "What are we going to do there? And why did you have to hide it from me?"

He couldn't help regretting not taking Halo along with him. Now he was trapped. How could they do this to him? He thought they were... they were teammates... did they not see the need for each other now more than ever?

Trace and Kaos laughed.

"Look," said Kaos, pointing at Kire's face. "He thinks we're going to kill him."

"You should've seen the look on your face, Kire—the look of absolute betrayal!" said Trace.

Kire was relieved but didn't show it; instead, he wore a stoic expression on his face.

"Why are we going to the White Forest?" he asked.

"Come on, we'll talk about it on the way," said Trace, pulling a backpack out of the car. "We won't hurt you."

Soon they were stepping into the thick carpet of leaves and twigs that had woven in and out of Kire's dreams for the last couple of weeks. The forest felt even colder than usual.

"That new boy you were talking to earlier today," Kaos began.

"Stephan Krause?" asked Kire. "What has he got to do with anything?"

"Everything, Kire," said Kaos. "I heard him talking about top dogs and stuff with you earlier."

"He was just upset," said Kire. "Did you hear him say his cousin wasn't the same?"

"I heard him say Alfred wouldn't talk to anyone or leave the house," said Kaos, flicking a spider off of his shoulder. "I also heard him say he wanted to beat Trace so he could become the new top dog in school."

"Yeah," said Trace. "He would probably take Amberly from me, too. I'm not going to let that happen."

"Are you both nuts?" Kire exclaimed. "We have *death* in the form of *aliens* staring us in the face and you're worried about how people see you at *school*?"

"This is just a side mission! I get to beat up this Stephan who has come prepared for me and the momentum will go a long way if and when we meet Heno."

"You won't gain any momentum from this fight, Trace," Kire said raggedly. "Only a broken nose, rib, and tooth."

"My goodness," Kaos chuckled. "Kire does paint such vivid pictures."

"Yeah, he's always just worried about Heno," Trace said, snorting.

"You think Heno won't come?" asked Kire.

A large owl hooted loudly from above, spread its large wings, and took off into the sky.

"We beat his pal, Jago," said Kaos. "I think he'll think twice before rushing at us."

Kire sighed. "He's going to be prepared for us! He's going to come at us with everything he's got!"

"You're being paranoid, Kire. Heno won't attack us because we don't have the mirror; the mayor does. And the mayor's place is probably the safest for the Djigi."

There was nothing more to argue about. As much as he hated to admit it, Kire knew they were right. The Djigi was probably safer in the hands of the mayor than in Marilyn Moe. But there were only eight days left, and Heno must have been getting desperate.

They arrived at Trace and Kaos' shack and much to Kire's surprise, they were not the only ones there. Several students of St. Bernard had gathered to witness what was sure to be a legendary fight. Kire could count at least thirty kids who must have nothing better to do than to watch two boys fight each other.

"This is wrong on so many levels," said Kire angrily. "What is this? Don't you have enough to worry about right now? Don't we have more important things to worry about?"

Trace walked up close to Kire and hissed, "This is important. Your opinion doesn't matter here."

Kaos slapped a hand on Trace's shoulder and pulled him back. "Easy now," Kaos said. "Little Kire is just watching out for us."

"Stephan called for this fight, didn't he, Kaos?"

"Yeah," said Kaos. "The dude called me and said he wanted to repay you for what you did to his cousin. He thinks he's an angel of vengeance or something."

"He challenged me, and you expect me to run away like a coward? Give up without a fight?"

"Some things aren't worth fighting for," said Kire. "Especially not such an insignificant, worthless title."

Trace stepped away from Kire. "You're free to go home to your mommy," he called as he walked away. Kaos just shrugged at Kire and followed Trace.

The students formed a circle outside the shack surrounding Trace and Stephan.

"Who do you think is going to win?" a girl asked Kire as he reluctantly joined the circle.

Kire snorted and moved away from her. He could see Stephan kneeling on one side of the circle facing out, wrapping his hands with rags.

"These guys are really going to do it," Kire sighed. He saw Stephan wave a hand and motion for him to come over.

"Hello, Kire," said Stephan, smiling. "You don't look pleased with the arrangement."

"I'm not pleased with the whole nonsense," Kire replied

through gritted teeth. "Why do we keep coming up with new ways and reasons to hurt each other?"

Stephan scoffed and chuckled. "Okay," he said mockingly.

"What? Is it funny to you?"

"Yeah," Stephan replied lazily. "I mean... Did you try telling all of this to your pals? As much as I want to knock their teeth out, it was them who called the fight."

"What?"

"Your boy fixed the fight. You know that, right?" said Stephan. "Aww, looks like you didn't know about it."

Kire blinked rapidly and tried to clear the surprise off his face.

"You..." He pointed at Stephan. "You're lying, aren't you?"

Stephan simply shrugged.

Kire walked about the crowd in search of Kaos. "There you are," he muttered when he found the kid taking bets from students.

"You slimy worm," Kire roared hoarsely. "What have you done?"

"What do you mean 'what have I done?'"

"You said Stephan called you to fix this fight!" asked Kire. He could feel fury rising up in him, like a pot of water about to boil over.

"Yeah?" Kaos replied casually.

Kire grabbed Kaos by the collar and pulled him close. "Don't you lie to me? Did Stephan call you to fix the fight or not?"

Kaos closed his eyes. "He didn't call me," he said, "but we needed the fight."

"You idiot!" Kire roared angrily.

Kaos slapped Kire's hands off his collar and pushed Kire so hard that he fell on his butt. Kire roared and pushed himself up before landing a hard punch on Kaos' face. The latter staggered backward and tripped over an exposed root. The students noticed the altercation between Kire and Kaos and shifted their attention from Stephan and Trace.

Kire saw Kaos put a hand to his cheek. "You little devil."

Trace ran over just in time to stop Kaos from throwing a punch at Kire.

"What happened between you two?" Trace snapped.

"He lied, Trace. He lied about Stephan challenging you; this fight was called by neither of you. It was all that lying snake's plan."

A loud murmur broke among the students at this revelation. Kaos rose to his feet and brushed the dirt off his pants. He looked at the ground, refusing to meet anybody's eyes.

"Kaos? Is that true?" asked Trace.

"Yeah," Kaos mumbled without looking up. "We needed the money, you know, for your mom's medication."

The anger in Kire began to simmer down. "Your mother is sick?"

"It's none of your business," Trace shot at Kire before returning to Kaos. "You told me you had it all under control, that you could lend me the money."

Kaos threw his hands into the air. "Don't be ridiculous, Trace," he said. "Where do you think I can get that sort of money?"

"Your parents are rich!" Trace yelled.

"Yes, they're rich. But they don't give me their money; they keep it all for themselves and just buy me what I need. They wouldn't just *give* me money."

"You could've at least told me," Trace bellowed.

"But he didn't," Stephan spoke for the first time. "But since we're already here—"

"Stephan, no," Kire said.

"How about we just get it done and over with?"

Trace sneered and cracked his knuckles. "Let's just get it

done already because, frankly, you're starting to get on my nerves."

"You don't have to do this!" Kire yelled.

"Your mother needs that money, and you have to earn it," Stephan said.

"Don't you dare talk about my mother," Trace growled.

"Make me," Stephan taunted.

Just then, Kire felt his phone vibrate and saw that Rose was calling.

"Rose," he began impatiently. "This isn't the time to call. Can we talk later?"

"The mayor was attacked!" she exclaimed over the phone.

"What? Just now?"

"The mayor was attacked on his way from the school," Rose said. "The Djigi is gone!"

A loud cheering noise boomed from the kids watching the fight and Kire moved away from the circle so he could hear Rose better.

"Rose, are you sure about this?"

"Of course, I am, Kire. He's being interviewed on TV right now. He says it's Andrew who attacked him."

"Andrew?" he repeated. "But Andrew is..."

"Kire, I think Heno is in Andrew," Rose said bluntly.

Kire's mind immediately flashbacked to the time he saw Andrew ransacking the lockers in the locker room during soccer practice—it was Heno looking for the Djigi! That would explain the speed with which he cleaned the place back up. The change in character, his reluctance to hand the Djigi over to the mayor, and the amazing strength he showed—Andrew was Heno. Kire squeezed his eyes shut as facts began to pile up in his head like a stack of crates.

There was a loud scream from the crowd and Kire saw Trace fall to the ground, bloody and bruised.

"Kire, where are you?!" asked Rose, with fright in her voice.

"I need you to come up to the challenge shack in the White Forest, you know it, right?"

"Yeah, I do. But what are you doing at the challenge shack?"

"Not me, Rose; it's Trace and Stephan fighting for some stupid top dog position. And please, come with the first aid kit, will you?"

"Okay."

Kire slid the phone into his pocket and ran over to the fight scene. He pushed through to the front to find Trace kneeling on the floor. His face was swollen and bloody. Stephan looked far better; save for a red spot on his right cheek, he looked fine.

"Is that all you've got?" Stephan taunted. "Come on, Trace! Give me a fight worth my time. Don't you want to save your mother?"

"Don't..." Trace started to say. "... don't you dare talk about my mother."

"What, like how she gave birth to a worthless son who she doesn't even want? Who can't even stand up in a fight?"

"Shut up," Trace growled and pushed himself up from his knees.

"Your father must be disappointed in the boy he calls son," Stephan said. "I heard he got so tired of seeing you and your mother's faces that he *left*."

"Shut up," Trace growled again. He had an expression on his face Kire had never seen before—it was so human, so real. Kire could tell Stephan hit a nerve.

"Isn't that why you need medication for your mother? Because she fell into bad habits after your father left? That's funny considering the fact that he always beat her like she was a punching bag."

"Shut up!" Trace roared before charging at Stephan like a wild beast. The latter smiled and threw a punch that landed on Trace's face. But he might as well have planted a kiss on his opponent, for Trace showed no sign of a hit. He grabbed

Stephan around the waist and slammed him onto the ground. Trace then sat over him and began to rain punches on him.

"Die! Die!!" he yelled. Kire had actually never been so frightened by Trace before. He was only thankful that he wasn't on the receiving end of those punches. Kire grabbed Trace from behind and tried to pull him off of Stephan, but it was no use. Trace was blind with rage and showed no sign of being aware of the world outside of himself and Stephan.

It's so commonly said that love is blind, but then so are rage, anger, hate, envy, jealousy, and vengeance. All of these feelings become masters of their carriers when given the opportunity. And when these feelings get the chance to wreak havoc on their host, the streets are strewn with blood and ash.

It took three boys to pull Trace off Stephan. The latter wasn't moving, but Kire hoped he was only unconscious, nothing more.

After an hour, everyone had mostly left except Kire, Trace, Stephan, Kaos, and Rose, who had joined them later on.

"This is all your fault," Kire barked at Kaos. "You're the most selfish person I have ever met. How could you have manipulated them into fighting each other?"

"Manipulation is sort of my thing," said Kaos coolly. "I can't help it."

"Don't give me that. Everyone can work on their faults," Kire retorted furiously.

Rose was cleaning one of the particularly nasty wounds on the still unconscious Stephan's face. "That isn't going to heal before school tomorrow," she said, dabbing antiseptic on the wound.

"You still have to treat my wounds, too," Trace winced.

"How about you go to the hospital?" Rose said. "You might have a concussion, you know."

"I don't want the police finding out about this or anything," he replied, all of his bravado gone. "And besides, I can't afford that."

Rose stood up when she was done with Stephan and went over to Trace. Wordlessly she began cleaning his wounds.

Kire felt uncomfortable for some reason when he saw Rose tending to Trace's face. It was strange because Kire knew Trace was wounded and she was just tending to his wounds, but he couldn't ignore that pang of jealousy in his chest—that cold liquid steel running through his veins and making him feel nauseous. He took out his phone and searched for the attack on the mayor in the news to distract himself.

"Andrew ripped the mayor's car door from its hinges?" Kire said, surprised.

"Wow, in the parking lot at school?" asked Trace.

"No, it looks like it was at the mayor's house when he got back from school," Kire read. "I wonder how Andrew got there so quickly."

"What are you guys talking about?" mumbled a very woozy Stephan.

"I forgot he was there," Trace said.

"Easy for you to say—you were going to kill him," Rose said coldly. She began cleaning one of his wounds a bit harder than necessary.

"Ow!" Trace yelped and pulled his face away from her touch.

Kire frowned at this; he wished it was him, not Trace, who got injured so Rose could be devoting all of her attention to him instead. Maybe he should've put his face between Trace and Stephan.

"Why do you keep looking at her that way?" Kaos whispered. "Do you have a thing for Rose?"

"You should get yourself some rest," said Kire. "All that lying must wear your brain out."

Kaos waved a hand in dismissal. "I'm just saying that if you like her, then maybe you should let her know. I've seen the way she looks at you. You're the only one who can make her smile."

"Shut up," Kire hissed. It would've been nice to ask advice from someone experienced in heart-related matters like Kaos, but Kire was still angry with him. Kaos raised both hands in surrender and backed off. He pulled out a wad of crumpled dollar bills and began to count them.

"Here," he said, handing over the money to Trace. "It's all yours."

"I don't want that money," Trace said, looking away.

"I know you don't want it, but you need it," Kaos countered. "She needs it. And I'm sorry for doing this to you. I just thought you would never agree to it if I told you what was at stake."

"So, what happens now that you won?" Kire asked. "Does Stephan have to go find another school?"

"There's no need for that," Trace said. "I'm tired anyway."

"Stop talking so I can finish cleaning this wound on your chin," Rose ordered sternly.

"Yes, doctor," Trace said with a grin.

Kire felt like someone had stabbed him in the heart with a knife. At that particular moment, he hated Trace more than anything in the world.

"Hey, can I talk to you for a second?" Kaos nudged him with a leg.

Kire sighed and followed Kaos a little ways away from the shack.

"Trace isn't going to steal your girl. He likes Amberly way too much for that."

Kire scoffed and kicked a rock. "I don't know what you're talking about," he said.

"Well, if you say so," said Kaos, raising his brows. "Can I let you in on a secret?"

Kire searched Kaos' eyes for any signs of trickery. "What?"

Kaos' eyes flicked over to Trace and Stephan to make sure

nobody was listening. "The reason Trace fights as much as he does was because he had a difficult childhood. He's like a pressurized can filled with too much air. He's always trying to keep all the anger and hate he's had with him since childhood down. But..."

Kaos rubbed the side of his face with a hand and took in a deep breath.

"Many times, the pressure is just so much that he has to let it out."

"So, you instigate people to fight Trace? Use them as a pressure outlet of some sort? That's really sick, man."

"Kire, what would you have me do?" Kaos asked, desperation in his voice.

"Get him help? Take him for counseling and therapy?"

Kaos scoffed. "He can't afford to get counseling. And Trace has to be there to look after his mother."

Kire's curiosity grew considerably at this. "Why? I heard Stephan mention something about Trace's dad the other time. What is it?"

"That's a long story, Kire," Kaos sighed.

"Then make it quick."

"Okay," said Kaos, "his dad was really abusive, he would always beat his mom and you know what that can do to the mind of kids, right? Anyway, his mother really wasn't able to leave because she had nowhere to go, and she was afraid of what he might do if she left. So, she developed an... unhealthy habit to help her cope with what was happening to her."

"What unhealthy habit are you talking about? Didn't you say the money was for medicine?"

"Oh," Kaos cleared his throat. "She would drink as an escape, and it caused her to develop liver disease. Trace has to pay for the medications. Whenever he gets money, she finds a way to get it to buy more alcohol, and the cycle continues."

"What are you two talking about over there?" Trace shouted from the shack.

"We'll continue this conversation later," Kire murmured. "Listen, I only told you all that because I don't want you hating Trace and me. I did Trace a favor by fixing this match; he gets to let some steam out while getting paid for it."

"You're ruining his life and allowing his mother to continue ruining hers—there's no favor here," Kire said.

It was selfish, but the biggest thing Kire took from that conversation was the insight about Rose.

26

Trace didn't come to school the next day but showed up at soccer practice to yell from the sidelines.

"Why is Connor moving like a snail? You there, are you cross-eyed? Why do you keep passing sideways?" he would say. He kept yelling at his teammates until Coach finally told him to shut up.

After school, the quintet team gathered at Aunt Marg's for tea. Old Aunt Marg beamed at them when she saw them walk in.

"She looks so happy we're here," Rose said.

"And she should be," Kire opined, "we're the only young people who come here. We brighten up the place a bit."

The crew took their seats at their corner table with a sober atmosphere hanging thick over them. But their moodiness was soon cured by the scent of tea and freshly baked scones.

"Which should come first?" asked Trace, holding a scone in his hand. "The fruit jam or the cream?"

"Spread the cream first," Kire suggested.

"I agree with Kire," Kaos said. "The cream should come first."

"No way, the jam first, and the cream follows," Amberly said.

"Amberly is right," said Rose. "The jam should be spread over the scone first and the cream on top of that."

"So, this is a case of boys versus girls then," Trace declared. "How about we try both methods side-by-side and see which one is the most successful."

He took a scone and spread cream on it, but when he tried applying the jam next, it wouldn't stick to the cream and ended up all over his hand. It was a different story when he put the jam first on the second scone, followed by the cream—everything stuck to one another perfectly.

"Women are always right," Kire bemoaned.

"This is great," said Amberly. "We have an alien on the loose, and here we're debating whether the jam or the cream should come first."

"I don't think there's much to worry about just yet," said Kire.

"Did that book tell you something again?" asked Trace.

Kire shook his head. "No, I just analyzed what we already knew."

"Kire knows something," said Kaos. "Tell us now. You don't want Trace beating it out of you."

"I think I stand a decent chance against him," Kire said coldly. "He looks like a broken toy right now."

"Okay," said a badly bruised Trace. "No need to practice a war of words on me. Tell us what you know."

Kire sighed. "Two factors are important in Yash's plan: time and location. Fortunately, we know both of them. The time is seven days from now, and the location is at the top of Kula Mountain in White Forest."

"This is good information, Kire," said Amberly, "but not all of us have the luxury of spending twenty-four hours on top of a mountain waiting for an alien to come."

"I figured that one out," Kire said. "I went back in time, this time with my watch, and I took some measurements and did some calculations. I assumed the ship and peak were already aligned when Yash was marking a line on the mountain top."

"If you know the position of the ship, then the problem is half solved," said Kaos, "But there's still the shift in time, possible change in speed of the revolution of Earth and stuff like that. Are your calculations correct? Yash happened six thousand years ago."

"They should be correct, roughly," said Kire, "and if my guess is right, Yash has an army waiting on the other side; it'll be an all-out war on both fronts."

"When you say 'both fronts,' you mean the Albusus as well, right?" asked Amberly.

"Yes," Kire said. "Yash will be trying to distract them so they can't send help here while he wreaks havoc on our planet."

"Well, I have bad news for him," Amberly said after swallowing a huge chunk of scone. "That party won't be happening because we're here. Kire, did you figure out the time?"

"Yeah, it'll happen at midnight," he said, raising the tea cup to his lips.

Kaos groaned. "Of course, it is. Another sleepless night," he said. "No way am I doing that again—I *need* my beauty sleep. And won't the alignment only last for a minute or so anyway?"

"I think that once it matches, they can simply fix it, so the ship matches the speed of Earth's revolution," Rose ventured. "That way, they can keep the portal open for as long as they want."

"Oh my gosh, we really have mad men in this world, so many of them," said Amberly.

"Why do you assume Yash is a man? What if he's a woman?" asked Trace.

"If there's one thing men love to do, it's destroying things they're unable to build, like courage and a happy home," said Amberly.

"If you've judged me already, why do you still keep me around?" asked Trace, feigning annoyance.

Amberly chuckled and cupped his face with a hand, looking into his eyes. "It's because I hope you will be different, Trace."

Trace held her hand to his face and kissed it. "I will be, for our sake."

Kire glanced in Rose's direction and Kaos groaned. "Hey, Kire," he said, "can you ask Halo if we have got room for one more quintet gift? I know a pretty girl who I'd like to bring along."

The team laughed and Kire saw Rose's cheeks turn pink. Then, Aunt Marg came over to them with a golden loaf of freshly baked bread.

"Oh, no, Aunt Marg," said Kaos, rising from his seat. "We didn't order bread."

A smile spread across the silver-haired lady's wrinkled face. "No, you did not. But since my husband died, this place has never been as lively as you all have made it every time you come by. And I'm so happy about it."

"Looks like it doesn't take a quintet gift to put a smile on people's faces," Kaos said.

"No," Kire admitted. "It doesn't."

After the meal, the team left Aunt Marg's place, thanking her for the golden loaf on their way out. Rose was dropped off at home, and Kire managed to give her hand a gentle squeeze as she got out of the car.

"That was lame," said Kaos, rolling his eyes. "*I* would've kissed her by now if I were you."

"They haven't had any outings yet, so cut it out," said Amberly, in Kire's support.

"Aren't we coming from a double-date plus me right now?" said Kaos, with an eye on the road ahead.

"Most double-dates don't involve discussing how to avoid the demise of Earth," Kire groaned.

That seemed to settle the argument. Amberly asked to be dropped at the spot where Kire had met her mom the other day, and Kire got out there, too, since his house was only a few blocks away.

Trace wasn't altogether pleased with that. "I hope you don't get any ideas, Kire," he growled. "That girl is eternally off limits to you—" Kaos grinned and Trace shot a look at him, "—or anyone else for that matter." The grin on Kaos' face fell.

"And here I was thinking as best friends, whatever is yours is mine," he said as he drove away.

"Uh," Kire began. "Okay, bye."

"Kire," Amberly said, looking into Kire's eyes with her icy blue eyes. Kire assumed it must be taking her quite an effort to do that, and sure enough, after a moment, she looked away as though staring at him hurt her, like it was a strain on her. "Do you have anything to say to me?" she asked.

Kire swallowed and searched his brain for what she could be talking about. "That..." he stuttered. "About that... I just... I guess I wanted to tell you... and your mom that whatever it is that you think I did wrong, I know nothing about it."

"You're amazing at pretending," Amberly snapped and turned to go home.

"I'm not pretending!" Kire barked at her. "That's one of the problems I've got with you; you seem to think there's some secret I'm privy to. There's none, and please, stop assuming you know about my life. Because you don't! Just like I don't know what you've been through."

Amberly stopped walking and sighed. "I thought you might say that," she said.

Kire felt anger charge through his body like electricity. His pleading expression hardened into a snarl.

"Fine," he threw at her. "You know what? I don't care what you think. I don't care what your mom thinks either! You have no idea what my life is like. You have no idea what it's like having a father like mine!" He then turned and stormed home.

When he got home, he stood outside his front door for a moment and collected himself. He took deep breaths, wiped the tears from his eyes, and forced a smile.

"Hey, Mom," he said when he walked in the front door.

Emma was wearing an apron, her hands were covered with flour, and she was staring into a cookbook sitting open on the counter amidst a messy kitchen full of baking ingredients and tools.

"This is unbelievable!" she yelled at the book. "Why would you wait this long to tell me to add salt? It would've been nice to know a while ago!"

"Did you add salt?" Kire asked and threw his bag on the couch before slumping into it himself.

"Well, I was wondering why the dough was so watery," she said. "But I don't want to throw all this away." She groaned and went to work, trying to fix her disaster. Kire found himself dozing off on the couch.

A few hours later, the Hunter family was seated around the table with awkward expressions on their faces.

"It's not as bad as you're all making it seem," Emma admonished father and son.

"No, it's not as bad as we make it seem," Gerald growled. "It's worse. Far worse. What did you say this was again?" He pointed to the flaky pastry sitting before him.

"Spanakopita," Emma replied. "It's a Greek delicacy."

"Tastes like fried sand," Gerald grumbled.

"Kire," Emma called to her son. "What do you think of the Spanakopita?"

"It smells nice," Kire replied, crunching his teeth down on a piece of the disaster. The Spanakopita was decidedly tough and tasted like fried sawdust.

After the meal, Kire found himself sitting at his desk contemplating Halo. He missed being able to tell his mom everything and he was finding that he was growing rather lonely having to keep so many things from her all the time. Simply wanting somebody to talk to, he took out a pen and wrote, 'Hello, Halo.'

The words sank in slowly, like a sinking ship into the black depths of the sea.

'Hello, Kire, how are you today?' Halo replied in bright golden letters.

Kire smiled. 'I'm fine. I have a question to ask, and I need you to answer me truthfully.'

'You want to ask if there is any chance Rose would say yes if you asked her out?'

'Are you reading my mind?' asked Kire.

'No, I am reading your face, young man. I advise you to stop grinning like a clown. It makes your situation obvious. And you humans are incorrigible, there is a life-threatening situation out there and you are worried about asking a girl out.'

'Well, it's not my fault,' Kire scribbled furiously. 'I can't seem to get her out of my head. The girl basically lives rent-free in my mind.'

'Oh well, you can always squash thoughts of your sweetheart with thoughts of Amberly,' replied Halo.

'Don't you talk to me about her. She's a witch!'

'Kire, do you have feelings for Amberly?'

'You disappoint me, Halo,' Kire wrote. 'How could I ever have any feelings for that girl? And besides, she's Trace's girlfriend. Trace is all she sees, not that I care about that anyway.'

'That is a relief. You can absolutely not fall in love with her. Understood?'

'What? Why not?' he asked out of curiosity,

'That is something you will find out sooner or later. Now back to your question.'

Kire thought Halo was trying to change the subject, but he was happy to go back to talking about Rose.

'That wasn't a smooth transition, but I'll take it. Will Rose say yes?'

'She is a girl, Kire. I do not understand the female gender any better than you do. What are you asking me that question for?'

'You see the future, dear Halo. All I ask is that you see if there's one scenario where Rose says yes to me.'

'You want me to predict a woman's heart, is that it? Well, I cannot. Do you have any other impossible requests to make?

Kire sighed. 'No.'

'I will be calling it a day then. And Kire? You are a wonderful person. I think anyone can see that without straining their eyes.'

'Right, like Amberly.'

'Be good to that girl, but you absolutely cannot date her. It would be immoral.' And with that, the lights on Halo's pages went out.

Kire found Halo's remarks about him and Amberly odd. They weren't related. What was immoral? Maybe it was because she was Trace's girl? His boggled-down mind swam with thoughts of Amberly and Rose until his restless body finally fell asleep.

KIRE once again found himself on top of Kula Mountain in the White Forest thousands of years before it was the forest he knew today. It was night, and the darkness that enveloped him was as thick as ash and heavy as a wet blanket. Up in the night sky, he could see just a few twinkling distant stars.

Kire was in the same spot he and Halo had visited the last time, the same spot Kire found himself in during that nightmare. Halo wasn't around tonight, which led Kire to believe he was dreaming again. Halo never seemed to appear in his nightmares—maybe he didn't get the memo. Kire knew this scene too well; two hooded figures in black flowing cloth approached the peak of the mountain with a long, narrow cylinder in hand. One of them was Yash; Kire had seen his red eyes, two narrow slits that bled hate. He stepped aside for them to pass, but he was very well prepared for what was to come. Yash would try to attack him and then he would fall off the mountain only to wake up screaming in his bed in a pool of sweat.

Kire clenched his fists tightly as the figures approached. One of them continued to the top of the mountain while Yash stayed behind. But something was different about him this time. He was so... conscious.

"So, it is you," Kire heard someone hiss. He looked around to see if there was anyone else around the mountain. Surely it wasn't Yash speaking to him.

"I stand right before you; why do you look around?" the voice hissed again.

"Halo?" Kire tentatively said, hoping perhaps his friend would come out and help.

"You are all alone," said Yash. "I see that you wish to try to hinder my plans. If you think you can win, I would like to assure you that your efforts will be in vain. Another stupid idea that fills the heart of you humans. Hope." Yash walked slowly around Kire. "You all say hope is the evidence of things not seen. I say nothing that is not seen should be relied on. Hope is a mere lie you tell each other to keep expectations flying. You are welcome to bring all of it, but my warrior will destroy you.

And when your planet burns, you will see your hopes burning with it."

Kire swallowed. "That was a very scary speech," he said, ready to wake up from his nightmare. "Can you do me a favor right now?"

The slits narrowed further. "What?" Yash spat.

"Push me down the mountain," said Kire. "I have to wake up early tomorrow."

Kire thought he heard Yash laugh, and he wondered if asking him to push him off the peak was a sensible idea after all. Long, thin, cold hands pressed against his chest and pushed him with such force that Kire was sure his ribs broke. He fell off the mountain and tumbled down the steep hill until he landed on the rocky plateau below.

"No..." he gasped. "I'm supposed to wake up..."

He tried to move but ended up roaring in pain; it felt as though every bone in his body had been broken and was now stabbing him from the inside. His breathing grew heavy and troubled. Kire heard something land beside him and managed to turn his head. "Why aren't I waking up?" he croaked.

A deep, wicked laugh came from Yash. "You do not wake up until I say so." He bent over and grabbed Kire by the collar. "Come, let me show you what to hope for."

He dragged Kire over that rocky flatland and Kire screamed and yelled as his broken body was pulled along mercilessly. Finally, Yash stopped and sat him up against a boulder. "Now, watch," he hissed.

Kire saw the rocky plateau break up and the trees suddenly surround it; he was now in the modern White Forest. Suddenly, a loud explosion rang at the east end of the forest and Kire saw a yellow burst fill the land below. Then came the screams from all around him, but he couldn't see anyone; fire razed the forest. This wasn't the kind of fire that could be put out by firefighters and extinguishers. It was alive, like a monster, and it raged like a wild beast, devouring the forest and everything in its path.

"I will now leave you here to burn," said Yash. "Experience firsthand the heat of Yarra—the fire that lives. This is the only thing your world has to hope for, Kire—fire and death." Then he was gone, like the blowing wind.

The fire seemed to notice Kire and began to burn furiously towards him, charging as a bull does at a matador. Kire tried to move, but he couldn't feel his legs or any of the bones in his body. All he could do was watch as the fire devoured the green trees in his path before finally engulfing him. He let out a blood-curdling scream as he felt every nerve in his body burn.

"Kire! Kire!!"

He woke up shaking and out of breath. His throat was raw from screaming.

"We should take him to the shrink," Gerard said to his crying wife.

27

It was Friday, which meant there were only four days until Heno had to be stopped on Kula Mountain. Trace and Kaos and his other nightmare-free teammates were excited about the coming soccer match, but Kire was filled with dread and fear.

Needless to say, his meeting with the shrink his parents took him to ended up being a colossal failure. If he even admitted that he was on a team of five people with powers they didn't yet understand and that there was an alien planning to send a living fire to devour the planet, the shrink would've had him admitted to a hospital.

So, he lied that he was just a bit stressed about school and soccer and was having nightmares about forgetting to turn in assignments. The shrink eyed him suspiciously but didn't press him further.

Kire now found himself in the locker room preparing for his soccer match. St. Bernard had the advantage of the home ground, but Bowell High was a tough team to beat. To put it in perspective, every time St. Bernard had played against them over the past ten years, the latter lost every time without scoring a single goal in the process.

"Coach will probably keep you on the bench," said Trace to Kire as they changed in the locker room. "We need to win this match to qualify for the championship."

"How can you even worry about soccer right now?" asked Kire. He slammed his locker shut.

"You worry too much about everything," said Kaos, "and that's why Yash specifically chose you for his VIP torment. You even earned yourself a shrink."

"Yeah?" said Trace, pulling his jersey over his head. "How was it? Revealing, I hope?"

"Shut up, both of you," Kire said raggedly.

"Someone is peevish," Kaos said, stifling a laugh.

Kire chose to ignore them and tried to focus his mental energy on soccer. They got dressed, laced their soccer cleats, and stepped out into the green field outside. St. Bernard's team wearing white and red stood on the eastern and southern sides of the field while Bowell painted the west and northern side with their butter yellow and lime green jerseys.

As both teams filed out of the locker rooms, a loud cheer erupted from the stands. The school's respective cheerleading squads came out for their performances. The Bowell High cheerleading squad composed a song that reflected the relationship between St. Bernard and Bowell High:

"ST. Bernard has been crucified,
    Ten times more than we remember,
    St. Bernard will be crucified,
    One more time for all to remember."

· · ·

"Looks like we got lucky this time," said Jeremy, the guy who was benching Kire. Kire was the third choice for the right-back position, but big Jeremy was the undisputed starter for the team.

"And why is that?" asked Kire.

"Well, they did forget to mention we were large toothless dogs that never bite," Jeremy replied, flashing yellow teeth.

"And why don't the officials do something about it?" asked Kire, clearly displeased.

Jeremy chuckled. "We're not any nicer," he said. "You'll see."

After the Bowell High cheerleading squad finished their cheer, they were jeered and applauded away from the field, and it was time for Amberly's team to perform.

St. Bernard's girls began by showing off their acrobatic skills, which earned excited screams from even some of Bowell's students. The next item on the list was a well-concocted jibe arranged into a chorus.

"They beat us one, two, three,
    They beat us a good ten times.
    But their trophy cabinet,
    Is just as full as ours."

"Our trophy cabinet is full?" asked Kire.

Jeremy laughed. "That's the fun part Kire," he said, snorting. "Our trophy cabinet is full... full of dust, just like theirs."

It all made sense to Kire now, but he wasn't pleased with it. Something had to change.

"If we wanted to add to our trophy cabinet, what would we need to do?" asked Kire.

"Oh, I've never considered that because we never get past

this stage. What's the point anyway? Hope is useless at this point."

"Hope isn't useless," Kire said, storming off to the bench stand for St. Bernard substitutes and team officials.

The game started after the coin-tossing ceremony, and off the team went. St. Bernard was outplayed grossly, and twenty minutes later, Bowell netted their first goal against St. Bernard.

"That was a long time coming," a substitute that would probably never be used said. "I checked the last record, and we always conceded the first goal after five minutes. It looks like we broke that trend this time around."

Coach Turner was on the touch-line rubbing his smooth bald head in stress. He looked tired, fed up with the whole affair.

"I heard they'll be firing him if we lose this game," the substitute said.

"That's not surprising," Kire noted. "Our team is playing like they have lost the game already. People with a loser mentality don't believe in winning."

"They have tried and failed. Do you blame them?"

"No, I'm just saying we might as well not play at all if we believe we've lost the game already."

Just then, the whistle for halftime sounded and the team marched with their heads down to the locker room. Kire got up from the bench and hurried to join them. Coach Turner leaned against a corner of the wall with his arms folded across the chest. He wasn't talking, just watching his team with empty eyes. Kire pounded a locker three times to gain his team's attention. "Hello, boys, I believe the scoreboard clearly says that we're trailing in the match by two goals to nothing."

"Yeah, so what?" said Jeremy, the culprit for the first goal. "They're always going to beat us, Kire, always."

"Then I shouldn't have said, 'Hello, boys,'" said Kire coldly. "It should've been, 'Hello, losers.'"

"Easy there now," said Elton, the team's defender and captain. "I won't let you insult my team."

"Coach, if we lose this game, you'll get fired, right?" said Kire, ignoring Elton.

The locker room went silent.

"I suppose so," grumbled Coach.

"And we're losing by two goals already," said Kire, "which means your termination letter is probably being typed as we speak."

"Kire, why are you being like this?" said Jeremy.

"Yes, Kire, you're probably right," Coach replied, ignoring Jeremy's outburst.

"Then you can make one more mistake, right? I mean, since you're going to get sacked anyway."

"What do you want? You want me to put you in?" asked Coach.

"Yes, I want you to put me in," Kire replied.

"And who do I take out for you?" asked Coach.

Kire turned to face Jeremy, and the latter staggered backward. "Take him out, Coach. He thinks we're going to lose anyway, and I think the team can do without one more loser."

"Coach, you can't do this to me," said Jeremy, looking like a frightened cat. He saw Coach Turner bow his head in surrender and knew that instant he was going to get substituted. Almost immediately, the begging wimp in him was replaced by a mischievous devil.

"Fine," Jeremy snarled, eyeing everyone on the team. "Let me remind you, my father makes these draws, and he can help us when we qualify."

Trace sniffed and crossed his strong arms across his chest. "That's kind of awkward, especially now that we're trailing behind by two goals."

Jeremy's lips quavered in fear and unexpressed anger. As

much as he wanted to lash out at the team, Trace's stare held him back.

"I'm not getting substituted. Take someone else," Jeremy declared.

"Well," Trace began, inching closer to Jeremy. "Kire is a right-back, and there's only one right-back on the team," he stabbed Jeremy in the middle of the chest with a finger. "You."

"I don't want to leave," Jeremy whined.

"You don't have a choice," Trace said in a low, threatening voice. "When I say you leave, then it's time to leave. Remember who's the top dog here. Your father will have a hard time drawing you out of my grasp if you annoy me further."

Jeremy shot one last look at Coach, who averted his eyes. "You will regret this. Every one of you will," he said and bounded out of the locker room.

"That was pretty intense," said Kaos, drinking water from a bottle. "Kire, you have to make it count, or that guy is going to laugh at us the rest of our lives."

"Even if he's the reason we're two goals down?" asked Kire, looking from Kaos to Trace.

"Even if we're *ten* goals down because of him," said Coach Turner. "But don't you worry, everyone prepares for what happens when you win. No one tells you what to do when you lose."

Kire set his jaws stubbornly. "We're not losing," he said. "Now, everyone, come together. Let's talk tactics."

"And I thought I'd have to endure that only at quintet meetings," Kaos groaned.

Elton raised his head. "What's a quintet?"

"Nothing!" Kaos, Trace, and Kire said at once.

Elton looked from Kire to Trace and finally to Kaos. "You three are definitely up to something."

"Can I have your attention now?" asked Kire, clapping his hands to relate the urgency of their discussion. "Bowell has enjoyed long spells of possession, but the few times they lost it, they didn't know what to do."

"They can attack, but they can't defend," Trace deduced. "How do we take advantage of that?"

Kire shrugged his shoulders. "We attack more than we ever have."

Coach grunted at this. "Those guys will rip us apart if we attack too much," he said.

"The scoreboard says we're already ripped apart," said Kaos. "What harm will a little more ripping do to us?"

"How do you want to attack?" asked Elton.

"Possession," Kire stated simply. "Trace and Kaos can cause enough damage when they get the ball; the problem is they never get the ball. So, we stack up the midfield and force the opponent to make mistakes, then punish them by either scoring or giving Trace or Kaos the ball."

Coach shook his head. "How come I never thought of that?"

"We switch to a five-man midfield, and everyone should attack as if their lives depend on it. Three men in defense led by Elton, Kaos, and Trace will lead the attack line, is that understood?"

"Yes," the rest of the team, including Coach chorused.

Coach hurried outside to tell the game officials the team would be making a halftime substitution. Less than ten minutes later, the team was summoned outside for the second half of the game.

Kire felt a surge of excited anxiety rush through his veins.

"Elton!" he called to the team's skipper. "I need you to cover for me when I make those runs inside, all right?"

Elton nodded and the whistle for the second half start went off. The entire team charged forward at Bowell, who had restarted the game. It was chaos for the opponents. Twice they lost the ball, only for Trace or Kaos to fluff it over the goal post.

"You won't get that many chances, Trace and Kaos. You

either bury those goals, or we can kiss qualification goodbye," Kire warned when Kaos kicked a shot right into the opponent's goalie's open hands.

Minutes later, Bowell skidded past the five-man midfield and added one more goal to make the score line three to nil in their favor.

"Hey! Call Trace," Amberly yelled at Kire from the touchline.

"Trace! Amberly wants to talk to you," Kire called to Trace.

"Hey, baby," said Trace, beaming. He jogged across the field as Bowell celebrated their last goal.

"Kiss me," Amberly ordered.

"Well, that's a girl who isn't afraid to ask for what she wants," Kire muttered to himself when he saw the steely gaze in Amberly's blue eyes.

Trace leaned down and kissed her. She then pushed him away roughly. "If you don't win this match," she said, "that will be the last kiss you'll ever get from me. You know what I just noticed?"

"Why are you talking to me like that?" asked Trace, looking hurt. But Amberly didn't seem to care at all what happened with his mood.

"I just noticed Kire running up the whole field trying to score while you're missing sitters like you were paid to do it. If you lose this match because of this defeatist attitude, you and I are through," Amberly announced.

Trace scoffed and chuckled. Then the smile slid slowly off his face like a load of mud. "Why aren't you laughing?"

"Because it's not a joke," Amberly barked at him and shifted her attention to Kire standing behind Trace. "You're single, right? Get ready to date a cheerleader." She turned around and stomped off.

Trace turned and gaped at Kire, who shrugged to show he

was equally as lost. A few minutes after Amberly promised to break up with Trace, he netted the team's first goal. Soon after, he assisted Kaos for the second goal. The pressure in the St. Bernard camp was high now; a draw had never seemed likely in their meeting with this particular foe. But with three minutes left to end the match, Kire and Trace worked together beautifully to net the third goal for the school. The crowd on the touchline burst into an excited roar; for the first time in years, they were going to beat this team!

"Trace!" said Kire, panting. The last goal had taken quite a bit of energy from him. "We have just a few seconds until the match ends. We can't let the match go into a penalty shootout." The St. Bernard team might be motivated, but they were inexperienced and might fluff the shootouts. They had to bury the game before then; only time wasn't on their side. "If we can get the ball on time," Kire added.

The referee blew the whistle, and Bowell restarted the game with a pass. They probably knew St. Bernard was a bunch of greenhorns at penalty shootouts and wanted to waste time. But where there was a will, there was a way. The entire St. Bernard team charged at once and Bowell crumbled under the pressure.

Kire got the ball and drove it toward the goalpost. But just as he was about to kick the ball, he felt something heavy collide with his leg and sweep him off his feet. He went down in pain and held on to his ankle, groaning. The referee pointed to Bowell's goal. It was a penalty! Even Kire rose to watch Trace take the one thing that would save them from certain disqualification. Trace took three steps away from the ball and breathed in. The referee blew the whistle and Trace trotted towards the ball and kicked it in the direction of the goal. The goalie dived in the opposite direction and the ball went right in.

Cheers erupted from St. Bernard's side and excited spectators flooded the field and lifted Trace into the air. Kire winced and hobbled off the pitch with his one good leg. Someone ran up to him and slid his arm over her neck; it was Rose.

"Hey," he breathed.

Rose flashed him a smile as sweet as honey. "Let's get you to the infirmary," she said.

"Kire! Kire!" someone bellowed from behind. Kire turned to see who it was and smiled.

"Coach," he said, still smiling. "Looks like we get to have you for a while longer."

Coach Turner laughed and said, "Not exactly. I was going to leave anyway, but I didn't want to leave a failure, and it was you who helped me achieve that."

Kire looked at the field behind; Trace and Kaos were carried on the shoulders by excited St. Bernard students.

"I wonder if the referee managed to end the game," Kire bemused. "Anyway, you have Trace to thank for the win. I'm just a defender."

It was a weird coincidence that his quintet gift, Halo, was also a form of a defense weapon rather than an offensive one.

"There's a saying in the soccer world," Coach began philosophically. "'Attack wins you games, defense wins you titles.' People who allow others to flourish are unsung heroes, Kire, and they're the true heroes."

"I'll be leaving for Barcelona after this semester; my family needs me there. Thank you for the honor, Kire." Coach grabbed his hand and gave him a firm handshake before continuing his way.

"That was sweet," said Rose. "I'm glad we won, even if I don't understand anything about soccer."

Kire snorted and allowed her to lead him to the infirmary. "What's there to be glad for then?"

"Well," said Rose, "when people try so hard, it's only right that they win once in a while, right?"

"Right," said Kire, "and I hope the same holds for our match with Heno next week. The quintet holders in the past gave their lives for it. I hope we don't have to do the same."

Rose sighed. "Me, too."

28

It was Saturday morning, the day after the memorable soccer match with Bowell High. Kire's sprained right ankle was wrapped in a brace, and he could barely move it without wincing in pain. He spread out on the couch in the living room, watching the news.

When his father heard that Kire had sprained his ankle playing soccer, he couldn't be prouder.

"Now, you're becoming a man," he said to Kire that morning. "I'm proud of your performance, son. Now that you've made me proud feel free to ask me any tip, any question at all, and watch me answer you. Including—" Gerald leaned in toward Kire and dropped his voice to a whisper. "—all the tips you need for the ladies."

"Gerald!" Emma called.

"I'm teaching our son to become the best version of himself!"

Emma appeared in the living room with a tray of steaming bone broth in a bowl.

"I saw a snake in the back," she said. "How about you be the best version of yourself and go kill it for me?"

Gerald guffawed and hiked up his pants. "I'll show you what a man I am," he said and marched off to the door.

"Gerald! Are you going to strangle the snake with your bare hands? How about you take the shovel along or something?"

"There's no need for that," he grunted, exiting through the door.

Emma sighed and set the tray on a small wooden table beside Kire. "Now, you take this while I prepare to call the doctor."

Kire frowned in perplexity. "What for?" he asked. "I've already got my cast on and everything."

"Not for you," his mother replied. "Your father. Hopefully, that species isn't venomous, but he'll feel pretty miserable for a long while after he's sure to have been bitten."

Kire drank the thin broth. "A little meat will take nothing away from the broth, you know."

"Ah well, the broth isn't for your enjoyment," Emma replied. "It's to help you heal faster, and you boys should please stop trying to kill yourselves."

"Ahhhhhh!" came the unmistakable scream of Gerald.

Emma, who had already dialed the number, called the doctor and told them they were on their way to get treated for a snake bite.

"Mom, you could've just stopped dad from going out there," said Kire.

"And how was I supposed to do that?" asked Emma. "Your father is as stubborn as a mule, and if I'd told him not to go out and fight a snake with his bare hands, it'd hurt his inflated ego. I can't be his mother, Kire. He has to learn to grow up and take people's advice, even if it's from women."

"What about the lamb and the goat story?" asked Kire, raising an eyebrow.

Emma smiled. "Well, the lamb letting the goat go for a dive cools the mind and soul, you know? How's that ankle?"

"I think it's healing fast," said Kire. "I think the brace will be coming off sooner rather than later as long as I rest for the weekend."

Just then, Gerald came running into the house and Emma wordlessly led her husband out of the house and into the car.

A little while later, Kire heard someone knocking on the door. He got off the couch, barefoot and in his pajamas and hobbled over to the door. It was Trace and Kaos.

"Pew!" Trace shot at him with his hand.

"Ha-ha, very scary," said Kire sarcastically. "Come inside, both of you."

He returned to the couch with his legs stretched on one side. Trace and Kaos sat in the chairs in the living room.

"How is that?" asked Trace, pointing to Kire's ankle. "Healing well?"

Kire nodded. "The school nurse suggested I stay off it for four weeks, but I think I'll be good to go by Monday." He said, running a hand through his disorderly hair.

"You're *super* healing," Kaos said matter of factly.

"Super healing?" Kire repeated. "Is that even a thing? We carry gifts; we don't super heal like vampires."

"Vampires aren't real," said Trace.

"I don't know about that now," Kire objected. "Aliens weren't real until we stumbled on those quintet gifts. If you ask me, I'll say there's a fair chance vampires, werewolves, and tooth fairies are roaming the streets as we speak."

"I'm not asking you then," Trace murmured. "Although, I have to agree you have a point there."

"Kaos, are you being serious about this super healing?" asked Kire.

"Yes," Kaos replied. "Remember you told us the last quintet holders that survived lived a long time? I think super healing had something to do with it. They lose cells slower than most and heal from wounds faster than normal."

"You may be right about that," he admitted to Kaos, touching his ankle. "But I'm thinking the two of you didn't come here to discuss super healing."

"No, we didn't," Trace said proudly. "We're very busy people. Even sitting here with you is costing us money."

"What is it then?" asked Kire.

"There was a meeting in school this morning, and as you know, my father is a rather important member of the committee," began Kaos.

Kire rolled his eyes. "More like a generous member of the committee."

"He's right, don't argue," Trace said quickly when he noticed Kaos was going to debate Kire's last words.

"Fine!" Kaos barked at Trace. "Five boys are missing from their homes. All of them are students from St. Bernard. All the disappearances happened between midnight and five o'clock this morning and were carried out by the same person."

Kire was troubled by this new information, but what was the quintet team going to do about a possible ring of kidnappers? Engage them in sword fights? Teach them how to tend to flowers?

"Listen, both of you," said Kire. "We still have to defeat Heno first. After that, we can go on a vigilante trip and save the rest of the world, but Heno is our top priority. We'll let the police do their jobs on this one."

"Kire," said Trace, shifting in his seat. "The kidnappings were confirmed to have been carried out by Andrew, or Heno as we know."

"You both are talking nonsense," said Kire, looking from Trace to Kaos.

"Trust me, Kire," said Kaos, "I wish I was talking nonsense."

"The mayor was at the meeting. He was so mad when he found out it was the same kid who stole the Djigi from him," Kaos said.

"What in the world does Heno need five kids for?" asked Kire.

"We'd have to be Heno to know the answer to that," Trace said and glanced at his watch. "It's time we got going. I have plans with Amberly when she gets off work in ten."

Trace and Kaos rose to their feet. "You should be more careful," said Trace. "Close your windows, lock your door. Basic security tips can save your life."

Kire nodded and got up to see Trace and Kaos off to their car. "Send my love to Amberly," he said sarcastically.

"I'd rather not do that," said Trace. "But, Kire, are you *sure* you never did anything wrong to her? I mean, Amberly is a bad girl through and through, but she doesn't hate anyone like she hates you."

"She sure does hate me," Kire said, groaning.

"Actually," Trace said out of the car window, "she loathes you. I'm always advised to try and break something in your body every time she's around."

"I have no idea what your girl hates about me, Trace," said Kire.

Trace just shrugged his shoulders.

29

Kire stood in front of the old signboard that used to read St. Bernard but was now burnt to a crisp. The signboard was the only thing that wasn't actively on fire. The school burned in front of him, and he could hear the haunting screams of the people inside but didn't see anyone. The trees, black, charred, and choked of their leaves, were still smoking. They stood like sinister ghosts in this apocalyptic world. The sky burnt and exploded with blackness. Everywhere was burning, everything was burning, everything was ash and darkness: fire and pain.

Kire walked toward the school and saw five bodies lying side by side. The bodies looked as though they took a stroll through hell—they all suffered from horrible burns. Despite the suffering written boldly on them, Kire's stomach lurched when he saw who they were. There were two girls and three were boys. Panic set in and he felt his heart beating so fast he was sure it was about to give out. Lying on the rough ground were the lifeless bodies of Kaos, Trace, Amberly, Rose, and himself? How was that even possible?

"Did you think you could escape what is coming your way?" a voice boomed behind him.

Kire spun around to face the intruder, and he froze when he saw who it was.

"Andrew?" he called, squinting his eyes in disbelief. But it was Andrew all right, a larger version of him. The arms of the dirty white shirt he wore had been ripped off.

Andrew laughed a scattered unnatural laugh that sounded like a hyena ready to pounce on its prey. "Tell me," he hissed. "Do you really think you and your band of children stood a chance against a six-thousand-year-old being? I think not." He scratched the side of his face with a fingernail that looked like a claw. He continued, "In a couple of hours, the gate between Yash and Earth will be opened, and the universe will be purged of humanity once and for all."

"Why do you want the human race to become extinct?" Kire yelled.

Andrew chortled and exhaled. "Breathe in," he said. "How is it that you cannot smell your own vileness in the air? You humans are a rather hopeless folk. First, you make weapons to kill each other, and then you go on to complain when someone generous wants to help you get the job done in one painless sweep."

"And by generous, you mean that mad man, Yash," said Kire.

"Man?" asked Andrew, screwing his face as though the word was a bitter pill he had to swallow. He gave Kire a wide berth and started circling him. "Yash is neither man nor woman. He is a god sent to wipe the universe of its wickedness. We want to rid the universe of corruption, evil, and death. Tell me, Kire. Do you not see the corruption that abounds among your kind? Do you not see the evil in your own mother and father?"

"My mother isn't evil!"

"What about your father? Tell me, can you say for certain

that your father is a good man? You will grow up, become a father, have a child, and subject the newborn to the pains you were forced to kneel to as a child. You will be just like your dad. You already are."

Kire felt anger rising in him. "You don't know anything about me or my future."

Andrew growled in displeasure. "Such insolence. You humans with all of your terrible manners will be burned off the surface of the universe."

"Did you ask Andrew kindly when you took his body? Did you use your manners then? How about now, burning down things that don't belong to you?" spat Kire.

Heno chuckled. "I see you have figured out my little plan." He sighed tiredly. "Andrew was a big loser when I found him. He was still beating himself up for betraying a friend. You see, Andrew has a little issue in his childhood that makes him cave in at the slightest pressure now. That's how Trace and Kaos got him to sell you out. All of you kids are all so broken. It is pathetic."

"You should get out of that body," Kire warned. "It doesn't belong to you."

"Oh, the limitations of this weak body remind me it is not mine, Kire," Heno growled. "I am tireless in my own body, relentless. But this body is... temporal... like its use will be.

"When Yash sends the fire of Yarra to Earth, it will burn up the sorrows and pains, the hurts of a failed childhood that haunts your days. It will consume your unfulfilled dreams; your sorrowful memories will perish. Everything will be made new again."

Kire woke up to find himself sobbing. His face was slick with tears and tiny beads of sweat had formed across his forehead. There was no screaming that night, so his mother wasn't woken up to come and comfort him. He wished he could scream now; all the pent-up sadness he felt would merge with his voice and escape from his body.

He rose from the bed and went to wash his face. The boy in the mirror looked older and strange to Kire. Save for his unrepentant hair that sat like dried twigs on his head; there would've been no resemblance between who he was now and who he knew himself to be. He made his way back to his room, sat at his desk, and opened Halo.

'Hey, Halo,' Kire wrote in the book. The words lingered for a while and then sank into the pages—one of the few miracles Kire never got tired of.

'Hello, Kire,' Halo replied. His words glowed like hot gold. 'Looks like you had a bad dream.'

'Yeah, I did. How come Heno knows who we are already if he's never seen us?'

'Heno does not know who you are,' Halo replied. 'Only you know who you are.'

Kire frowned; it would seem Halo wasn't as informed as he hoped. 'Well, in my dream he knew exactly who I was.'

'He does not,' Halo insisted. 'There is a bond between the quintet gifts and their holders. What Heno does is summon the bond of a quintet gift and the owner sees the things Heno wants him to see. Although, all Heno sees is an illusion of the book.'

'He doesn't know me then?' asked Kire.

'No, he does not,' Halo replied. 'But he knows you can see him. Heno is trying to tire you out, do not let him succeed.'

'I'm so tired,' Kire wrote

'I know,' replied Halo. 'How is the Rose matter?'

'Well,' Kire bit the end of his pen nervously. 'She said she's going to think about it.'

'What's there to think about?' asked Halo. 'It's a yes or no question.'

'Don't ask me, Halo. It seems customary for all women to think about things first,' Kire replied, satisfied with himself.

'You are lying, Kire,' Halo said, at last. 'You did not ask her out.'

'Okay, Halo, bye.' Kire slammed the book shut before it could reply and fixed the strap back on it.

I'm sorry, Halo, but I can't have my nonexistent love life probed by a book that will never have one, thought Kire.

It was a bright morning, absolutely devoid of the darkness that plagued his night. He could hear plates and silverware clinking downstairs and a tempting scent wafted into Kire's room. He took a hurried shower, got dressed, and limped down the flight of stairs. He met his father spooning from a bowl of soup and his mother doing something at the stove.

"Good morning, Dad. Good morning, Mom," Kire said and pulled out a chair from the side of the table. "There's meat in dad's bone broth? Wait, this isn't plain broth; this is chicken broth."

The bowl before Gerald was filled with soup and chicken. In fact, there was more meat than soup in it.

"Be quiet. A man needs this to heal properly," Gerald said, and lifted a piece of chicken with his hand, opened his mouth wide, and dropped the chicken in.

"I have a sprained ankle and got boneless bone broth for it," Kire said, annoyed. "How come dad gets meat for a snake peck?"

"Peck?" Gerald roared in disbelief. "That wasn't a peck! It was a bite. A snake bit me. And it was venomous."

"Yeah, garters don't even have enough venom to harm humans," said Kire. His mother returned with a bowl of oatmeal and milk.

"He paid for the chicken, Kire," said Emma as she walked to the sink. "If you want meat in your broth, you might want to consider buying your own chicken as well."

Gerald chortled and snorted. "This kid is still in high school. He can't afford anything," he said. "Hurry and be off to school."

Kire quickly ate his food, murmured a goodbye, and hurried out of the house, only for his mother to call him back.

"I think you're forgetting something," she said, putting a finger to her right cheek.

"Fine," Kire said, groaning. He planted a kiss on her cheek and turned to leave.

"You should consider using your father's gel," she called after him as he went.

"I don't want to go back in there just for him to remind me I'm *only* a high school kid."

"I'd have thought you would never forget it," his mother said, calling after him. But he pretended to not hear her, just like he pretended the following day wasn't the unwanted appointment with Heno.

St. Bernard was in high spirits when he arrived at school. Everyone had suddenly become a figure to consult in matters of soccer and related activities. When he stepped into the corridor, Kire could feel the weight of the eyes resting on his body. A few people were kind enough to pretend they weren't staring, while many others were blatant with their effort.

"Look who we have here," Kaos hollered as Kire stepped into the class. "It's the guy who kicked Jeremy Langley off the team and out of the school."

Celebratory cheers broke from the seated students, leaving Kire confused. "What do you mean off the team and out of the school?" he asked. "I only substituted for him at halftime; he's still the team's number one right back."

"The team has enough technique, and while I hate to admit it, you bring attitude and character to the field," Trace said. "No coach will ignore that."

Kire sighed and walked up to his seat at the back of the

class. "Whatever," he said. "Coach is gone anyway. The new guy will kick me out like a soccer ball."

"And they would be right in doing so," said Amberly, who was standing in the doorway. "You deserve to be kicked around the same way I was."

The whole class fell silent.

Trace rose to his feet. "Amberly, we need to talk."

Scarcely had the words left his mouth when Mrs. Goody stepped past Amberly into the classroom.

"Another morning with you folks looking gloomy," she said to a class still shell shocked by Amberly's words. "Look alive, people!"

Someone coughed.

"Can I help you?" Mrs. Goody turned to Amberly, who was still in the doorway.

"N-no," she said before sauntering off.

During lunch, Kire tried as hard as he could to avoid the quintet team, except Rose. Seeing that she wasn't in the lunch-room, he went to the place she was certain to be: the greenhouse.

Rose was tending to the Edax Animae plant when Kire entered the greenhouse. Its ordinarily pink traps were now brown and dry.

"Is it dead?" he asked as he got close to her.

"Oh, hey. Huh, yes, no. I mean, it's dying," she said at last. "The fight with Jago must have had something to do with it. None of the plants here have been quite the same ever since."

Her soft brown hair was gathered into a ponytail held together by a green band. He wanted to touch it but decided that Amberly had given him enough letting down for one day; better not to earn another.

"I thought Albus fixed it after," said Kire, walking past the pots of exotic plants and flowers. "Everything looked fine."

"I guess it goes to show that some things can't be fixed," said

Rose, her eyes still fixed on the dying Edax Animae. "They're either whole or broken."

"Like we can't be fixed if anything happens tomorrow," said Kire, sighing. "Maybe you shouldn't come tomorrow night."

Rose raised an eyebrow. "I thought we were supposed to stick together," she said.

"We did well enough against Jago when Amberly wasn't among us," Kire said.

"Jago underestimated us then," said Rose. "And Heno won't be making the same mistake. You don't think having Amberly will make fighting Heno easier? We have an extra person." Rose dug at the roots of the Edax Animae.

"How about you just pull that out?" Kire spat, frustrated, motioning to the Edax Animae.

"I'd destroy the roots," Rose countered and continued to dig. "So, you don't want me or Amberly at the fight?"

"You deserve the day off," he said. "And, ugh, Amberly needs to be there because it wasn't fair that she got to skip the first one." He stared at her struggling with the plant. "Oh, why don't you just yank that thing out!"

"There you go," she said when she dug the plant out. "A little bit of patience and I don't need to destroy something that didn't have to be."

"That's a wicked thing to say," Kire said. "I might get destroyed myself."

Rose wiped the sweat off her face with the back of a gloved hand. "I'm sorry," she said. "I know you don't like what she—"

"Would you like it if I started hating you for no reason?" asked Kire breathlessly. "Everything I do happens for a reason—we like people for a reason, and we hate them for a reason. There's got to be reasons for the emotions we feel."

"Maybe she does have a reason then," said Rose. "I mean, how come she hates only you?"

"I asked her, I asked her what it was she had against me,

and she couldn't tell me. And do you know even her mother feels the same?"

"You've met her mother?" asked Rose. She put the dead plant in her hand on the slab top.

"Yes," Kire groaned, moving away from the Edax Animae; he thought he saw a movement from the wilted plant.

"I just think you should try to settle this before tomorrow, and there's nothing you can say to keep me out of the fight, by the way," she said. "Last time, I was scared, and it nearly cost us all our lives. This time, something has got to change about that."

Kire smiled warmly at her. "That's the team spirit we all need," he said. "But I have a premonition that we're dealing with a far more cunning customer. That reminds me, you can control plants, right?"

Rose shook her head. "Not control," she said. "I can urge plants to react a certain way, but I can't control them. No one can." She said with the air of a philosopher.

"Ah, I see," said Kire, with a hint of sarcasm. "Then you can *urge* animals too?"

"What?" said Rose, chuckling. "No, I—I can't do anything to animals."

The bell rang, and they had to leave the greenhouse to go back to class.

On the way to class, he went to the school library and borrowed a hiking map of the White Forest. The librarian, however, an ancient little man, was unwilling to give it to him.

"Mr. Schaefer says five of our boys have been carted off. We can't risk any more of you," the man wheezed.

"Mr. Grant, did Mr. Schaefer also mention they were taken from their rooms and not the White Forest? That place is the safest we have right now."

Mr. Grant seemed to consider this for a while. "Fine," he said in a frail voice. "But you can only read it here."

Kire frowned. "It's a map, not a storybook. Why would I ever 'read it here'?"

"That's the deal," said the librarian. "You either take it or leave it."

The rest of the day passed rather uneventfully, but it could've been different had Kire not been so worried about their chance of beating Heno. During his last class of the day, Mr. Schaefer made an announcement over the PA explaining what happened with Andrew and urging everybody to be extra cautious. When class was over, Amberly ran up beside Kire in the hallway.

"Hey," she said, "I'm sorry for what I said earlier; I didn't mean it."

Kire took one long stare at her and nodded. "It's all right," he said.

"I didn't mean it, you know, or maybe I did," she said, "but Trace wanted me to come apologize, so here I am."

Kire sighed. "Oh, well, in that case, you're forgiven."

"Are you certain about that? I mean, I might have broken your fragile heart."

"Amberly, I get that Trace forced you to come and do this and it was absolutely not your desire, but I'd rather be alone right now."

Amberly scowled and turned to walk in the opposite direction. Kire, not wanting to go home quite yet, decided to venture into the White Forest. He hiked up into the forest and looked at his phone—he'd managed to take a picture of the map. According to the map, the shack was halfway to Kula Mountain. He planned to stop there for a bit of rest before the final lap to Kula. He sighed at the sight of the shack, thought of Stephan Krause, and wondered where he was now.

"Rest at last," he murmured and made a mental note to take water the next time he was coming there. But just as he was about to settle on the patio, he heard strange, muffled sounds coming from the shack.

Kire jumped to his feet and looked around the forest. Save for the endless assembly of trees growing and ferns, there was nothing else to be seen, which meant the sound had to be coming from inside the shed. He was about to make a terrible decision, and there was no one but himself to blame for whatever happened after. The wooden floor of the patio creaked under his weight, and the muffled sound grew louder.

Kire crouched low, snuck to an open window, and peeked through. Five boys were in the cabin, blindfolded and in pajamas. The muffled sound was coming from them as well. There was a rag tied around their heads in such a way that it formed a huge lump in their mouth. That way, they wouldn't be able to close their mouths or do anything more than make hopeless, muffled sounds. Their hands were tied to a wooden pole behind them. Kire didn't remember the shack having so many pillars.

Suddenly, there was a rustle in the woods behind him and Kire ducked around to the other side of the house to hide from whoever was coming. But he knew if the boys in the shack were the same ones that had been kidnapped, the only guest to the shack would be none other than Heno.

And he was right; Heno, still housed in Andrew's body, emerged from the clusters of trees with a sack slung over his shoulder and continued toward the shack. Kire could hear the sound of boots against the shack's wooden floor. Kire made his way to another window and peeped through it to see what was happening.

Heno dropped the sack on the floor and oranges and apples rolled out of it.

Heno pulled the blindfold from the boys' eyes and removed the gag. "There," he said to them, "eat and gain your strength back."

"I'm not eating! I'm not doing this again!" one of the boys yelled in defiance. "You let me go right now, or else."

Heno didn't seem pleased by the rebellion. "Or else what?" He stared hard into the boy's eyes. "Now, eat."

As though enchanted, the boy bent to the floor and picked up a green apple. There was a distant look in his eyes and a purplish glint, and his prior facial expression was replaced by a blank stare.

Heno growled in satisfaction. "Good boy," he said. "Now, will the rest of you do the same, or would you have me force you?"

The other four boys scampered for fruits and sank their teeth into them hurriedly. Heno smiled as he watched them eat. Why did he want them to eat so badly? And what was the boy talking about when he said he wasn't doing that again?

Kire didn't have to wait long to get his answers. As soon as the boys finished eating, Heno tied them up again, but that was only the beginning.

Heno then knelt before the first boy, the one that rebelled, cupped the sides of his face with his hands, and pressed his forehead to the boy's. Suddenly, the boy gasped and convulsed but was held in place by Heno's powerful hands. It lasted for about ten seconds, and when it was over, the boy's head fell limp like he was a sleeping drunk.

The other boys were trying to disappear into their poles now, struggling and trying their hardest to escape, but Heno still managed to have his way. One by one, he held them by the sides of their faces while they gasped and convulsed in his grip until they fell into some terrible kind of sleep.

Heno stood up and flexed his arms and hands like they were new. He looked physically stronger and healthier, as though he had stolen all of the strength, health, and energy from those poor boys. Kire watched Heno go to a corner of the shack and pick up a cylindrical object. Kire groaned; he had been so close to getting that mirror and stopping Heno's plan all along! Heno wedged the cylinder under his arm and exited the shed. He then disappeared into the forest in the direction of Kula Mountain.

Kire dialed 911 and informed the police he found five unconscious boys in a shack in White Forest. Once he hung up the call, he stepped into the shack and felt their pulses just to be sure they were still alive.

Of course, they were, but barely; they were all pale and cold. He vaguely recognized the boys, having seen them in the halls at one point or another, but assumed they were all freshmen because of how young and small they looked. Perhaps that was just because of the current state they were in.

Kire wondered why Halo had chosen these boys—was there any particular reason? And why didn't he kidnap any girls?

Kire untied them and put them on the floor beside one another. The police would be there soon, and they would be safe. He took pictures of their faces and jumped out of the shack, making a beeline home and not looking back or stopping once.

When Kire was safely home, he sent a message for everyone to meet at Aunt Marg's for a conference. Kaos replied with a message saying Kire wasn't the leader of the quintet team and that he wouldn't be present and was speaking for Trace as well. But that answer changed when Kire sent him pictures of the boys at the shack: pale faces with saliva dribbling its way out of their mouths.

30

"Oh, no!" Rose gasped.

Kire had explained his encounter at the shack to them and was positively thrilled to see the smirk disappear from Trace and Kaos' faces. As expected, Amberly wasn't among them again because she had to work.

"And he went to the mountain after that?" asked Trace.

"Yep," Kire replied. "And he had the Djigi with him."

"Why didn't you try to grab it?" asked Kaos. "That way, we wouldn't have to face him tomorrow night."

"I'll remember that the next time I face a monster strong enough to subdue Andrew and five other boys," said Kire darkly.

"The cops have found the boys," said Rose, reading from her phone.

"Why didn't you stay with them anyway?" asked Trace. "You could've become the hero of St. Bernard! Of Montgomery!"

Kaos sighed.

"I like how you think, Trace," Kaos said. "We'd make the front cover of a magazine one of these days. Probably after we catch sneaky Andrew."

"How many times do I have to tell you Andrew isn't Heno," said Kire, frustrated. "He's a *victim* in this case."

"Yeah, tell that to the cops that caught him kidnapping boys," said Trace. "He's done for. No one will believe him anyway, so why not take a little bit of glory?"

"Don't be selfish," said Kire, glancing at the clock of cups on the wall. Time seemed to have picked up speed since his sighting of Heno earlier.

"I think he's taking strength from them," said Rose, looking at her phone. "The cops said when they found the boys, they were seriously malnourished. We know Heno has been feeding them, but somehow, he's able to sap their strength out from them again."

"That's scary," said Kaos, shivering. "It's like a soul transfer thing."

Kire sighed. "I'm glad you're finally taking this seriously. And meanwhile, the only person who has never used her abilities is Amberly. Trace, have you seen her use it before?"

Trace swallowed. "Not exactly," he said, clearing his throat.

Kire's eyes narrowed in suspicion. "There's something you're not telling us, Trace," he said, leaning forward.

When Trace saw that all eyes, including Kaos', were on him, he groaned. "Fine," he said and rubbed his face down with a hand. "She said she wanted to defy you or whatever."

"So, she hasn't taken her gauntlet out of her wardrobe this whole time because she was saving it to hurt me?" said Kire, steaming with anger.

"Maybe she's saving it for her wedding," Kaos suggested, earning himself a glare from Trace.

"She won't have a wedding if she doesn't survive tomorrow night," Kire said bitterly. "You know what, I'm out of here." Kire rose to his feet and snatched his phone up from the table.

"You don't want a ride?" asked Kaos.

"No."

"Wait, let's go together," said Rose, rising as well.

Trace and Kaos stared at the pair with mischievous grins spread on their faces. "Looks like something hot is cooking here."

Kire ignored the sniggering duo and stepped out of Aunt Marg's place into the fresh open air outside.

"You should stay back tomorrow, Rose." He sighed.

"Why?" she asked.

"Isn't that obvious?" said Kire. "To keep you safe? Protect you from Heno? You saw what he did to those kids; he's gathering energy to defend the Djigi, and he'll do it for as long as he can."

"So... you want me to quit?" asked Rose. "What about Amberly? Is she allowed to stay back?"

"Is there a time Amberly hasn't stayed back?" snapped Kire.

"That's because she has to work all the time, unlike you," said Rose. "And I know she doesn't make it any easier, but let's be the reflection of what we want others to be, even if it hurts. If we die tomorrow, you'll perish with all that resentment."

They had stopped walking and she placed a soft, warm hand on his chest over his heart. "Let only good things live inside here."

She was staring kindly into his eyes with her own sweet honey brown eyes. He felt his heart begin galloping. Was this his moment to kiss her? Even though they were in the middle of the sidewalk and there were kids in the yard beside them screeching and playing with a soccer ball?

"Kire? Are you all right?" Rose asked.

Yes, this is my moment to kiss her, Kire thought. He grabbed hold of her hand sitting on his chest and put his other hand on her back and pulled her closer. He put his lips gently on hers and he was pleased to notice her kissing him back.

They pulled apart, still in each other's arms. Kire laughed

quietly, nervously, and Rose simply kissed him once more on the cheek before she said, "I'll see you tomorrow."

Before Kire could gather any number of words to string together in response, she was gone.

31

Kire, of course, didn't sleep a wink that night. Between the anticipation of his certain death the following day combined with his kiss with Rose, his heart raced all night and he could hardly get his body to sit still, let alone his mind. Kire couldn't help wishing he could speed up time with some magical spell and be done with all of this so he could just focus his worrying and anxiety on Rose like a normal teenager. Even if Heno was going to kill them, there was a good chance that they'd have died of anxiety before the fight even started.

Kire felt sick to his stomach when he listened to the principal's announcement about the found boys and the anonymous tip-off. The boys were all still in the hospital but were expected to go home later that day. Kire spent his lunchtime alone in the library, mostly just to avoid the cafeteria. He seethed with envy overhearing conversations of students who didn't have to fight an alien that night.

At the end of the day, Amberly, Trace, and Kaos were waiting outside the front doors of the school for Kire. They moved toward the greenhouse, where they'd have a bit more privacy to talk shop.

Finally, Rose joined them, sweaty and panting. This was the first time Kire saw Rose since they kissed, but she did a good job hiding what had happened the evening before. Kire thought he saw Amberly nudge Trace as though it was time for a pre-planned arrangement but dismissed it as a product of his heightened nervousness.

"So, what's the plan?" asked Trace.

"The plan is to distract him and take the mirror away from the position," said Kire. "All we have to do is ensure the Djigi isn't aligned by midnight. And to do that, we have to beat Heno the same way we did Jago. We'll all converge here at eleven," said Kire. "And make sure you each bring a bottle of water."

"Will there be a fire on the mountain?" asked Kaos.

Kire shook his head. "No, but after the strenuous hike up the mountain, there'll be a fire in your chest."

Rose then let out an ear-splitting scream all of a sudden. It was so surprising that Kire found himself covering his ears just at the same moment Rose jumped on him, wrapping her arms tight like a noose around his neck with her legs locked behind him.

Kire staggered backward and tried to regain his footing. "Rose! What is wrong with you?"

A white rat ran between their feet before darting off into the hedge nearby.

Amberly laughed, and Kire frowned. But everyone, including Trace, who had been privy to her plan, looked shell-shocked.

"Why did Rose react so wildly to the rat?" said Amberly, with an expression that said she wasn't at all surprised by Rose's reaction. "I guess she's just afraid of animals."

"You knew she was afraid of rats, so you brought one here to scare her? On a day that's already the most frightening day of all our lives?" Kire snarled. Rose was still holding tightly to him. Her face was buried in the side of his neck.

"She wasn't going to tell anyone about her fear of rats," said Amberly, combing her golden hair with her fingers. "It's all over now, though. No secret between us all."

Kire swelled in indignation and then glared at Trace, who quickly crossed his heart. "I swear, I didn't know anything about it."

"It's all right, Rose." Kire glared at Amberly. "The rat is gone now."

"I want to go home," she said, sniffling.

"Sure thing," Kire said, leading her away. "Meeting is over!"

He was able to settle Rose in a cab with a kiss on the cheek, and when he arrived home, he called her to affirm she had arrived home safely. Now, all he wanted to do was force himself to get some sleep.

Kire got lucky that evening and was able to get a few hours of sleep before dinner. Usually, when he tries to sleep when he isn't tired, his eyes refuse to close, and his brain wouldn't cease pumping imaginations through his mind. So maybe this was the end after all, and even his body knew it.

All too soon, dinner was over, and his parents retired to bed. He picked out the same all-black outfit he wore the last time there was an occasion as such. Rather than put Halo in his bag, he held on to the book as though he expected Jago to leap out at him again.

His mother wasn't in the living room this time, although a part of him wished she was. She'd send him back to his room and lock him in. Kire got outside without needing to sneak and started his death walk to school. It was a few minutes to eleven, a little earlier than he told the rest, but it was fine anyway.

Overhead, the moon and a few cloaks of clouds decorated the peaceful night sky. Scarcely had he arrived at school when he heard the screech of tires behind him. It was Kaos and Trace playing music loudly as they pulled up to fight aliens once again.

Trace and Kaos got out of the car. They were both in red leather jackets that reflected every single light in their surroundings, white pants, white shoes with inch-thick soles and red laces, and a red baseball hat on their heads.

"You like what you see?" said Kaos, throwing up a pose.

Amberly then stepped out of the backseat. She was also wearing red leather; only hers was a dress that stopped a few inches above her knees, accompanied by a pair of silver heels that went well with the silver gauntlet gleaming up to her elbow.

"Dressed for the occasion, I see," said Kire rather spitefully.

"Where's *your* girlfriend?" asked Trace.

"She's not here yet, I guess," Kire replied and bit his tongue after.

"Ohhh, so you guys *are* an item now?" asked Trace, laughing aloud.

"I-I thought you asked about my girl*friend*, you know," Kire quickly stammered. "A *friend* that's a girl."

"Hey, guys, sorry I'm late," Rose said, running from the opposite end of the road.

"Speak of the devil," said Amberly, chuckling.

"We have only one devil here, and you know who it is," Kire shot back at Amberly.

Rose was in a pair of green pants and a green hoodie. Her Pendantix glistened in the moonlight. There was a backpack, green as well, hitched up behind her.

"Shall we?" she said, smiling at the rest of the team.

All the bravado disappeared from Amberly when they started up into the White Forest. Her heels kept sinking into the soft soil, and Trace had to cut them off with his flaming sword for her to walk properly. They all marched in silence, a solemn assembly heading toward an unknown fate. The shack where Trace and Stephan had fought was now fenced off by the police, given that it was a crime scene. The team went around it, making their way further into the depths of the White Forest. Even if Heno didn't attack them, there was a good chance a wild animal or snake would do the job. But Kula appeared before them; the rather small mountain covered densely in trees.

"Well," started Trace, "here goes nothing."

The five started up the mountain, trying to find a way through the trees and thick bush, all while keeping their eyes peeled for Heno. None of them said anything, but the very real prospect of dying had them whipping their heads up at every little sound. If he survived this, Kire wasn't looking forward to the next therapy appointment.

Trace walked in front, grabbing at the leaves as he trampled a path for the others to follow. He was muttering to himself and was about to draw his sword to start hacking away at the branches in his path.

"Don't be ridiculous!" said Kire. "You'll burn the forest down and would be doing Yash a favor."

Trace looked like he was about to snap back at him but sheathed the sword at the logic in his words.

"He's right," said Kaos. "We're not trying to give the other team a goal here."

"I can't see anything," Amberly said, stumbling over a root and making enough noise to alert anyone within a mile radius.

"Fine," said Kire, taking out his phone. "I'll walk in front, and you all just follow behind me. I think we are more than halfway to the top anyway."

None of them complained as Kire trudged up the mountain, slapping branches and leaves out of his way while shining the flashlight on his phone in front of him. They probably wanted him to be the first to be attacked when they found Heno.

The ground was finally starting to level out again and he

could just make out the crest of the hill up ahead when they all froze at the sound of rustling leaves and feet running on the ground. Kire's heart raced and he gripped Rose's hand just as hard as she was gripping his. Just then, a mountain goat bounded out of the darkness and ran right past them down the mountain without giving them a second glance.

Kire relaxed for a moment until Kaos said in a terrified voice, "What was the goat running from?"

"It was headed *away* from the direction we are going," whimpered Amberly. "We're in trouble."

They all stood without moving, looking around for what had chased the goat. Trace pushed Kire forward. "You wanted to be in front," he said, but only fear was in his voice. "Go on, hotshot."

The light from Kire's phone was shaking as he took a few tentative steps forward, Rose squeezing the life out of his other hand. When nothing popped out of the darkness, they inched forward again slowly until they saw the edge of the tree line. The top of the mountain was just bare rocky ground up ahead and they saw something glinting in the moonlight.

"The Djigi!" Rose cried, pointing straight ahead.

It looked like the mirror had been stood up at the very top of the peak, and from Kire's dreams, he knew that on the other side was a near-vertical slope down the other side of the mountain. But if the Djigi was there, then where was—

"MARTYRS OF THE EARTH REALM," they heard a booming voice out of the darkness.

They all froze again and looked around at the sparse trees surrounding them. Coming out of the darkness was Heno in the form of Andrew. His body looked worse for the wear, like an old sweater worn too many times. "Welcome to death," he said, a sinister grin spreading across his face.

"Point of correction," interjected Trace. "*Defenders* of the Earth realm. You have to die to be a martyr."

"And you don't think you're already dead? Surely, your friend must have delivered my messages to you," said Heno, smiling at Kire.

"We're here to kill *you!*" shouted Amberly, forgetting her fear when she had a chance to be spiteful. "To send *you* to hell!" She took a step forward and Trace grabbed her arm, holding her back.

Heno scowled. "So few breaths left in you, and you choose to waste them shouting needless taunts at me. You should be asking if your untimely deaths will be swift and painless or slow and gory. Why am I surprised that you are so pathetic?" He looked at Amberly like a bug that had wandered into his house that he planned on squishing.

Trace growled, and Kire knew what was going to happen next. "Don't talk to my girlfriend like that!" Trace pulled out his flaming sword like a knight ready to defend the honor of his fair maiden and ran straight toward Heno. His form was mediocre at best, but he charged up the hill toward the enemy.

"Trace!" screamed Amberly, flinging out her gauntleted hand in his direction. To the group's astonishment, a massive fallen tree branch weighing roughly fifty pounds lifted into the air and hurtled toward Heno. They all gasped as it collided with him, but it seemed to do as much damage as a small stick. In fact, he wasn't paying attention to Amberly at all and had all his focus on Trace, who was barreling toward him with his flaming sword. As if having calculated this move down to the millisecond, Heno simply stepped aside at the last possible moment when Trace swung with all his might and fell to the ground in a pile behind him. It looked like Trace had been nothing more than a small child throwing a tantrum.

Heno turned to Trace and, lightning-fast, raised his fist and was ready to deliver a colossal hit. Amberly screamed again, but suddenly, vines shot out of the forest from several directions and wrapped around Heno's raised arm, halting him in place.

Rose stepped forward with a hand outstretched, a mixture of fear and concentration on her face.

Heno growled in anger. "You think this will stop me?" he yelled. "I've killed hundreds of you. Thousands!" Behind him, Trace had gotten to his feet and Kire was frozen in place, watching as Trace swung toward Heno again. His sword went sailing right by as Heno twisted to rid himself of Rose's thorns. "Argh!"

They definitely should have had some sort of plan before doing this, but it was too late now. More vines kept coming out of the forest and roots came up to trip him, but Heno kept his footing. Trace got in a few good swings but had more luck hitting Rose's vines than Heno himself. Kaos had moved a safe distance away and Kire was about to shout at him when he realized the intense look on the other boy's face was because he was trying to get into Heno's head.

Kire watched the team and tried to think of a way out of this. How were they supposed to stop Heno? He was easily holding his own against them and Kire didn't have much in terms of the offensive. He had pulled out the book and gripped it in one hand. Now was not the time to be asking Halo questions, but what was he supposed to do?

He looked around wildly for an answer. There had to be something! Rose and Trace were the only ones keeping Heno distracted and Amberly looked like she was panicking. She wrapped her arms around herself as she watched Trace and Rose battle the creature. She hadn't practiced with the gauntlet and now they were all paying the price. The branch had lifted on accident and she didn't know how to do it again and wasn't even trying.

Her wide, panicked eyes whipped to Kire. "Don't just stand there, you coward!" she screamed venomously. "*Do* something!"

Flames rose inside Kire's chest. *Amberly is calling me a coward?* he thought, his anger increasing. The anger he held at bay was coming to haunt him at the worst time possible.

Was she really blaming him right now? She was the one who was balled up, crying in the cave that first night. She was the one who didn't show up to fight Jago with them. And now she was the one standing on the sidelines while her boyfriend and the rest of the team were about to die as she blamed Kire for everything, *again.*

Halo had said they needed to find love and unity, but how was he supposed to do that when Amberly would rather chew him out instead of trying to help?

"What is your *problem*?" Kire bellowed, stomping up to her while dodging Rose's vines as they flew by. Heno had shoved Trace back, but Rose had lifted another root and sent Heno stumbling backward. About fifty feet past them was the mirror and an idea struck Kire, but he had to get away. He felt like he could hit Amberly right now for distracting him. "We're in the middle of fighting a literal alien, and you want to fight with me? Now?! If you didn't notice, you're not doing anything either!"

"Coming up here was your idea!" she shouted back in his face. "And Trace is going to get killed because of you. It's always you! Everything bad that happens is because of you!" She had tears welling up in her eyes and looked at him like he was the bane of her existence. He had had enough of her attitude and her bullying.

Kire stepped up to her. "I don't know what I ever did to you, Amberly, but I'm sorry!" he shouted, and before she could reject him, he continued. "You can hate me all you want if that makes you feel better, but I want you to know that I don't hate *you.* You annoy me to my wit's end and make my life a miserable hell, but I don't hate you. I won't live my life like that and I don't think you deserve it either, despite everything. Now excuse me while I go save us all."

He left the hurt expression and unshed tears on her face as he turned and sprinted up the mountain. Since Amberly was going to be of no help, he put her out of his thoughts and ran as hard as he could, thankful for all the days he missed the bus and had to sprint to school. Kaos was still intensely focused with the crown on his head as Kire ran past and no one noticed as he snuck passed the fight up the hill.

He suddenly tripped over a rock, knocking one loose and causing others to roll down the hill in a shower of stone. The commotion caused Heno to spin around and find Kire picking himself up from the fall.

"You slimy, cunning humans!" Heno roared furiously. He was wrapped in Rose's vines and let out a roar before lifting his arms with impossible strength, ripping through them like they were nothing more than string. He picked up Trace and flung him to the side and started to run up the mountain.

Kire's heart pounded wildly as he turned and set off at a full sprint again. Heno burst after Kire, who responded by picking up speed toward the Djigi sitting at the mountain peak. They were just passing the last few trees and the terrain was really becoming more loose rock than grass, making it hard for Kire to find a purchase. He just needed to get to the mirror, but he was no match for Heno, who caught up with him in a matter of seconds. A powerful hand slammed down on Kire's shoulder and ripped him backward, sending him flying partway back down the hill.

Kire yelped in pain as he collided with the rocky ground. His shirt was torn and there would surely be a massive bruise there later if they made it that long. His plan was looking more difficult by the second as Heno came thundering back toward him. The others were coming up the hill but what could they truly do?

"Stay down and I will make your death swift," said Heno, marching vengefully toward Kire. The sinister look on his face had turned to one of wrath and Kire knew there was a very good chance it was going to be the last thing he would ever see. The others were shouting, vines wrapping around Heno but he only ripped them off, stomping forward. Kire scrambled backward, unable to get to his feet and he heard Rose's scream as Heno reached him, gripped him by the throat, and raised him into the air.

A victorious smile split Heno's face as Kire struggled to breathe at the crushing pressure on his windpipe. This was how he was going to die.

"Hey!" he heard Amberly's banshee shriek as a small stone bounced off the side of Heno's skull. His enraged face turned to Amberly, who was outside of Kire's dimming vision. Heno's face went slack at something Kire couldn't see as he heard Amberly yell, "LET GO OF MY BROTHER!"

Kire fell from Heno's grasp a split second before a bus-sized boulder sped toward Heno at seventy miles per hour, slamming into him hard enough that he and the boulder leveled tree after tree before coming to a stop twenty feet away.

Kire pulled himself to his feet, but Heno had already shoved the boulder aside and was running back toward him. Kire sent an incredulous look toward Amberly, "Brother?!" he asked, mind whirling. She stood there, gauntleted hand outstretched and a shocked look on her face as if she hadn't expected that from herself. He remembered Mrs. McHenry's story then, about how her husband had fallen in love with another woman and left them.

I have a sister? He didn't have time to think it over now.

Kire's mind was racing, and it took all his strength to focus on the task at hand. He began to run back up the hill when Heno barreled into him from the side, sending him back down the hill again. He realized then that he was too slow and Heno was just too fast. He was never going to make it. Heno came at him again and Kire's legs felt as heavy as lead like he was moving through a swamp.

"Kire!" Rose shrieked.

Amberly stretched her covered hand toward another boulder, this time being the size of a small car, and it hurled itself at Heno. Heno leaned sideways and the boulder missed by less than half an inch. The alien paused and turned around at this. "Nice try again, sweetheart," he sneered at Amberly.

The distraction gave Trace the opportunity to raise his flaming sword again and launch a flying attack at Heno while Kire backed away to catch his breath. Heno caught Trace's sword with both hands and to Trace and everyone's surprise, was unhurt by the fire.

Heno grinned. "Fires burn better when the wet wood of hate and anger is pulled out. Sadly, you learned that too late." He grabbed Trace by the collar and hurled him like a broken toy at a tree ten feet away, which he slammed against and fell onto the ground with a loud crack and a scream—he'd definitely broken his leg.

"Why are they always throwing him?" cried Kaos.

"Shut up and use your stupid crown," Rose yelled, straining to get her vines to wrap around Heno again. Sweat was beading on her forehead from the exertion.

While Heno was distracted again for a moment, Amberly rushed over to Trace's side, but he waved her away with a wince. She turned around and her blue eyes flashed icy indignation—she wanted revenge.

"Now, ladies. Do you want to give up?" said Heno, cackling. He flexed and cracked his fingers, grinning wickedly. It was evident in the way he spoke that he enjoyed the horror he saw in their eyes, the pain that coated their screams.

"I'm still here and I'm not a lady," said Kaos, in injured pride.

Heno scoffed. "I see," he said. "I wonder what devil

possessed you to make you think you stood a chance against me." He cackled when Trace hobbled to his feet to standoff with him again.

"He's going to try to hold us down here until the time is up," Kaos yelled to the others. "We need to stop him before that."

Rose managed to get some vines wrapped around Heno's ankles again, which temporarily kept him from moving.

"Rose can do it for us!" Kaos said. "The key to beating Heno is destroying his purpose. You see, if the mirror is destroyed, Heno and Rezin will be destroyed as well."

"How do you know this?" asked Amberly.

"His mind," said Kaos, breathing heavily. "My crown lets me read his mind. Only a bit, though. You don't want to linger in there."

Kire nodded. "Halo told me that as well. If we destroy that mirror, I think that should do it," he said panting, hands on his knees. He couldn't stop looking at Amberly, but she refused to meet his eyes.

"Okay, where does Rose come in?" asked Amberly impatiently.

"That mountain goat from earlier can easily outrun Heno and us. All you have to do is make it go up there and knock the Djigi off the mountain while we keep Heno busy."

"But—but it's an animal. And it's probably far away by now. How am I supposed to make him do anything?" Rose asked, continuing to strain as she tightened the vines.

Trace made a half-hearted attempt at distracting Heno, his strength weaning.

"Don't think of it as an animal, Rose," said Kaos desperately when he saw Heno approaching, making a beeline for Kire. "It's a vine with four legs and two horns!"

"That makes no sense," Rose whimpered.

"None of this makes any sense. Now be quick, or your boyfriend dies," Amberly hissed.

Amberly and Kaos worked together to hurl rocks and debris at Heno as Rose shifted her attention from her vines to the goat who had only traveled just a little further down the hill.

Was this the love and unity that Halo was talking about? They might still be bickering, but they were doing it to protect one another. When Kire had tried going up the hill on his own, it hadn't worked. But if they all worked together like this, would they win?

In Rose's mind, she urged the goat to run as fast as it could back toward them. The goat raised its head and dashed for the mountain top. Within seconds, it burst through the trees at full throttle and with its head lowered, sped past the ground and up the mountain.

Heno frowned, still unable to understand what was happening, and then he saw Rose crouched a small distance behind Amberly and Kaos; her eyes were closed, and she put two fingers to her temple.

He growled dangerously as realization dawned on him. "You cunning humans!" He turned around and chased after the goat, the others running after him to slow him down. But the goat was built for this and Heno wasn't. When he saw he wouldn't be able to catch up with it, he became desperate and stopped to conjure the same purple ball of destruction Jago had, its darkness swirling between his hands.

He threw the first ball toward Amberly and Kaos to keep them off his tail. They had to throw themselves to the side to avoid being vaporized on the spot. The ball hit a tree behind them and shattered into a thousand pieces, sending a boom through the mountainside. Then he created a bigger ball of purple fire, narrowed his eyes for better aim, and launched it at the little goat leaping up the mountain.

Kire, having been watching from the side, held out Halo with a sudden force, mentally begging for the shield to come out. If it didn't, they were done for. He had screwed his eyes shut but at the cry of rage that came from Heno, he knew it had worked. The shield parried the blast away from the goat and it ran free to the top.

Heno let out a vengeful roar, realizing that he wasn't going to make it before the goat got to the mirror.

"Kire!" Kaos yelled happily.

Heno watched helplessly as the goat reached the peak and continued running until it slammed into the mirror with its horns. The mirror shattered on impact and flew off the opposite side of the mountain to crash down to the rocks below in a far-off, pitiful thud.

All was silent for a few moments.

"NO!" Heno screamed into the night, the sound carrying like a demonic exorcism.

The team held their breath as bright light seemed to have attacked Heno, swarming around him like angry bees. They watched in horror as he fell to the ground, spasmed, and then lay unmoving.

They held their breath, waiting to see if anything else would happen, but nothing did. That was it. Only the goat made any sound as it galloped back down the hill, bleating the whole way down.

They quickly made their way back down to Trace, who had collapsed by a tree. Aside from the broken leg and sheer exhaustion, he seemed to be doing all right. Amberly, Kire's sister, hugged Trace tightly and was crying, so the others decided to give them some space.

"Hey," Kire said to Rose. "That was a good job you did out there. It's all because of you that Heno is dead now. You kept your head level when the rest of us were fumbling around."

"Really?" she said with a blush. "Thanks, Kire. But, uhh, let's not overlook the fact that *Amberly* is your *sister!*" her voice rose to an exclamation. Was that really what she wanted to talk about, seeing as they almost died several times?

"Yeah," Kire said, scratching the back of his head. "I'm not going to worry about that just now. I just want to appreciate that great work you did with the goat," Kire said with a grin. Despite his nonchalance, Kire's mind was going a million miles an hour. They had just defeated an ancient, powerful alien—with the help of a goat—and all his mind was doing was replaying every interaction he had ever had with Amberly. Was she really his sister? His half-sister?

Rose smiled radiantly at Kire and pulled him into a sudden passionate kiss and a warm embrace. He was shocked at first but then relaxed when he realized what was happening; teenage hormones taking over. He started to feel something vibrating on his chest where her chest met his. They pulled away from each other and looked down—her necklace was glowing and shaking before it disappeared completely.

Kaos' crown was doing the same, as well as Amberly's gauntlet. Trace's sword burst into flame before seeming to burn itself to oblivion. The items vanished into nothingness as if they had completed a job well done.

"Looks like the stupid gifts are leaving," said Kaos, rubbing his head.

Kire frowned. "I don't think so," he said, pulling Halo out; Halo was calling Kire's name. He quickly opened the book to read in flaming golden letters, 'Don't let your guard down. Someone here is angry.'

After reading the statement to the others, they all looked around at one another with puzzled expressions. They had just defeated Heno. What could possibly be happening now?

"Who?" Kaos finally asked, looking toward Kire and the book. Kire looked down at new writing scrawling across the page as his friends watched him anxiously.

'The last of Yash's minions... Rezin.'

EPILOGUE

They heard the crunch of footsteps, and they all held their breath.

The footsteps came from a man in a smart black double-breasted tuxedo and sunglasses. His hands were in his pockets and his footsteps were certain and determined. Kire thought the man must be an FBI agent. Or worse...

The man stopped walking and bent down and picked up a purple gooey mass lying on the ground.

"So," the man began in a voice both cold and low. "You failed to kill them, did you not?" he said to the gooey mass.

Kire broke into a cold sweat.

"Looks like I'll have to do it myself," the man said, tossing the purple mass behind him. Then he turned and looked straight at the group. He took off his sunglasses and they saw two red flaming balls where his eyes should be. Rose screamed and the others tried to hide.

"Hello, Kire," the man said, looking directly at him and ignoring the others.

Kire squeezed his eyes shut. He assured himself that it was

just a dream. When his eyes opened, the man was standing before him, white-faced and eyes red with hate. There was no expression on his face; he showed no emotion whatsoever.

"Kire..." said the man in black. "My name is Rezin, the last of Yash's three. And I'm here to kill you and your friends."

AUTHOR'S NOTE

Dear Beloved Reader,

I'm so thankful and grateful that you chose to read The Unchosen Ones! It is the first book in The Unlikely Defenders Series, where each of the five "defenders" will have their own book. I truly hope that you enjoyed The Unchosen Ones. If you did, I would be so thankful if you would consider leaving a review. Reviews help other readers find my work, and each review means the world to me.

Grab the next book in the series here! View the entire series here!

https://swiy.co/UnlikelyDefenders

Click here to visit my website and interact with me on social media. There's awesome merch available for each of my series. Also, make sure to sign up for my mailing list to be the first to know about new releases and special happenings such as previews and give-a-ways!

I love getting feedback from my readers, and if you'd like to stay in touch (or discuss my books), join me over at the Lily Skyy Readers' Group. I'd also love to connect with you on Instagram, TikTok, and Twitter! Feel free to reach out to me directly via email at social@lilyskyy.com.

Again, I thank you for reading, and I can't wait to join you on the next adventure!

Sincerely,

Lily Skyy